WHAT WOLVES KNOW

WHAT WOLVES KNOW

Kit Reed

CONTENTS

WHAT WOLVES KNOW

The creator of Buffy the Vampire Slayer *et al. (a lot of al.) the original Lemony Snicket and I were walking to a screening of* Valentino, the Last Emperor, *with producer/director Q&A to follow, which led us to imagine which dumb questions... Spontaneously cranky, we chorused, "Where do you get your ideas?" Um, I dunno, where do you get yours? In fact everything is made out of something, writers just don't necessarily know what, and if they do, they don't always want to tell. This one's easy: I read an ad for a high-end app which for self-protective purposes, I'd rather not name. Basically, it explained that with nothing more than an investment in their software you could perfect your novel—and sell it, recouping the cost with your first, pretty-much-guaranteed sale. I looked at the splash page, which as I remember it included examples from* Moby Dick, *and "Monkey Do" was born. Unlike most of my stories, it happened in one very short day.*

MONKEY DO

Every writer wants to be famous, at least just once. I've been at it since before the dog died, but it's an animal planet, so what do you expect? If a hundred monkeys typing for a thousand years would probably produce a novel, what could one monkey do with a computer and the right software?

That is, a computer-literate monkey like Spud.

I never liked the monkey. I brought it home because I was stuck on certain points in my monkey planet novel and needed a specimen to observe firsthand. In a one-room apartment, gorillas are out of the question and chimps are too annoying to have around. Plus, baboons are

3

evil incarnate, which you'd know if you'd ever looked one in the eye. Ergo, Spud.

He was quiet, he was small enough to fit in a shopping bag, if he scrunched, so what could go wrong?

He had bad habits, his breath was vile but I thought, cool. Bestseller at any cost. Instant movie. Fame! I finished the book OK, I even got paid. I did all the right things to promote it even though they weren't paying squat. I touched all the miserable bases, up to and including being snubbed at cons and sitting at bookstore tables for hours, waiting to sign *Rhesus Planet* for fans who never showed up. Nice poster featuring Spud attracted a few ladies, but they awwww-ed and moved on.

My novel tanked but the monkey is still around.

It's not like I wanted to keep the monkey. It sat around scratching its belly and mocking me, and I could swear it was grunting, fleabag of a failure. I saw pity in its eyes.

You bet I was over Spud. In fact the first thing I did after the book was done was take him back to the pet store for a refund but the dealer said he didn't accept returns. I tried to trade him in for an anaconda, but a sarcastic, second-hand rhesus monkey with white eyebrows and a white goatee and white hair on its butt like a second beard around its asshole turns out to be a drug on the market.

So I donated him to the local zoo. They took him on a trial basis. We hugged goodbye. I thought good riddance but he was back on my doorstep in less than a week. There was a note attached to his carrier: BAD INFLUENCE. I was embarrassed, but not surprised.

I tried to take him out in the wild and set him free, and he was OK in the car until I turned off the freeway. Stupid jerk, he started to cry. Never mind, I found him a nice field with lots of growing things that he could eat if he wasn't so fussy, a nice pond and trees he could jump around in. God knows I tried to turn him loose. I put him down and gave him a little pat on the butt. "Go, be free!" Instead he locked his arms and legs around my shin and no matter how hard I kicked to shake him off he clung, going ook-ook-oook so pathetically that I picked him up and we went home.

As a result Spud is still around, a constant reminder of whatever is the most recent failure and believe me, there have been a few too many since

Rhesus Planet, the unsuccessful *Cockatoo Nation* being one. At least the dealer let me turn in the bird for a goldfish, which mysteriously disappeared the day I brought it home.

Never mind. I did what you do in the wake of failure, which pretty much happens every time I try. I sat down at the computer and started another novel, but when nobody likes you it's hard, thinking up new words to push around the screen.

You get distracted, and the monkey was no help. Spud got bored or jealous or some damn thing whenever I sat down to write. Worse, every time I walked away to get coffee or look out the window for inspiration, which was often, he hopped up on the table and started bopping away at my keyboard with his little fists, bonka-bonka-bonka, and one day when I came back from gazing into the bathroom mirror, I found words.

HELO BILY

Well, he spelled it wrong, but I'm here to tell you: never condescend to a monkey. It turns out the little fuckers are clever. Plus they are easily bored and idle hands can delete an entire chapter just while you're in the bathroom, examining your zits.

I had to come up with a distraction if I was ever going to finish this rotten book. If I could just get Spud onto something that kept him busy, he wouldn't have to spring up on my keyboard every time I turned my back, like, when I came back to work I wouldn't have to deal with him crouching on top of the bookcase with that reproachful look, oook-oooking every time I quit typing because I was trying to think.

It was inhibiting, all that judgmental hopping and oooking and worse, knowing that he was watching my every move with those sober eyes. I could swear he knew every time I switched screens to see if my Amazon figures had improved or went looking for signs of life on my Facebook page; if I started to blog the ook-ooking slipped into a positively spiteful screeeee.

The monkey was judging me. If I wanted to get anywhere with *Koala Galaxy*, I needed to get Spud the sententious rhesus monkey off my case. Monkey see, monkey do? Fine. I would create a diversion.

I dragged out the laptop Mom bought me when she first found out that I was going to be a famous writer. If it takes a hundred monkeys a thousand years to type a novel and I only had one, how wrong could it go?

I gave my old klunker to the monkey.

Oh, he bonked out a few words but he was no threat to me, for I am an artist. While he was plinking away I managed to crank out *Gibbous Moon*, 3,000,004 on Amazon last time I looked, and *Screaming Meemies*, my first horror novel which, in case you're interested, is in its fifth year on offer, for mysterious reasons, and therefore still available.

And Spud? Oh, he banged out a few hundred words, no big deal, but pretty damn good for a monkey. At least his spelling improved. His little screeds weren't worth squat, but seeing how lame they were compared to my work absolutely cheered me up. I would pat him on the back and praise him and I don't think he knew for a minute that my tone was maybe a little bit condescending, for he is the monkey and I am the pro.

He got good enough that I started printing out some of his stuff and at night, after we'd both eaten and I was sick of playing World of Warcraft and fluffing up my MySpace page, I workshopped the stuff with him, or I tried to. If you want to know the truth, Spud's always been a little too thin-skinned about criticism to be a real writer. One harsh word out of me, one little suggestion and he started ook-oook-ooooking so loud that we had complaints from the neighbors and the super gave me an or-else speech.

"Very well," I said to the monkey finally, and I'm sorry to say that he took it very badly, "if you can't handle a little constructive criticism, shut up or get out of the kitchen."

How was I supposed to know he was so thin-skinned that he would sulk? When I next looked at his laptop screen the ungrateful brute had typed—never mind what he typed, it was insulting and unprintable. I shouted, "language!" but he didn't care.

I told him what he could do with his copy and went back to work, and if the next time I peeked Spud had written a villanelle, well—never mind. "Oook-oook-oook," I said to him after I printed it. "This is what I think of your villanelle." He cried when I tore it to bits and threw the pieces away. At least I think that's what he was doing. I sneaked a peek at his screen, which is how he usually communicates, but it was blank, so I never found out what he was thinking.

For the next few days he pretty much abandoned the laptop. Whether I was working or not, he sat in a corner and kept his back to me. He wouldn't eat, at least not while I was watching, and he wouldn't touch the keyboard—plus, every once in a while I could swear I heard him moan, but with monkeys, you never know. He was sulking for sure.

In a way, it was a relief. It was a lot easier to work without him watching. I managed to finish *Dam of the Unconscionable*, my first literary novel. My feeling is, I never sold many copies because I've always been a hybrid and the world resents a literary novelist, but I could gain respect. I thought *Dam of the Unconscionable* would make me famous. I wrote my heart out on that book! It was so intense that I just knew it would win a couple of prizes; this was going to be the novel that would break me out.

Meanwhile Spud was languishing. He wouldn't type, didn't write, wouldn't celebrate with me when a small press gave me a contract for my novel. He wouldn't touch the laptop even though I gave him inspiring speeches about perseverance. Frankly, it was depressing, seeing him dragging around with his shoulders hunched, and I would do anything to buck him up. I even told him he showed promise and slid the open laptop in front of him, hoping to lure him back to his escritoire. The ungrateful bastard just sat on the windowsill, looking into his paws. I hate the sober little jerk but that expression made me feel bad for him and a tad bit guilty too, for letting him type away on that laptop with nary an honest or even a hypocritical kind word.

"You're good," I told him, and I tried my best not to sound condescending this time. "You're really good." But he just looked at me the way he did, and I knew that he knew.

Then *Dam of the Unconscionable* tanked. The small press wouldn't even give my money back. I brought home the only copy they printed and I shook it in Spud's face. I'm afraid I shouted: "Well, are you happy now?" I could tell he was still sulking. He wouldn't even oook for me.

So for months Spud sat around and brooded; he was shedding, like every clump of fur was a little reproach. Have you ever tried to sit down and get serious about your novel in the presence of a living reproach? It's like typing on the deck of the Ark the day it starts raining in earnest. Everything shorts out.

If I was ever going to finish *Screed of the Outrageous* and get famous, Spud was a problem that had to be solved.

I couldn't get rid of the guy, too much has gone down between us, so I had to make him happy. Whatever it took.

Then inspiration struck. I was surfing—OK, I was mousing along thinking, the way you do when things aren't going well inside your head, and I came upon this amazing product.

I clicked on this page and it said in big letters all the way across the top, **NOVEL WRITING WAS NEVER EASIER**. I thought, oh boy, lead me to it, for if I haven't mentioned it, a writer's life is consummate hell. The ad read:

Create and track your characters.

Invent situations that work.

Consummate climaxes.

Triumph over conclusions.

Pay for our software out of your first royalty check.

Everything you need to be a successful novelist for five hundred dollars.

Naturally I clicked through to find out more about this miracle and on the next opening in Ta-DAAA print I got its name:

Success guaranteed with . . .

STORYGRINDER

Lead me to it, I thought. Of course electronic miracles are not for me, for I am an artist, but given that Mom had just sent me one of her inspiration bonus checks, I thought it might be just the thing for Spud. Plus, if I downloaded it for him, I could look over the monkey's shoulder and see if **Storygrinder** knew any tricks, like five hundred dollars, is there anything in that black bag for me?

So I read the fumpf out loud, thinking to get Spud's attention. "Success guaranteed," I read. "Spud, get a load of this. They can show you how to write *Bright Lights, Big City*," I told him, which, unfortunately, didn't get a rise out of him, not so much as an ooook.

Then I said, "Or if you wanted, maybe even The Bible."

Nothing. "Or . . . Or . . . " Then I was inspired. "A book like Animal Farm."

8

Bingo. Spud's head came up.

I thought, if a hundred monkeys typing take a thousand years to write a novel, this software ought to be enough to keep this one off my back for thirty years, which is about as long as these labor-intensive rhesus guys are supposed to last.

I bought **Storygrinder** for the monkey. One look and it was clear the software was not for me. It was, frankly, simplistic. One click and I could write *The Last of the Mohicans*, which, hel-LO, has already been done.

"Here you go, dude," I told him, and on the premise that monkey see, monkey do, I walked him through the first stages.

"It was the best of times, it was the worst of times," I wrote, like Charles Dickens, although the application gave me options that would let me write like one of the Brontes. A flag popped up:

DID YOU MEAN TO REPEAT YOURSELF? FIX.

So I wrote, "Call me Ishmael." Naturally it questioned my spelling, but what the hey, Spud sidled over to watch.

Then I started writing a book that began, "It was love at first sight. The first time Yossarian saw the chaplain he fell madly in love with him," and the monkey's interest in life came back with a jerk.

"Oook!" Spud said, and he hurtled in and shoved me out of the way with the force of his entire body. "Oook-ooook!"

"Good boy." Although it would have been fun to play with the software at least a little bit I backed off, relieved and delighted to see him distracted and busy for a change. "Go to it, little dude. Onward," I said, "and upward with the arts."

His eyes lit up.

I said helpfully, "I'd click on the button that says, Start my book."

For the first time since I brought him home to my apartment, Spud sounded positively joyful. "Oook!"

It did my heart good to see him pounding away with both fists, and better yet, given the nature of the buttons and whistles attached to this new application, which not only tracks your spelling and punctuation but also tells you when you're depending too heavily on certain verbs or using an adjective like "magnificent" more than once in your whole entire novel, the little bugger is a genius with the mouse.

A month with **Storygrinder** and Spud bounded past the pound-and-click method and into proper keyboarding before I noticed what was up. For the first time since I gave him the laptop he started using his tiny fingers. To my surprise the animal has a stretch that any concert pianist would envy and man, you ought to see his attack! After a month he was up to speed and the next thing I knew he had outrun me, typing so fast that there was no telling where it would end. Next time I checked his output almost matched mine, and as I was in the final third of my next attempt after *Screed of the Outrageous* and frankly, my best shot at going for the gold, so what I had thought of as a gimmick to keep Spud out of my hair ended up with us in a footrace for fame.

He was hard at it and instead of being relieved by my first weeks of freedom from his constant sulking—to say nothing of the fierce, judgmental attention I got back in the days when I was working well and he was bored—I was proud, but I was also a little bit afraid.

The worst part was that where we used to print out every night and talk about what he'd done, now at night when Spud was done for the day he would slam the laptop shut with this don't-even-think-about-it glare. And do you know, he had the thing password-protected? I ask you, who taught him that? Either he was jealous of **Storygrinder** and afraid I'd siphon off a copy and get the jump on him, or he didn't want me finding out what his novel looked like.

What it looked like, it looked like it was a thousand pages long and I had to start wondering whether it was *War and Peace* he was writing, only with rhesus monkeys instead of Russians, or this century's answer to *Gone with the Wind*. Monkeys, you never know, and he wasn't tipping his hand. Naturally I'd started out with this thinking I would keep close tabs on him, of course he'd want me to print it out so we could workshop what he was writing the way we did in the good old days, but I'd do it better this time around. Like, more praise for what he was doing, but definitely constructive criticism over cookies and cocoa like we used to do, late at night.

How sharper than a serpent's tooth is the ungrateful protégé. The one time I tried to hook up his laptop to the printer cable, Spud latched on to me like that thing out of Alien and plastered his smelly body to my face. I went lunging around blindly with his legs in a stranglehold so tight that I couldn't breathe and his fists clamped on my ears. I had to stagger into the kitchen and duck my head in the dirty dishwater to make him let go. After that I had to make certain promises, like you do when you have to get somebody off your case because they're all up in your face.

I retreated to my corner and he stayed in his forever typing, typing, typing, and when I tried to make things better with a tactful smile or an inoffensive remark—even when I came at him with bananas and candy he would get all defensive and slam the laptop shut with that look. He was what you'd have to call vindictive, so after a while I backed off and tried my best to get back to *Deranged All Over Town* which will rival *Bright Lights, Big City* if I can ever get it back on track which given what happened with the monkey's novel, gets harder and harder to do.

The little bastard sent it off to an agent without even telling me it was done.

I'd just as soon spare myself the details of what happened next, but since the monkey can't open bank accounts or deposit checks not to mention endorsing them convincingly, I've benefited a bit. Prada and Gucci everything, as Spud could care less about outfits and frankly, he's careless about his looks. A specially fitted car seat for trips to public appearances and book signings, where he has generously allowed me to stand in for him. In fact, as far as the world knows it is I, Billy Masterton (that's the renowned W.B. Masterton, Pulitzer Prize-winning author) who did the deed. The monkey has nothing to complain about. He has his very own room in our Brooklyn town house and I bought him three computers loaded with **Storygrinder** in his own special work area that I've fitted out so he can write his miserable, best-selling potboilers three at a time for all I care. Between us, the monkey and I put James Patterson so far behind in the popularity sweepstakes that the man can put his entire staff to work 24/7 and still never catch up on any bestseller list. And if I get the money and the credit?

What Spud doesn't know, he doesn't have to know.

The trouble is, this whole mad success up to and including best-sellerdom, has me working day and night on the little bastard's behalf, which means that since it all hit the fan and sprayed money on us, my cherished *Deranged All Over Town* is advancing at the rate of one line a day, and I'm sad to say the line I finally manage is one I'm so pressured to write that I don't get time or space in my head to think it through, which means first thing next morning, I have to delete.

Plus, Spud has me answering every single piece of his fan mail, sending thank-yous for those endless and insultingly expensive gifts and maintaining his pages on MySpace, where he has ten thousand friends, and on Facebook, where he has a mere eight thousand, although my carpals are seriously tunneled just from scrolling through the stuff, never mind the hours I spend virtually sitting in front of W.B. Masterton's virtual bookstore on Second Life.

And the monkey? I think he just finished this century's answer to *The Brothers Karamazov*, but with more sex and a lot more guilt. Where does he get off, thinking he knows anything about guilt? He, who smothered my brilliant career like an infant in its crib.

But what's killing me, if you want to know what kills me, is the blog. I don't get to see what the monkey writes until he posts it. I sneak looks at his printed works while I'm waiting for his platoons of fans to flood the auditorium where I am speaking, or for booksellers to unbar the doors to let the next wave of frantic admirers in, but that isn't enough. His work is pretty good, which, frankly, is depressing, but not half as depressing as discovering from one of these gooshy-eyed teenagers or inspired surfer dudes that the son of a bitch has been dissing me on his blog.

If you want to read what Spud says about me, go ahead and read it, you'll find more than you want to know about our relationship plastered on my author page at: *http://www.wbmastertonauthor.net*

I only looked the once. After everything I've done for Spud, the software and the encouragement and the plush cover for his rotten car seat in the Beemer and the patent leather evening slippers because after he saw mine he wouldn't stop oook-ooking until I had some especially made for him; in spite of me buying him his very own organ grinder the ungrateful little bastard had the nerve to write this very day: "Those of you who think I know the way to happiness might as well know that success isn't everything. You may think I am happy because of the American Book Award and all, but as long as I am the prisoner of a shitty writer, happiness is forever and eternally out of reach; and if any of you care about me ever, you have to come to my house and GET ME OUT."

That to his eight million hits a day, forwarded to all their friends and acquaintances all over the English-speaking world!

OK, if that's how it is, that's how it's going to be.

Well, if that's what he thinks of me . . .

I'll show him.

The ape's got four more novels banked in those computers, and even if I can't crack his passwords, he's already raking in so much that it's no skin off my butt if he crashes and bursts into flames, so, cool. I'm fixed for life. I don't want to hurt the monkey, really, and I won't hit him with a bill of particulars. I won't even do the gratifying thing and smash his head in with an axe.

Given the pillow, which I've soaked in chloroform, the little fucker won't feel a thing.

In South Africa I heard the story of Happy Sindane, the child who walked into a police station and told the officer on duty that he'd been abducted from white parents and raised in a black South African township where he was treated like a slave. More than one Afrikaner couple who had lost children rushed to claim him. Opinions on the true story as well as how Happy is doing today vary, and me? I thought it was time to write the story I'd always wanted to write, about a boy who had been raised by wolves.

WHAT WOLVES KNOW

When you have been raised by wolves people expect better of you, but you have no idea what they mean by *better*.

Happy comes out of the crate panting and terrified.

When you have been raised by wolves, you expect better of people.

Injured in the struggle before the dart bit him and his world went away, Happy blinks into the white glare.

A dark shape moves into the blinding light. Sound explodes, a not-quite bark. "Welcome home!"

This is nothing like home. Then why is the smell of this place so familiar? Troubled, Happy backs away, sucking his torn paw.

He hears a not-quite purr. "Is that him?"

"Back off Susan, you're scaring him. Handsome bastard, under all the filth." The dark shape gets bigger. "Hold still so we can look at you."

Happy scrambles backward.

"Wait, dammit. What's the matter with your hand?"

The not-quite barker is not quite a wolf. Pink, he is, and naked, except for fur on top, with all his pink parts wrapped like a package in tan cloth.

A . . . Hunter is the first thought that comes. Happy has never been this close to one, not that he chooses to remember. He looks down. His body is choking. There is cloth on Happy too! It won't come off no matter how hard he shakes. He tears at it with his teeth.

The not-wolf yaps, "Stop that! We want you looking good for the press conference."

Happy does not know what this means. With his back hairs rising, he gives the wolf's first warning. He *grrrs* at the man. Man. That's one of Happy's words. And the other? Woman. The rest, he will not parse. The man grabs for him even though Happy rolls back his lips to show his fangs. The wolf's second warning. Now, wolves, wolves know when close is too close, and they keep their distance. With wolves, you always know where you are.

Wolves don't stare like that unless they are about to spring and rip your throat out, but unlike the wolf, man has no code. If Happy bolts, will this one bring him down and close those big square teeth in him?

"Hold still! What happened to your hand?"

Happy does as taught: he snarls. The wolf's last warning.

"Now, stop. I didn't bring you all this way to hurt you."

"Brent, he's hurt." The other voice is not at all like barking. "Oh, you poor thing, you're bleeding."

The man growls, "Come here. We can't let the people see blood."

Happy bunches his shoulders and drops to a crouch, but the man keeps on coming. Happy backs and backs. Oh, that thing he does with his face, too many teeth showing. Just stop! The more Happy scrambles away the more the man crowds him. At his back the walls meet like the jaws of a trap. He tips back his and howls. "*Ah-whoooooooo . . .* "

"Quiet! What will people think?"

"*Ah-whooooooo.*" Happy stops breathing. He is listening. Not one wolf responds. There is an unending din in this bright place but there are no wolves anywhere. Even though he was running away when the humans caught him, Happy's heart shudders. He is separated from his pack.

"Shut up. Shut up and I'll get you a present."

There are words Happy knows and words he doesn't know, but he remembers only one of them well enough to speak. "Oh," he barks bravely, even though he is cornered. "Oh, oh!"

"That's better. Now, hold still." When a human shows its teeth at you it means something completely different from what you are taught to watch out for, but you had better watch out for it.

The woman purrs, "Brent, you're scaring him!"

Woman. Another of Happy's words. The sound she makes is nothing like a howl, but he thinks they are kindred.

"Are you going to help me or what?" The man lunges. Should Happy attack? Other words rush in. Clothes. Arms. Clothes cover the man's stiff arms and he is waving them madly. How can Happy tear out the throat with all that in the way? Can he bring the man down before he pulls out his . . .

Another of Happy's words comes back. Gun. It makes him shudder.

"Brent, he's shaking."

"I'm only trying to help him!"

"Oh, you poor thing." Sweet, that voice. She sounds like his . . . Another word he used to know. *Mother.* Parts of Happy change in ways he does not understand. She says, "Look at him Brent, he's shaking!"

"Oh," Happy barks hysterically. "Oh, oh!"

"Come on, now. Calm down or I'll give you another shot."

The man makes a grab for him. In another minute those hands will close in his fur. Grief touches Happy like a feather, for like the man with his grasping fingers and not-quite barking, Happy is more pink than fur. It is confusing.

"Don't be afraid," the woman says. "Come on, sweetie, come to Mother."

Happy will not know exactly who he means when he thinks, *This is nothing like Mother.* It does not explain, but measures the extent of his confusion. In this and every other circumstance, Happy's position is ambiguous.

This is not one of Happy's words: ambiguous. He has been pulled out of a place he can't explain into a world he doesn't understand and it makes him sick with grief.

He doesn't belong anywhere.

"Oh," Happy yelps. Then more words come. "Oh, don't!" Although he has outlived his mother Sonia and half his litter-mates, in wolf years, Happy is still a puppy.

He does what any puppy does when cornered and outnumbered. He rolls over and shows his throat.

"For God's sake, kid, get up. What will people think? Get him up, Susan, they're staring."

Others come. Men. Women. People with—how does he know this—cameras! People are pointing their cameras. Kept out by the rope that protects the live baggage claim area, strangers jostle, straining to see.

There are words Happy knows and words he does not choose to understand. She growls, "You should have thought about that before you snatched him."

"Not snatched," the man says firmly. He says in a loud voice because they are not alone here, "*Rescued*. This is not what you think," he shouts to the onlookers. "This is my long-lost brother, I went through hell to save him."

"Stuff it, Brent. They don't care who he is or what you did."

"I rescued him from a wolf pack in the wild!"

She says, "They aren't interested, they're embarrassed."

He shouts, "They stole him from our family!" He is trying to get Happy on his feet but Happy flops every whichway, like any puppy. Brent tells the crowd, "When they found him, the police called me."

Happy gnashes at his hand.

"Ow!" Brent shouts over Happy's head, "Olmstead. My name is on the dog tag!"

Dog tag. It is confusing. Is he less wolf than dog?

"Hush, Brent," the woman says. "Let me do this."

Flat on his back with his paws raised, Happy lifts his head.

Unlike the pink man, the woman is gentle and she smells good. Hair. Not fur. Nice hair. Clothes like flowers.

"Sweetie, are you all right?"

Oh, that soft purr. Happy wriggles, hoping to be stroked, but there will be no stroking. What was that word he used to have? *Ma'am*. It doesn't come out of his throat the way it's supposed to. At least this part comes back: if you can't speak when they make a question, you nod. Happy nods. She shows all her teeth ("See, Brent?") and he shows all his teeth right back to her in . . . Oh! This is a smile. You do it because they expect it. You always did. From nowhere Happy can name there comes a string of words: *Songs my mother taught me.* Now, why does this make his heart break? He doesn't know what it means and he doesn't want to know where it's coming from. *Songs my mother . . .*

She touches his hair. Parts of Happy go soft and—oh! Another gets hard. Smile for her, she is soft in interesting places. At eighteen Happy feels like a puppy, but he isn't, not really.

Then she prods him with her toe. Her voice drops so he will know she is serious. "OK then, get up."

Slowly Happy rolls over and rises on his hind legs, although he is not all that accustomed. Susan shows her teeth at him, but in a nice way, and her voice lightens. "That's better. Let's get him in the car."

With wolves, you are always certain. Your wolf mother loves you. Get out of line and she will swat you. Grey Sonia did it as needed. Get too far out of line and your father will kill you. Happy bears the marks of Timbo's fangs in his tender hide—this torn ear, that spot on his flank where the gash is healing.

If you are male and live long enough, you will have to kill your father. It is the way of the pack.

The wolves aren't Happy's real parents. In a way this is news to him, but from the beginning he had suspicions. Happy's captor—er, rescuer— doesn't know what Happy knows, and what the boy knows is buried so deep in early childhood that it is only now coming to the surface. All his life Happy has run after the hope that the next thing will be better.

He only left the woods after Timbo tried to kill him.

He thought his real family would be kinder, although for reasons he only partially understands, he had forgotten them.

In fact, he was the last child in a big family. Happy made one too many, and the mother put him in clean clothes when they went out but at home he was forgotten, sitting for hours in his own messes. She yelled at him for being in the way. One did things that hurt, but he will not remember which person. When he cried nobody cared. They didn't much notice. He wasn't supposed to hear his mother snap, "And this one's my mistake."

Words are like weapons, no wonder he forgot.

The night the wolves took him, Happy was alone in his little stroller in a mall parking lot, hours after the family car pulled out with everyone else inside. He was so thoroughly combed and scrubbed that it may have been an accident, not neglect that found him there in the dark, crying. A central fact about Happy is that he doesn't know.

He cried and cried. Then the wolves swarmed down on Happy in his stroller, and the bawling toddler lifted his arms to them. The big males paced, slavering. The child didn't read their watchful eyes but Sonia knew. She turned on them, bunched and snarling. They backed away. Then she nosed Happy. He looked into her yellow eyes and clamped his arms around her magnificent neck. He buried his face deep in her thick white ruff. Timbo picked Happy out of the stroller and dropped him at Sonia's feet. The pack took the message and backed off. He has been running with them ever since.

The first thing Sonia did was rip off his little outfit with her teeth and lick him raw so he would smell of her and not the other pack, the one he quickly forgot. The only thing left of them was the scrap of metal dangling from his neck. Timbo wanted that off too. Even though he was the leader, Sonia rolled back her lips and snarled. It stayed. Happy ran with the wolves but the cold square tap-tapped on naked flesh, a sign that he was different. Sonia fed her new pup off her sagging belly and licked his tears away. Then she dragged him through dirt and rotting dead things until he was fit to run with the other cubs and from that night on she was his mother. The rule of the pack: never get between a cub and its mother. He knew he was loved.

Timbo did not love Happy, but he protected him.

In time the pack forgot that he was not one of them. Howling to stay in touch, they ran at night, *ah-whooo*, ranging wide, *ah-whoooooo*, and with the knife he found on a dead man, Happy was as good a hunter as any. Even Timbo came to respect him. This, he thought, was all there was to life. The howling and the hunting, Happy and his litter-mates running free in the night.

When you are raised by wolves but are not one of them, time is never what you think. You do not age at the same rate.

Happy he was, yet living with the wolves, nursing injuries when his litter-mates grew up and the challenges began, Happy thought: *This can't be my real family. Some day my father the duke and my mother the movie star will come for me.* Where did these words come from? Who were his people, really?

The litters he ran with grew up much, much faster than Happy.

It was a mystery. The other cubs grew tall and rangy while he was still an awkward pup. They flirted and rutted, things Happy thought he understood and longed for vaguely but was not built to do. He was shaped all wrong, too young in ways Sonia would not explain to him; she was, after all, a mother and there are things mothers keep from you until it's time. His litter-mates frolicked and did things Happy was not yet old enough to do. When he tried to play they snapped: *don't bother me.* In time, he played with their cubs. Their cubs grew up. Sonia got old. Then Sonia died, and with Sonia gone, craggy Timbo began stalking him, licking his chops.

Now Happy was old enough to do all those things he had been too young to do before, and Timbo?

Timbo had to die. Happy had reached the age of kill or be killed. Wolves know that when you are grown, you have to kill your father. Kill him before he kills you.

He thought he could take Timbo in a fight so he scent-marked a tree, making clear his intentions. The wolf's challenge!

He bunched himself as Timbo circled, snarling. Imagine his surprise. The gouge in his flank goes all the way from *here* down to *here*. Now, a wolf can lick all the hurt places, but Happy wasn't built to reach the places wolves can reach without trying. Pain drove him sobbing out of the woods.

When you have been raised by wolves, you know what to expect.

Foolish to expect better of people.

Nursing the fresh gash in his flank, he watched the building, men walking back in front of lighted windows. He heard a sound like a forgotten lullaby: human voices. He limped out of the woods, whimpering, "Oh, oh, oh." Then, when he least expected it, a word came to him. He pointed his nose at the sky. "Oh, help!"

He expected helping hands, kind words, but big men clattered out shouting, "Stop where you are!" They were nothing like he expected. Happy froze.

Somebody yelled, "What *is* that?"

Somebody else yelled, "Some kind of *animal*."

They were so angry! *This is nothing like I thought.*

Happy did what wolves do when they are in trouble. He howled. *Ah-whoooo.* One by one his brothers responded but the howls were scattered, the howlers far away. Wolves know never to come out of the woods, no matter who is calling. *Ah-whooooooooo!*

The men pulled shields over their faces and raised their guns. Guns: a word Happy didn't quite know. In the struggle, the chain around his neck parted, and the only scrap of his old life fell into their hands. Why did he imagine it made him special?

He limped back into the woods. The other wolves—his brothers!—smelled men on him. He was ruined for life in the woods and there was as well . . . what? The curiosity. When the men fell on Happy, he felt his flesh smacking into human flesh and there was no difference between them. Even clothed, his attackers were more like Happy than Happy was like the wolves. Like the missing limb that hurts at night, he felt the ghost family. Wolves run in packs or they prowl alone; they kill and are killed and that's the end of it. Men have families.

Night after night Happy doubled back on the clearing. He was drawn by half-remembered smells—hot food, the scent of bulky, not-wolf bodies—and sounds: music and forks clattering, the buddabuddabudda of low, not-wolf voices. Circling, Happy yearned for something he missed terribly. As for what . . . He was not certain.

Alone, Happy howled to the heavens. He wanted to bring out Timbo, even though he knew Timbo would kill him. *Ah-whoooo.* If they fought to the death, one way or the other it would end his confusion. Happy's howling filled the woods but not one wolf howled in reply. *Ah-whooooooo!*

The loneliness was intense.

This is why Happy did what wolves never do. For the second time, he left the woods. For a long time, he circled the police station. Then he dropped to his haunches on the front walk and howled to heaven. He howled for all he was worth. Unless he was howling for everything he was losing.

Now look.

The needle Brent used to get him out of the airport left Happy inert, but aware. They are riding along, he and Brent and this Susan, he can smell her. The car is much smaller than the van that took him to the hospital after the fight at the police station. They sewed him up and Brent came. Happy did not know him, but he knew him. He rolled off the bed and fell into a crouch, ready to lunge. Guards came. He struggled but the doctors gave him to Brent anyway. They said he was next of kin. Family.

. . . Brent?

It was on the dog tag. That's Brent's word for it. But why was Brent's name on the dog tag? *Am I his pet?* Happy wonders. *Do I belong to him?* He is no dog. He runs with wolves.

He does not like Brent. Keep your eyes shut, Happy. Keep them closed and he won't know you're in here.

He is riding along between them. The nice soft woman is soft, but not as nice as he thought. She says over Happy's head, "Why in hell didn't you hose him down before we got in the car?"

"It's not my fault he stinks."

"You could have put him in the trunk!"

Smelly breath mists Happy's face as Brent peers at him, but he keeps his eyes clenched. "Lie down with wolves and you smell like one. You hear?"

"Save your breath, he's out cold." The woman riding along next to him, what does this Brent call her? Susan. Susan gives Happy a little shake; his head rolls back and settles on her arm. "If you want him smiling on TV, you'd better revive him."

"Not now, Suze. Live at Five next Thursday."

"Like they aren't already waiting at Chateau Marmont?"

"No way! We can't go public until Dad makes the deal." *Dad.* The word Happy refused to remember. His teeth clash and his hackles rise. It is hard to keep from growling.

"You should have thought of that at the airport. Mr. Show Biz." She goes on in Brent's voice, "'I rescued him.' Like you didn't see the camcorders. Screen shots. Everybody knows!"

"Well, tough. Nobody sees him until the press conference. Dad is talking eight figures."

Happy's insides shift. He is confused. Wolves don't think in figures.

Brent barks, "Driver, get off at National."

"What are you *thinking?*"

"Gonna hide him!"

"Not in this town," Susan says. Distracted, she's let parts of herself flow into Happy. She thinks he is asleep. Parts of him flow back and she lets him.

"Outskirts. Inland empire. The valley."

She says, "Too close." Happy leans a little closer; she shrugs him off, but he slips back and she lets him. It is hard for him to keep from smiling. They ride along like this for a while. At last she says thoughtfully, "Your mom stayed back in Caverness, right?"

"She did," Brent says, and then he just stops talking.

The car rounds a corner and Happy leans into the body next to his, but only a little bit. He can feel her voice vibrating in his bones. "Then take him to your mom's."

Warm, she is so warm.

"No way. She hasn't forgiven me for losing him."

Something changes in the car. "You lost him?"

Happy's ears prick.

The woman has asked a question that Brent won't answer. He says instead, "Come on, Susan. What are we going to do?"

"You lost your very own brother?"

"Not really. Well, sort of."

Happy is trying to make his mouth into the right shape to frame the big question. Even if he could, he knows not to bring it out. It is disturbing.

"Brent, what were you *thinking?*"

The fat man whines, "Mom *said* he was a mistake. I thought she would thank me, but she freaked."

Mom. Another word Happy can't parse. Oh. Same as mother. That word. Soft, he remembers. Other things. He will not remember other things.

"She never forgave Dad either."

"So he lives in L.A. Got that." Susan adds drily, "Too bad you can't divorce your kids."

"Could we not talk about this please?"

She stiffens—*is it something I did?* "Back there." Her voice goes up a notch. "Look. Tell me that's not a mobile unit."

"Holy crap, it's TV Eight. Driver, take Laurel Canyon."

The car goes around many curves and up, up, higher than Happy remembers being, and whenever they round a curve too fast he bumps against Susan's soft parts like a sleeper with no control over what he is doing, but in all the uphill and downhill and veering around corners he never, ever bumps Brent, not even accidentally.

He is aware of a hand waving in front of his closed eyes. A pinch. He wants to play dead but he can't stop himself from flinching. The needle bites. The world goes away again. He can't be sure about the days or the nights, which they are or how many.

Happy sleeps and he wakes up, then he sleeps again, and in the hours they drive he can never be certain which is which, or whether the woman is touching him by accident or because she intends it.

At last the car crunches uphill and stops for the last time. Happy's head comes up. The smells when Brent hustles him out of the car and hauls him to his feet on the hard, hard street are terrible and familiar. They are climbing steps to a wooden . . . porch. Happy knows almost all the words now. Brent slaps the door and a remote bell rings. Footsteps come.

Terrified, he begins to struggle.

"Brent, he's waking up!"

"Not for long."

Happy yips as the needle goes into his butt. What they do and say when the door opens is forever lost to him.

When he wakes everything is as it was and nothing is the same. Will his life always be like this? Happy is curled up in his room. He knows it is his room because it used to be his room in the old life, and he knows from the sights and smells that nothing has changed here. It feels good and bad, lying in the old place. From here he can see the pretend bearskin rug in the center of the room with its plastic fangs and empty glass eyes, and lodged in the corner, the faded pink volleyball that he remembers from his very first time on the floor in this room, and his very last day here.

When wolves quit the lair they stalk away leaving it untouched because they are done with it forever; they do not expect to come this way again. Is this what not-wolf mothers do?

Not-wolf mothers leave the lost son's room exactly as it was in hopes he will come back, but there is no way Happy can know this. He has no idea who he is or why he feels both good and bad about being back here, although he is a little frightened. He doesn't know why all this makes him miss Sonia so terribly or why, on that night so long ago, his hateful big brother slammed the door to the family car and let them drive away without him.

Brother. That's what Brent is.

Oh.

Happy would throw back his head and howl for Sonia but his hideout is constricted, the woods are lost to him and Sonia is dead now. He could howl for this other mother but before, when he was small and crying out lonely, she was a long time coming and when she did . . . There are things you don't remember and things you don't want to know.

Can you want to belong in two places at once and know you don't belong in either?

At least Happy is safe. When he came to, instinct sent him off the bed where they'd dumped him and under here, where they won't see him before he sees them. Holed up, he counts the cobwebs hanging from rusting springs. He wants to weep for the blue dogs and pink teddies cavorting on the plastic mattress cover. He is under his old crib.

When you can't go back to being what you used to be, you go back to what you were in the beginning. You were safe because she loved you, and Happy does not know whether he means the old mother, or Sonia.

The sounds in the house are so different from the crackle and whisper of the woods that it takes time to name them. The hum of the refrigerator, the washing machine grinding because—Happy looks down— they have changed his hospital rags for gray stuff like the clothes— clothes!—he used to wear when he was a . . . The bark of the furnace kicking in. A telephone ringing, ringing, ringing and soft voices: women talking, a strange man's voice downstairs in the hall. Brent is arguing with the other.

The smells in this house at this moment in his life are enough to break Happy's heart. He can smell mold in the foundations, laundry products; dust, in this room in particular; there is the residue of memory and oh, God . . . *God?* There is the smell of something cooking. Whatever else is going on in this place he used to know so well and had forgotten completely, *Mom* is baking brownies. Everything waters. Happy's mouth, his nose, his eyes.

It's getting dark, but nobody comes. Cramped as he is, stuck under the crib for too long when he is used to running free in the woods, Happy is restless and twitching. He thought by this time Brent would be in here raging; they could have fought. He could have killed the brother. Unless Brent jabbed another dart into Happy before he could strike and dragged him out. Instead the shouting stayed downstairs, sliding into the low, grating whine of a long argument. Then doors slammed and the cars roared away. Now there is no more talking. The machines have stopped. There is almost-silence in the house, except for the stir of a body he knows, approaching. What does he remember from the last time he heard her footsteps? Nothing he chooses to remember. Trembling, he pulls himself out from under the crib just long enough to run his hand along the bedroom door. He finds the lock. He loves the click.

There is a long silence in the hall outside his room. Then there is the soft footfall as she goes away.

Alone in the tight space he has created, Happy considers. Wolves are taught to lay back in this situation, and he is more wolf than anything else. He's been out cold for a long time, and there are problems. Wolves

27

wake up ravenous. Happy hasn't fed since he came to in the crate and emptied his dish. Another thing: a wolf never fouls the den where he is sleeping. When the old house has been still for a long time he eases out from under the crib, unlocks the door and leaves the room.

Where Happy loped along on all fours when he ran with the pack, race memory kicks in, now that he is here. This place he hoped to forget was not built for wolves. He stands and prowls the house on bare feet. She has left food: some kind of meat on the kitchen table, brownies. He empties the plate, pulling strings of plastic wrap out of the half-chewed chocolate squares before he swallows them. Now, the other thing? As Sonia's cub he never fouled the lair. There is a bathroom just off the kitchen. Happy cringes. What was he supposed to do back then, when he was small and trapped in here? Who used to hit him and hit him for forgetting?

He touches the nail where the belt used to hang, and the ghost family rises up like the missing limb miraculously restored. Growling, he quits the house.

Can you ever walk out of your old skin and back into the woods where you were so happy, running with the wolves? There are no woods outside this house, just streets and cement sidewalks and metal fences around house after house after identical house; there are few trees and no hillside which means no caves, no undergrowth and no place to dig, where he can pull in brush to cover himself; it is worrisome and sad. The urban sky is like a cup with Happy trapped under it. He relieves himself and goes back inside. The old room is safe, now that he knows he can lock it.

His days don't change.

At night he goes out to eat what she leaves and to relieve himself. One night it was a meat pie, another, a whole ham.

People come. Sometimes they call outside his room, but Happy will not answer. The wolf doesn't howl unless there is another like him out there, howling or yipping the reply. Brent comes, but not Susan. In the long periods he spends curled under the crib, Happy thinks about this. Her body, expanding with every breath as they rode along in the car. The way it felt, and how he misses it.

If he can't do what wolves do, he understands, he wants to do what he *can* do with Brent's woman. How the parts go together remains a mystery; he only knows what he needs. Brent comes with a doctor, a talking-doctor, he says through the locked door. The doctor talks for a long time, but wolves have no need for words. The doctor goes away. Brent comes with a man who promises money. When you have nothing, you need nothing. Brent comes with another man, who makes threats. Wolves will not be threatened. When you are threatened, you go to ground and stay there. They go away. Brent comes back. He shouts through the locked door. "Just tell us what you want and I'll bring it! Anything, I promise, if you'll just come out so we can get started."

There is one thing, but Happy will not say it.

The brother hits a whine that Happy remembers from the time he refuses to remember. Oh. *That* Brent. This one. Same as he ever was, just older.

Brent snarls, "Dammit to hell, are you in there?"

No words needed here, either. None spoken.

Brent comes back with a woman. The scent brings Happy's head up. It is a woman. "He's in there? Why is he in there when he knows I'm out here?" She goes on in a loud, harsh voice. *Do you know who I am?"*

It's the wrong woman.

"Listen, baby brother. This is your new agent standing out here in the cold. If you know what's good for you, come out and say hello to Marla Parterre. She can make or break you."

Time passes.

"She's from C.A.A.!"

The agent goes away.

The mother comes. *Mhmhmmm.*

Brent shouts. "How can we sell his story if he won't come out? Dammit, Mom . . . "

She says in the old tone that makes Happy tremble, "Don't you dare talk to your mother like that." He knows her voice, but he always did. He just doesn't know what she used to say to him.

"I'm calling Dad," Brent says. "Dad will get him out."

Then his mother says, "Your father is not coming back here, Brent."

"But Mom, he got us front money in six figures, and we have to . . . "
Figures. Happy is troubled by the figures. Skaters, he thinks, short skirts,
girls gliding in circles, and wonders how he knows. Women, he thinks,
trembling. With their pretty figures.

"No." Her voice is huge. "Not after what he did. No!"

Brent brings a locksmith. There is talk of breaking in. She says, No.
She says, over her dead body. Will Brent kill her? Happy shivers. They
argue. She uses that huge voice on Brent and they go away. She bakes.
Sometimes now, she leaves the food outside his door, hoping he'll come
out to see. Happy lies low until she sighs and takes the untouched tray
back to the kitchen.

At night she lingers in the hallway outside the room. She does not
speak. He won't, or can't. Sometimes he hears her crying.

Happy waits. Sooner or later she always goes away. She leaves things
on the kitchen table. Meat, which Happy devours. Fruit, which he
ignores. Something she baked. She leaves the door to that old, bad bathroom open so he won't have to go outside to relieve himself. What's the
matter with her, did she forget? The sight of the toilet, the naked hook
where the belt hung, makes Happy tremble.

Outside is worse than inside. Nights like these make Happy want to
throw back his head and howl. Alone in these parts, he could howl to the
skies and never hear their voices. The other wolves are deep in the old
woods, and he is far, far away. He wants to cry out for Sonia, for the
past, when everything was simple, but one sound will bring police down
on him with their bats and rifles, visors on bug helmets covering their
faces.

Happy knows what wolves know. You never, ever break cover.

Wolves know what Happy is only now learning. He can't go back!
Happy's feet are soft and his muscles are slack from days under the crib.
He'd never make it and if he did, Timbo would outrun him in seconds.
Timbo would kill him in one lunge, and even if he could kill Timbo? His
parts and the bitch wolves' parts don't match. They have forgotten he was
ever one of them.

He sits on his haunches and tries to think. He is distracted by the buzz
of blue lights on poles overhead, where he is used to looking up and

seeing trees; by a sky so milky with reflected glare that stars don't show; by the play of strident human voices in the houses all around, the mechanical sounds of a hundred household objects and the rush of cars on the great road that brought them here. Looking up at the house, he groans.

He doesn't belong in there.

He doesn't belong out here, either.

He gets up. Sighs. Stands back. Upstairs in the house, there is a single light. She is awake. Now he knows, and knowing hurts somehow. She doesn't go into her lair and sleep after she leaves Happy's door the way he imagined. She sits up all night waiting. He steals back inside and goes upstairs to his room. Inside, he closes the door. Tonight, he will not turn the lock.

After not very long—did she hear or does she just know?—the bedroom door opens. She says his name.

"Happy?"

He always knew Happy was his name. This is just the first time he's heard it spoken since he joined the wolves and made Sonia his mother. Does Brent not know? The name Brent calls him is different. Is this big, leaden woman who smells like despair the only one who knows who he really is? In the hospital where the police took him, Brent shouted at the doctor like a pet owner claiming a dog that had strayed. "Olmstead. It's right here on his tag! Olmstead. Frederick."

Her voice is soft as the darkness. "Oh, Happy. I'm so glad you came back."

There is another of those terrible long silences in which he hears her shifting from foot to foot in the dark, pretending she's not crying.

She says, "You don't have to come out from under there if you don't want to."

She says, "Are you OK?"

It's been a long time since words came out of Happy; he only had a few when they lost him. He isn't ready. Will he ever be?

She says, "Is it OK if I sit down on the bed? I mean, since you're not using it?"

Words. He is thinking about words. He knows plenty now, all that talk going on outside his locked door. He has heard dozens. He could spit out a word for her if he wanted, but which one? He waits until she gets tired of him waiting.

She says softly, "I'm sorry about everything."

Then she says, all in a rush, "Oh Happy. Can you ever forgive me?"

This is not a question Happy can answer.

There is a lot of nothing in the silence that follows. She is breathing the way Sonia did before she died. It's a rasp of pain, but the mother smells all right to Happy. Wolves know nothing of the pain of waiting, nor do they know anything about the pain of guilt.

Her voice shakes in a way he is not used to. "Son?"

Son. It does not parse. Happy rummages through all his words, but there is no right one.

The first morning light is showing in the window; Happy sees it touch the fake fur of the ruggybear; he sees it outlining the hands she keeps folded on her plump knees and he watches as it picks out every vein in her sad, swelling ankles. She says, "It's all my fault, you know."

What should he do now, bare all his teeth the way they do, to show her he's friendly? Beg her to go on? Howl until she stops? He doesn't know.

She says, "I never should have had you." Slumped on the edge of the bed she leans sideways and tilts her head, trying to see under the crib where Happy's green eyes glint. He makes no expression a human could recognize, although Sonia would know it without question. She says, "Poor little thing."

A sound stirs the air, a kind of shudder. He wonders but does not ask, *Mother, did you sob?*

Her head comes up. "Happy?"

Startled, Happy looks inside himself—*Did I?* There is nothing he has to say to her.

Then she just begins. "You don't know what it's like living with a man who beats you. I was pregnant with Brent and our parents forced the marriage, crazy thing to happen in this day and time, like it ruined his life to marry me, we had too many babies, and who—*who* got me pregnant every time? Do you see what I mean?"

32

Happy won't speak. The words come so fast that he chooses not to understand them. *Ow, it hurts!*

Never mind, nothing he says or does not say will stop her. "Hal hated his life so he drank, and the more he drank the more he hated it so he drank some more and the more he drank, the madder he got and nothing I could do or say would make him happy. Every little thing I did used to make him mad at me. The madder he got the more he hit me, but he never hit me when I was pregnant. Oh, Happy, do you understand?"

For another long time, they are both silent.

A long sigh comes ripping out of her. "You do what you have to, just to keep it from happening again. When anger takes hold like that, it has to come out somewhere. Look." She holds up a crooked wrist; even from here it looks wrong. She touches a spot on the temple; she doesn't have to tell Happy about the long white scar under the hair.

He tried so hard not to remember, but he remembers. On his belly under the crib, Happy watches her over ridged knuckles.

Again. She says it again. "He never hit me when I was pregnant." Her breath shudders. "So I had you. I'm so sorry!"

Happy strains to make out what she's trying to tell him but there is no way of translating it.

"I tried. I even named you after him!"

Frederick, he supposes. He supposes it was on the dog tag, but Brent says his name was on the dog tag, and Happy? Frederick is not his name.

In the still air of the bedroom, her voice is sad and thin. "My four big boys fought back when he hit them, so I had you. Anything to stop him. But this time." That sigh. "He didn't. Forgive me, Happy. I did what you do to make it through. I couldn't take it!"

The story she is telling is sad, but it's only a story. Wolves know that fathers aren't the only ones that hurt you.

"You cried. You cried so much. He got so mad. He came at me. He kept coming at me and oh God, oh, Happy. I put you in front of me."

Happy flinches.

"I couldn't watch. I left him to it." Relieved, she says in a light voice, "And that was it." As if it's all she needs to do.

Fine. If she is done, then, she'll leave. As soon as she leaves he'll get up and lock the door.

Then, just when he thinks it's over and he can forget this, she groans. "I'm so sorry, Son."

There is another of the long, painful pauses that wolves prefer to using words. Silence is clear, where words are ambiguous.

She says, "I never knew what he was doing. I didn't want to know."

She says, "I know, I know, I should have left him, but where can a woman go with four little boys and a baby? I should have kicked him out, but how would I feed my children then?"

The silence.

"So you do forgive me, right?"

Forgive is not a word wolves know.

"Right?"

He won't move or speak. Why should he?

"These things happen, son. Things happen when people are stretched too far and their love is stretched too thin. Oh, *please* try to understand."

There is a long silence while she thinks and Happy thinks.

Just when he's beginning to hope she's run out of words forever, she says in a voice so light that it floats far over his head, "Then you got lost. And everything changed. He got himself a nice new wife and moved to Hollywood. After everything I did to make him happy. The others grew up and moved away. Until you came, I didn't have anything."

Happy doesn't expect to speak, but he does. The words that have been stacked in his head for years pop out like quarters out of a coin return.

"You didn't look for me, did you." It is not a question.

She sobs. "You don't know what it's like."

He does.

After a while she goes away.

Happy slinks to the door and locks it even before he hears her stumbling downstairs, sobbing.

"Can I come in?" Her voice is sweet. Just the way he remembers her. Even through the door, Susan is soft and he will always remember that body. He almost forgets himself and answers. Happy is stopped by the fact that except for the slip with the mother, he hasn't spoken. There are too many words backed up in him. He can't get them in order, much less let them out. He just doesn't have the equipment.

Instead he hitches across the floor the way he did when he was two and sits with his back against the door, putting his head to the wood. Feeling her. He feels her outline pressed to the other side of the panel, her heart beating. Susan, breathing.

"Don't worry," she says, "I understand. I just want you to come out so we can be together and be happy."

His fingers creep along the door.

"Happy," she says, and he will not know whether she is talking about their future or using his name, which is his secret. "You know, you're really a very lovely man. It's a shame for you to be shut up in there when you could come out and enjoy the world!"

Swaying slightly in time with that musical voice, he toys with the lock. He can't, he could, he wants to open that door and do something about the way he is feeling. With Susan, he won't have to wonder how the parts fit together.

Like a gifted animal trainer she goes on, about his bright hair, about how lucky she felt when she first saw him; she is lilting now. "It's sunny today, perfect weather, and oh, sweetie, there's going to be a party in the garden!"

Then he hears a little stir in the hall. Someone else out there with her, breathing.

"A party in your honor. Cake, sweetie, and champagne, have you ever had champagne? You're going to love it . . . " He does indeed hear music. Someone tapping a microphone. Voices in the garden. Behind Susan, someone is muttering. She breaks off. "Brent, I am *not* going to tell him about the people from Miramax! Not until we get him out of there!"

The brother. Happy shuts down. What else would he do after what Brent did to him? Things in this room, he realizes; Brent was that much older. Brent giving him a mean, sly look on his last night in this world he outgrew, letting their father hit the gas on the minivan and drive away without him.

35

After a long time, when it becomes clear that there's no change in the situation, Susan gets up off her knees—he can feel every move she makes—and leans the whole of that soft body against the wood. He stands too, so that in a way, they are together. She says in a tone that makes clear that they will indeed lie down together too, "Champagne, and when it's over, you and I . . . "

There is the sound of a little struggle. Brent barks a warning. "Ten minutes, Frederick Olmstead. Ten minutes more and we break down the door and drag you out."

He does not have to go to the window to hear the speech Brent makes to the people assembled. He can hear them muttering. He smells them all. He hears their secret body parts moving. They are drinking champagne in the garden. Then it changes. There is a new voice. Ugly. Different from the buddabuddabudda of ordinary people talking.

"Thank you for coming and thank you for your patience. OK, Brent. Where is he?"

It's him.

Brett whines, "I told you, Dad, I couldn't . . . "

"Then I will."

Another voice. The mother. "No, Fred. Not this time."

There is a smack. A thud. Under the window, the father raises his head and howls, "Two minutes, son. I'm warning you."

Happy's hackles rise. His lips curl back from bared fangs as in the garden under the window the mother cries, "I told you never to come here!"

There is a stir; something happens and the mother is silenced.

Him.

He commands the crowd. "Give me a minute and I'll bring the wolf boy down for his very first interview."

His father comes.

He will find that Happy has unlocked the door for him.

36

Big man, but not as big as Happy remembers him. Big smile on his face, which has been surgically enhanced, although Happy will not know it. Smooth, beautifully tanned under the expensively cropped hair, it is nothing like the angry face Happy remembers. The big, square teeth are white, whiter than Timbo's fangs. Even the eyes are a fresh, technically augmented color. Blue shirt, open at the collar. Throat exposed, as wolves will do when they want you to know that they do not intend to harm you. Nice suit, although Happy has no way of knowing.

"Son," he says in a smooth, glad tone that has sealed deals and gotten meetings with major players all over greater Los Angeles. "You know your father loves you."

This is nothing like love.

Caught between then and now, between what he was and what he thinks he is, Happy does what he has to.

He knows what all wolves know. If you are male and live long enough, you will have to kill your father.

It doesn't take long.

Brent finds the door locked when he comes upstairs to find out how it's going. He says through the closed door, "Everything OK in there?"

Although Happy has not spoken in all these days, he has listened carefully. Now he says in the father's voice, "This is going to take longer than I thought. Reschedule for tomorrow. My place."

There is a little silence while Brent considers.

Happy is stronger than Timbo now. Louder. "Now clear out, and take everybody with you."

It is night again. The mother knocks. Happy has mauled the body, as Timbo would, but he will not eat. There is no point to it.

"Can I come in?"

He allows it.

There will be no screaming and no reproaches. She stands quietly, studying the body.

After a long time she says, "OK. Yes. He deserved it."

When you remember old hurts you remember them all, not just the ones people want you to. Therefore Happy says the one thing about this that he will ever say to her: "He wasn't the only one."

"Oh, Happy," she says. "Oh God." She isn't begging for her life, she is inquiring.

It is a charged moment.

There are memories that you can't prevent and then there are memories you refuse to get back, and over these, you have some power. This is the choice Happy has to make but he is confused now by memories of Sonia. Her tongue was rough. She was firm, but loving. This mother waits. What will he do? She means no harm. She wants to protect him. Poised between this room and freedom in the woods, between the undecided and the obvious, he doesn't know.

What he does know is that no matter what she did to you and no matter how hard to forgive, you will forget what your mother did to you because she is your mother.

Geoff Ryman asked me to do a story for his anthology, When It Changed, *in which he matched writers with scientists from the University of Manchester, who would vet the chosen premise. Mine was based on the experience of a friend who had taken part in an experiment by the anthropologist Helen Fisher of Rutgers University. After intensive interviews, she put volunteers into an MRI to study brain activity. Parts of their brains lit up, indicating personal responses to images of men and women, from hotties to lifetime partners, indicating which, for them, were objects of lust and/or romantic love. I thought, hey, what if a parole board had one of these? Thanks to Steve Miller, Professor of Imaging Science, School of Medicine of the University of Manchester, who advised.*

DOING THE BUTTERFLY

Today I meet Tesla. It's our first date. She and I are scheduled to hook up bimonthly for... "Well," the clerk says brightly as she takes my particulars, "It depends on you."

In the cubicle where Tesla's subjects wait, each new aide takes me down the MRI checklist. By the time the kid with the gurney comes to wheel me to my assignation, I know the questions by heart. "Yes," I answer before he can choke out the first one. Anything to get in, get done, get it over with and get out. "No." I tick answers off on my fingers. "No. No, no and no. OK?"

In another minute he'll start to cry, so I have to let him ask all ten by the numbers as the gurney rolls along to the bay where the row of Department of Corrections Teslas wait.

"Are you claustrophobic?"

Are you kidding? Do you know where I've ***been?*** He does, of course. Which cellblock. Which tier. It's on my chart. "No," I say, although my year in jail took me apart and some pieces rolled away forever. "I'll be fine."

He's already asked did I remove my ring, belt buckle, what else did you have in mind, kid? Concealed weapons? Prosthetic leg? In a lab where six MRIs crouch like grazing beetles, you have to think ahead. The M in MRI stands for Magnetic. They claim the test is noninvasive, but these next-generation suckers are strong enough to yank shrapnel out of your gut.

I thought: If I claimed I had a steel skullcap, would they let me off? Then I thought better of it. These people will take any reason to put you back in the slammer.

He bends over, fixing me with watery blue eyes. "Are you OK?"

"Fine," I say, wiping where he dripped on my face. Tense, probably. Freaking, but determined to beat this thing. With an MRI, first impressions are so important. I need to come across as earnest, attractive and straightforward, a not-a-cloud-in-the-sky kind of guy. Tesla has to see a man clean of evil intentions, one you'd trust with your new puppy, kid sister, family fortune. That you'd feel good about unlocking his anklet alarm with the GPS, electrodes to jolt him if he strays. The kind of guy you want to release, so he can walk free in the world.

I've been quiet for so long that he says reassuringly, "There's no pain."

"No prob," I tell him. *Fluffy thoughts, Anderson. You need to think nice, fluffy thoughts while Tesla cross-sections your brain.*

I scare him so he rattles on. "Everybody's anxious the first time. Don't worry, they don't judge you on this one, even if the wrong parts of your brain light up."

Careful, Peter. "Which parts?"

"That show anger, um. Arousal?" He gives up and starts over. "They're looking for what's working and what's . . . You know. Shrunk."

I ask one question too many. "To find out . . . "

Which makes him frantic. "If you'll do it again! Look. This is only a dummy test. To establish a base line? Like, what's normal for you? You'll see scary stuff during the procedure, but don't worry, the images aren't loaded this time."

This makes me wonder which images, exactly, the D.O.C. thinks are loaded for me. So, what, do they start with something innocuous, like sunbeams and reindeer? Follow with Dumpsters full of body parts? Or is it belly dancing centerfolds, after which . . . My mind goes places you don't want to know about. That Tesla must never see. Wherever that is, my grimace scares the kid. He claps a damp hand on my arm and I jump. "Don't do that!"

"If you want Valium, I can ask Dr. Green," he offers. "Since it's your first time and all." Then, "But, just so you know? Once you're in the program they screen for tranquilizers, like, every time you come in for a scan? And if you don't test clean . . . "

"No thanks, I'm fine."

"This session is just to get you used to the procedure," he babbles, "so there's nothing, like, at stake here? Tesla 12 is cutting edge, so don't worry about getting sent up the river by mistake. In the Beta testing period these scans were, like, a hundred per cent accurate, so it's all good . . . "

He hits bullet points like a metronome but all I hear is, *She knows when you are sleeping, she knows when you're awake.* TMI, asshole, I think but do not say. "Fine."

"This time."

"Fine." *Chill, Anderson. Work on it. Can't show them what you're really thinking, ever.*

"OK then, um . . . Ah. OK. So, the technician will tell you all this before she starts the scan, but just so you know? Inside Tesla, it gets loud. They give you headphones to shut out the racket, pick your favorite CD, and there's a panic button. In case you . . . "

"I told you, I'll be fine."

Poor kid is too young to keep it impersonal. "You're not the type we usually get in here."

Please shut up.

"You know, the criminal type? Don't worry, you'll do fine."

If I shut up, will you shut up?

He's also too young to have opinions, but he can't stop. I am a captive audience. "Really. It's a clean test, you won't feel a thing. With probation, the government has to be careful, given recidivism and all. The T12 tells them who's in the right head to go loose in society. Some people object, but you've gotta admit it's cleaner than gazillion probation officers." For the criminal justice system, it's also cheaper. "I wouldn't know." "You don't feel a thing."

"I wouldn't know." I do know, magnetic resonance imaging is just that; I don't think it can read thoughts, but these Tesla 12s are sophisticated machines, and this is my first time. It's my first time for everything: jail, probation. Hell, the trial. Attempted manslaughter, charged at my first and only arraignment. The public defender tried to get me off after what I accidentally did to Tad Seaver. It was, after all, an accident. I wasn't trying to kill the guy, I just wanted him to pay for yanking my girl Stephanie out from under me like a rug in a cheap magic trick. I didn't even want him to pay for screwing her on his lunch hour at my place, on my Egyptian cotton sheets, I just wanted him to stop.

But that was before.

"No music, thanks," I tell the woman who taps in the code that unlocks the D.O.C. anklet, attaches headphones and slides me onto the tongue of the machine. I need the racket to keep my mind focused so it doesn't wander off and fall into one of their traps. Can't let the wrong parts of my brain light up. "I like the noise."

"Well, that's a first." Wow, look. I surprised a smile out of her. Lovely woman, how did she end up in this ugly job? "You may feel queasy going in; if you get twitchy, I can slow things down."

"Don't worry, I'll be fine." I'm beginning to feel good about this. At least I'm in the right head. Forget bureaucracy, invasion of privacy. Focus on that pretty face.

"OK, then. Use the buttons on this handset to rank your emotions— whether the images are good, bad or neutral, OK?" Our moment has ended. She's in high professional mode. "If goggles make you claustro-phobic, we can always use the mirror."

"Goggles will be fine." So she can't tell whether my eyes are open or not. I may peek, but since I've decided to choose *neutral* no matter what, who's to know?

"Don't worry, I'll be watching from the booth."

I slide into the maw of the giant beetle and the pounding begins. Cha-cha-cha-cha/cho-cho-cho-cho. I imagine a giant engine, pistons going up and down, until the racket intensifies. I'm surrounded by Einsteinian streetcars coming and going, gangs of them, that hypnotize. I zone out until the tech's voice comes into the speaker, "Now. In this sequence. Good? Bad? Neutral?"

Button under my thumb registers my first N.

"Wow." It's soft, inadvertent.

Never mind. I am safe inside the engine—not Tesla, which is imaging my head, slice by slice, serving up cross-sections of my brain for the D.O.C. I mean the one inside my head, where I let the racket drown out thought as I keep pushing N. N. N. Then the light assailing my closed eyelids turns red. Some new image. Push Neutral, dude. And don't peek.

Her voice is loaded. "What about this one?"

Chill, Anderson. Keep doing what you're doing. N. No, I'm not pissed, I'm not angry or lustful or anything that will light up my brain. N. I'm just a neutral, nonviolent kind of guy.

"OK. Responses to this montage?"

Don't look. N. In experiments, sometimes they deal you a wild card, but I'm beyond thought.

The sequence must have been a ringer.

I hear it in her gasp. N is not, apparently, the expected response to what she's showing me. The goggles render images up close and personal, 3-D high-definition LCDs. I'm scared to look. I have to look.

So much for the orderly's "unloaded images." The goggles fill with black-and-white photos taken as they liberated Dachau.

Lovely as she is, my handler's voice turns cold. "And these?"

One look and, B. I hit the button like a radioman on a sinking ship. B. Again, again, again. Anything to tell her, *What you are showing me is BAD.*

I'm so shaken that somehow, she knows. My handler's voice softens. "Are you all right?"

With my left hand, I give a thumbs up for the mirror: *fine.* I am. I have to be. I will be fine, I vow, until—does she feel sorry for me?—the slideshow slows down and turns benign. OK then, Peter. Settle. Let it play. I focus on the racket, which changes timbre as Tesla slices deeper into my brain. Don't think about Stephanie marrying rat-bastard Tad Seaver— Don't go there, Peter, no. Nice Seaver, OK person, Tad. N-i-i-ice. Rank images, not how you really feel, and do it fast, think *bland* . . . Remember girls before Stephanie, lovely things we did to each other and how good it felt, don't think too hard, *you are standing in a field* . . .

At last it ends. I slide out into the light, drenched and groping, steadied by my handler's touch. Gently, she lifts the goggles. "Are you sure you're all right?"

"Fine." I manage to sit. Standing? Not so fast.

She replaces the security anklet. "I'm so sorry." It locks with a spiteful *click.*

"You didn't do this." I'm not ready to say that in fact, I did.

"I'm sorry about all of it. Duane? Duane!" She hits her beeper. "Damn kid's supposed to wheel you back. Don't get up. I'm sorry it hit so hard. It's because you're not the type."

My inner demons leap for joy. "No problem. I'll be fine." But I'm staggered by *all that stuff.* The goggles produced horrors intercut with soft porn, and—weird! Photos from my life—at least it looked like my life. Some scenes, I remember being there. Others? Photos of stuff I don't remember, things I don't know about, but I was in them, so I must have . . . It's confusing, it's . . .

She checks her phone. "Hell with Duane. You're my last for the day. Let me take you." She offers her elbow.

"It's OK, thanks. I can walk."

"You need caffeine, something. I'll have Admissions send your valuables down to the caf."

We sit over coffee in the fading light until I stop jittering. I haven't said much. Neither has she, but we linger. "You don't do this for just anybody."

Her smile says: *you're not just anybody.* "No." I'd like to move into this girl's head and build a house in the part that lights her smile. "Most of our subjects don't . . . " She starts over. "You're not the usual type."

"So. Ah . . . Did I pass?"

"It isn't that kind of test. The computer calibrates, but somebody has to read the scan. Our psychoneurologists don't come in until Friday, and you only hear if your reading's . . . "

She doesn't need to finish. I only hear if Tesla tells the D.O.C. all the things I'm trying so hard to hide, and they start the drugs. Careful, I have to be very careful, or they'll bypass drug therapy and lock me up. "What. Agh. What are they looking for?"

"You know how this works, right? When you're angry, aroused, depressed, activity lights up different parts of your amygdala, and Tesla knows. The images are prompts, and with . . . " she chokes. "With our ex-convicts, Tesla looks for flareups. What angers you, exactly how angry you are."

"That's creepy."

"It's to keep everyone safe."

"Oh." I tent my fingers, trying for a neutral tone. I can't tell her the lie, so I do what I can. "That's great."

Too late. She knows I'm dissembling. The shutter clicks behind her eyes. "Two weeks, then." She gets up with an official smile. "See you in two weeks."

Once I clear the installation, I let go. It helps to curse them all as I kick an empty beer can along the sidewalk, once for the judge, once for the Department of Corrections, once for the guards on our cell block and once for the sanctimonious doorman in the complex where parolees live until they scan clean. I'm stuck here inside the perimeter until I convince Tesla that anger management classes have purged me of evil intentions and I am fit to walk free. As for Tad and Stephanie, well . . . That has to wait.

My apartment's not bad, but it's depressingly beige. Walls, generic furniture, carpeting, it's all beige except the display on the flat screen TV. Defying *feng shui*, everything's bolted down. It needs my own, humanizing stuff, books and photos and art, but my place is outside the perimeter where, until I'm off probation and because of the anklet and the restraining order, I can't go.

Vile Tad moved in with Steph the day I got sent up, and at this stage in my probation, the least offense . . . They're probably in there right now, just back from Walmart, taking down my oils and engravings to nail honeymoon pictures into my walls and crapping up the decor with flowered everything, which is Stephanie's tragic flaw.

Because my old office is within the perimeter, I could actually go back to my old job, except that I no longer have a job. As that video of me and Tad outside the Oyster Bar migrated from CNN to YouTube and went viral, I'm no longer welcome there. I didn't mean to shove him, I was just trying to make a point. I didn't even shove him very hard. It's not my fault the window broke, although I do wish the plate glass he got hung up on had finished the job by cutting off his head.

Oh, yes. I have a lot to keep from Tesla. As I'm basically trapped in beige limbo, terminally bored, I've done a little research. There are ways, I think, to fool Tesla, I just don't know what they are. Fail and I spin out my life inside the perimeter, on Public Work details, to be assigned after the next session, when they start measuring my progress. Unless they put me back in jail. I'm in stasis until the MRI, my new lover and— if I'm not careful—life partner, either declares me unfit for life anywhere but prison, or decides that my intentions are pure.

It's all about my responses; Google tells me so. The MRI's been used as lie detector (results questionable), mood detector, even a mood enhancer (proved). For the D.O.C., it's become a gauge of criminal potential which is, I guess, where I come in. Now, If I can just present as sweet-natured, innocuous . . .

They slide me onto the platform and Duane leaves. My handler says, "If you're thinking what I think you're thinking, Peter, don't bother. Don't even try."

"How did you . . . "

"Everybody does," she says as she positions my head on the block.

". . . Know my name?" I build a smile that makes her smile.

She taps my chart. "They all want to get even, it's natural."

"I thought I was good at . . . "

"Nobody's that good. OK, today we're going to count you down from two hundred, watch the numbers, every single one."

"No more Dachau."

"Promise." Her tone as I slide into the machine is warm, almost intimate. "It will help you get into the right head."

The numbers dwindle to one, but no amount of preparation will put me into the right head. The images go from general to specific, from innocuous to what I'd have to call occuous: photos of childhood disasters that I thought nobody knew about, things I didn't know, battle scenes from my time in the service, phone shots of Tad and Stephanie kissing outside my front door. Surveillcam digis of them having sex.

I don't have to ask my handler how well I did when the intolerable slideshow stops, and the goggles go dark. She lifts them and I sit up so fast that my head spins. "That was harsh."

"It's meant to be. Sorry, Peter."

I don't even know her name! "I'm sorry too. So, if you're done for the day, errr . . . "

She replaces the anklet. "Maia." *Click.*

Pretty name. "Can I buy you a drink?"

After the third session Maia's so worried about me that she lets me buy dinner. Until I lose the omniscient anklet, this is as far as it can go. An alarm sounds somewhere if you interface with a person from the D.O.C., Maia warned as we got into her car. "We can't see each other in any real way, but I just feel so *sorry* for you."

"It was pretty bad." It was. The scenes between Steph and Seaver are tight close-ups now, painful to see, fueling the urge to kill.

She taps my hand. "Get used to it, Peter."

"I'm trying."

"You have to, or they'll never let you go."

I cover her hand with mine. "And when they do let me go," I say with no intention of finishing the sentence.

She flows against me, just a little bit. "Then we'll see."

47

On our fourth—it isn't exactly a date, it's more like decompression after you come to the surface too fast and they're scared your blood will boil— on our fourth date she says, "You'll be OK, you just have to . . . "

"What, Maia. What?" Crap. How can I control this when I can't even control my voice?

She doesn't exactly answer. "It gets better, I promise."

"You mean, they stop showing . . . "

"No. That just gets worse."

I slam my fist on the table.

"You start to get used to it."

My heart goes out to her. "Maia, I love you."

"You can't," she says, and then my heart flies up because she adds, "Yet."

Maybe six weeks in, I'm almost getting used to it, but I can tell from Maia's greeting that last week's results weren't that great. We've progressed to exchanging lifestories and hand-holding at dinner, but it's not enough. She's the only person I've been close to since I almost killed Seaver and they cut me off from everyone in my old life. We've told each other everything, at least almost everything. Now Maia addresses the truth. She's known from the beginning. "You want to get out so you can go back and kill him."

Nodding, I tap the anklet. "Are you sure these things aren't bugged?"

"Like, they'd bug you when your scans tell everything they need to know?"

"Do they know . . . "

"That you want to kill him? Yes."

I swallow hard. I need this girl! "What else do they know?"

"That you have a sleeping libido and the fastest temper in the west."

"Working on it!" Maia says we're not bugged, but I pencil my next question on a napkin, in case. WHAT AM I GOING TO DO?

She thinks it's silly but instead of answering, she prints: IMPULSE CONTROL. Then she says, "Do you run? Play tennis? Any all-body thing?"

"I used to be a swimmer."

"Imagine you're swimming. Freestyle?"

"Butterfly. It's better than flying. I love the pool."

"Do this for me, Peter. For an hour tonight and every night until your next scan, get back in that pool inside your head. Perfect your butterfly," she says, and she wants me to read this on two levels. "Any time you're upset, start swimming. No matter what Tesla shows you next time, imagine the pool."

"Pretend harder," Maia says two weeks later. "One more like this and they'll start the drugs."

She waits for the rest until we're installed in a corner booth in a place where nobody goes. She slides a package across the table. "We're not supposed to do this, but I want to try something. These are the goggles. With today's memory card. Go home and do the butterfly while you run the sequence, OK?"

"You're a lovely woman," I tell her. She is. "Butterfly."

Our code word for whatever is between us. "Butterfly."

Progress. At ten weeks, the psychoneurologist who likes to hit on Maia lets it slip, and she tells me. "He thinks you're getting a grip on the anger."

"Does that mean I'm cleared?"

"No matter what you see, keep doing what you're doing." Her smile makes promises. "Maybe by spring."

"That seems like forever!"

"Compared to life back in the joint, it's a walk in the park."

"I love it when you talk tough."

"No matter what Tesla shows you," her fingers are crawling up my arm, a sensation I don't mind in the least. "Do the butterfly."

Lulled. I haven't been in the water since the day I came back from the gym and found them fucking, but I slide in and out of the MRI each time I'm tested as refreshed as if I'd just come out of the pool. Knots inside me unsnarl. A few more sessions like this and I can spend the time inside Tesla unmoved.

"Better, you're doing much better," Maia tells me, and ticks off a note on her pad. "Whatever you're feeling, the anger's under control."

When you're doing the butterfly, it's all you think about. I want to butterfly through the next session and into the zone but I can't, exactly, although freedom is close. The powers have slipped in ringers to wake me up. The usual is intercut with digis of A-list women, not stars, real people but so pretty that I can't help wishing they were here. Class portraits from high-end universities, or girls too pretty to need the online dating site they were posted on.

"This is interesting," Maia says, and I have to wonder how much she sees on the screen inside her booth. Fresh activity in the amygdala. "Your libido's back."

And the whole time, I thought she was tending the machine. *You watch Tesla as she scans?* I see the finish line receding. "Is that a bad thing?"

Her voice turns to satin. "Not to me. See you next week, Peter."

My heart staggers. "Next week?"

Satin, lace and velvet. "We can move a little bit faster now."

I can't help what happens when I stop doing the fly; the flood of new photos makes me roll over; I have to glide along on my back and let them wash over me. Maia naked, Maia in a silky shift, and the hell of it is—and these sweet surprises are scattered among the usual—for each Maia they show, there is a Stephanie. Now, I'm used to seeing Steph striking infuriating poses with Tad Seaver in these sessions: both of them clothed, naked, screwing this way, that, and I've learned to control my responses. That part of my brain stays cool, but now! Here's Steph without Tad: Stephanie when we first met, Steph and me in the pool that spectacular night, doing it naked; never mind Maia, I fix on Steph and me, just the way I want it, with Seaver dead, it's all planned. I don't want much. Him dead and Steph and me forever, that's all I want.

I try to keep my heart level.

Maia's face as she jerks off my goggles says it all. She snaps on the anklet. "I'm sorry. I tried to help you, but there's an irregularity. I'm afraid we'll need to start the drugs, which ones will be up to your psychoneurologist—your appointment is tomorrow, 6 a.m."

Make up with her, Peter, you've got to make up or you're here for life. I open my chest and rip out my heart to give her. "But tonight it's dinner together, right, Maia? Next week, the Rooftop Glade—great band. We can see the whole city from there."

She gives back nothing. "About next week. The trial period is over. Starting next week, you get a new handler. Goodbye, Peter. We're done."

I have a special interest in people born with the stupendously sublime sense of entitlement that somehow excludes everybody else in the world. This story is about one of those.

SPECIAL

Ashley Famous is coming to town and we're all excited and a little apprehensive. This is the last unspoiled village on the Hudson, one of those quiet places where nobody important ever comes, and the last thing we want is gawking disciples trampling our flower beds, to say nothing of gift shops and roadside shrines popping up all along Route 9. Still we get the shivers, thinking, *Ashley Famous. Here.*

Bill Anthony says although she's world renowned it's in a good way, no YouTube antics to embarrass us, no scandal, no paparazzi implied, she can only bring honor to Schuylerton. "Think people like us, but with the sheen of greatness"—Bill actually said that!—"when all she wants is to blend in and disappear." Well, she's picked the right place. We all mind our own business here.

She writes those sexy little books about God, so crowds collect like flies on a road kill because who wouldn't want to touch the hand that's been in touch with God? People do it, but not people you know. She can walk down our streets undisturbed, although when Gloria saw her out in front of Tazewell's Realty that first day, she could swear the woman had *look at me* written all over her.

Of course Gloria is not our most reliable witness. Even though she's a published writer, she is not all that popular, while Ashley Famous has all those fans driving her into seclusion. They follow her everywhere with misty eyes and wide, wet smiles. Bill says everybody has a cross and this is hers.

Our Reverend Anthony wrote a book about her, which is how they got friends. Bill fought his way to the platform when she got that medal, waving the book with her picture on the front. "Oh," she shouted, "how lovely," but by that time fans were stampeding like a herd of leeches and Bill had to rescue her. She thanked him with the saddest smile and said, "Sometimes you just get tired."

The thing is, if you've touched the hand of God and God just happens to drop in on you, the last thing He wants is to fight off gangs of rapt admirers, Bill says, so she's going into seclusion . . . here!

Bill is dean over at the college so he stepped up and invited her, to do what, we aren't certain, but there you are.

She's bought the Eversons' boathouse which is odd, since we will do anything to keep our houses in the family; we owe it to our children to say nothing of the generations that came before, but you'd have to be one of us to understand. We're not pointing any fingers, but this is the first piece of riverfront property to pass out of family hands in two centuries, and Grant didn't consult Bunk Schuyler at Historical Preservation before he sold.

Never mind. Schuylerton could use a little pizzazz, and it is well known that celebrities like Ashley Famous have creative, fascinating friends who would probably love a weekend in the country, especially with summer coming on. She'll want to invite gangs of poets and artists, who are bound to be more exciting than certain people around here, which will definitely perk up our social lives. We can't wait to be invited—that is, if she takes to us.

The question is, where to start with her? We won't intrude and we never, ever overstep—no screen captures in the IGA parking lot, we promise, no viral screen shots at Luther's Drug Store, even though we're dying for our friends to know. Uninvited drop-ins and cold calls are out; when a person's keeping the line open for God, who are we to interrupt? We don't go where we're not invited and our kind doesn't gawk, it's just not done.

When we do meet her we'll be discreet, we will! *Guess what. We have a secret. Guess what. It's you.*

54

Oh, but she said something odd to Jack Tazewell when he was showing the boathouse. "I think the most interesting things in the world are sex and religion, don't you?"

So, should we lock up our husbands or what?

We don't mean to fret, but if we happen to run into her, is it all right to say hello?

It's hard to know. But we *are* looking forward to meeting her, however it comes about, Ms. Famous and whichever husband she has this time around. We hear that there have been several, but never mind. We're very forgiving here. We'd let you into our hearts quicker than we'd let you into our homes.

We just haven't figured out how to let her know she has friends here in Schuylerton.

Beth and Gloria and Jeannie Chandler and I have been going home by the river road after lunch at the club, checking for signs of life. So far all we've seen is Grant Everson glowering over his rose bushes as we come through his gate; when he pops up with the hedge clippers we wave our fingers and laugh: la-la, Grant, you're the one who sold the boathouse, now look. Evanoaks is not your private property now.

Rich as she is, you'd think Ashley Famous would have the boathouse crawling with painters and decorators, God knows those books make millions, but the new mailbox and fresh geraniums in the cut-out truck tire planter are pretty much it. Well, that will all change once we're friends; we can tell her where to shop for all the best things. If only we'd come upon her planting something in the front yard; if only she'd hear our car in the turnaround and stick her head out the front door to see who's coming, then we could all smile and wave, hel-looo. Of course she'd wave back and if we caught her smiling we'd pile out of the car and make friends, but we've cruised the boathouse four times this week and we haven't seen a trace.

With anybody else, we'd start with the chess pie or the hot cross buns, but you don't take food to a star, not even the apple basket from Creech's Orchards with Elva Creech's jams and homemade maple sugar leaves; usually casseroles and deep dish pies are great conversation pieces, but even the mocha cheesecake from Tempest's Teapot is just wrong.

With a best-selling author who can't stop winning prizes, where do you start? It's not like Gloria would know.

We hear she's very reclusive. Maybe she's like us, standoffish, but only with people she doesn't want to know.

We hear she's a lot of fun at parties, if you can only get her to come.

We hear that sometimes she can get a little wild.

Then why is she so damn difficult, when all we're trying to do is welcome her to Schuylerton?

Bill warned us that she doesn't warm up to just anybody, but Bill is infuriatingly smug just because he happened to write a book. We're not *just anybody*, which he knows, and if he won't tell Ashley Famous who we are in this town, then how do we let her know?

Should we sidle up to her in the supermarket and start the discussion about cheeses or tell her which produce to avoid? A few words and she'll understand who we are. So, can we get friends by showing her the farmers' market or should we offer her our cleaning lady or should we just come right out in the open and give a party for her?

What if she hates parties and doesn't want to come?

What if she loves parties and doesn't want to come?

What if she wants to come, just not to our house?

Would she come if we gave it at the club? Does she really hate parties, and does she know what an honor that would be? Outsiders can live here for generations without seeing the inside of the Schuylerton River Club. Bill says the last thing she wants is to feel crowded and we don't want to make her self-conscious so it should sound casual, "If you happen to be around," even though we're putting on the dog. When she gets to the club and sees how much fun we're all having she'll know how lucky she is, like, *we know you're big and important but in our own way we're important too.* Of course she'll invite us back, if we can only get her to come.

We could probably start by reading her books, but who has the time? Should we fake it and send her admiring notes? Naturally we'll have them laid out on our end tables when she comes over and after she notices, of course we'll ask her to sign—unless that's gauche. We bought them all, what more does she expect?

Unlike my friends, who dropped theirs in the tub or left them out on the clubhouse porch in the rain, at least I tried. My Richard thought it was foolish, sitting up in bed improving my mind when he thought we should be doing something else, and was it my fault I got bored and fell asleep between the pages, or hers? To tell the truth, her stuff is all too airy-fairy for me—beautiful, but neither here nor there. So it just won't do to barge up to her on Broad Street with that gooshy Ashley-fan smile, babbling, "I just loved your book." I hate being false even when it's working, and if there was a quiz, I'd die.

Mirabile, Stephanie Parrish makes the big breakthrough. Yesterday our Ms. Famous tripped on the old boot scraper outside Fanueil Flowers and all her shopping bags went whoosh, so Stephanie got down and helped her pick up her stuff.

Of course she was grateful, and all the while Stephanie was taking note of the items: which face creams, what shade of lipstick, whose bread; hand-knit sweater from Erdrich's with those lambs on the front plus, from Ezekiel's of all things, canned smelts. She thanked Stephanie three times, but that was it. It wasn't like Ashley Famous invited her back to the boathouse for coffee, or to have lunch at Tempest's before she headed home.

In fact Beth was the first to speak to her, and it wasn't exactly a conversation. She saw her in Ezekiel's, lined up for bagels on Sunday morning just like everybody else but with dark glasses and a kerchief pulled down, so we wouldn't know. Beth just went right up to her. She smiled as nicely as she could without being smarmy and spoke. "Excuse me, but aren't you . . . "

And in the name of Edith Wharton, who used to live around here and I'm sure was a lot more gracious, Ashley Famous said, "No."

That set us back.

But we have discovered that she is a very sweet person and tremendously vulnerable, which Mariel Edmunds learned when she braved the Hudson in Jake's little boat after Beth told us about it at brunch. She cut the motor and glided in tactfully, so to look at her, you'd think she was quietly fishing in the marsh and accidentally drifted in without noticing how close she was, which is how she caught our world-class new neighbor weeping out on the end of Grant Everson's dock.

Well, one thing led to another—empathic grimaces, little waves—and Mariel scooted up the ladder and, respecting her privacy, sat on the end of the dock next to Ms. Famous, but not too close. She stayed quiet as the tomb while they both stared out at the channel until finally the sight of this *star* sitting there with tears streaming was more than Mariel could bear and she had to ask, "Are you all right?"

Imagine all that and then guess what this person with a brilliant career and gobs of honors and every man she ever wanted revealed in that thrilling, smoky voice she uses on TV. Not a damn thing. She said, "It's just so beautiful."

Although she's not one of our nearest and dearest Mariel is a master-piece of self-control; without turning a hair she dropped her own voice six feet to wherever Ashley Famous keeps hers and said, "Yes."

We all know you don't cry along, it's hypocritical. Mariel just sat there, and Ashley Famous just sat until she got over it and sprang up like a cat after a shower. She went skipping back to the house in her pink sneakers, calling back so carelessly that Mariel couldn't believe her ears. "Come again."

Mariel did not gush, "Oh, thank you." We're better than that. She put on our best Schuylerton River Club drawl, "But never without calling first."

So we were in. Well, not all of us and not that minute, but this was the start. Mariel waited a good long time and then she dropped by the boat-house and asked Ashley Famous to the River Club for brunch this Sunday after church, don't dress up, we're just country people here.

We'll all drift into church the way we do every week but we're a little twitchy: what to wear, what to wear? In addition to his duties at the Epis-copal college, where nobody knows what Ashley Famous will be doing for all that money, Bill Anthony is the rector here. When we told him she was coming he said of course, she'd already promised because it was his loaves-and-fishes sermon this week. So we could have seen her up close anyway, and without being beholden to Mariel, but who knew?

Besides if it hadn't been for Mariel, we wouldn't know that Ashley Famous and religion are . . . how did she put it? "Boy, is that a contradic-tion in terms."

When she dropped by to invite ("I would have called, but I went off without your number...") she scoped the boathouse interior, and she's not part of our foursome but Mariel is very good at detail. Tacky was only the beginning, she moved on to "neo-Goodwill." Patchwork quilts covering a multitude of sins, she said, inspirational motto painted on velvet, nicely framed and hanging over the fireplace and oh my God, a pillow needlepointed with praying hands. Plus, she told us, for an icon, she doesn't dress very well. She wore more or less what we wear except in all the wrong colors, Mariel said, borderline shabby, who would have guessed? Nothing went with anything else, and that was the least of it.

She positively exuded pheromones, how did Mariel put it? "She may be all about God but she talked like a sailor rolling into a bordello after years at sea, all that with her nice husband sitting right there!"

Indeed, we have to wonder. That tight T-shirt and flowered jeans she wore to church and to the club after, never mind the straw cartwheel hat and pink lizard clutch. She's the kind who can't tell when she's pitifully underdressed, and the husband was cute. Younger, in that obvious way, with a sensitive mouth and cultivated hair. There were so many people on the lawn around Ashley Famous that day, half my friends and all our men fetching this, offering her that, that I couldn't help feeling sorry for the husband, so I sat down next to him on the porch.

It didn't take much to draw him out.

A poet, he told me, smoldering nicely, he's one of those sandy boys who tan so fast that the body hairs shimmer, no question what she saw in him. He's adorable. I probably shouldn't have asked where to buy his books but when I saw his face I made up for it by reading the one poem he had tucked in his shirt pocket. Something to occupy him while Ashley holed up in the loft because, he said, and he wasn't complaining, she needs to get with God before she can face church. It's clear he adores her, but I could see how hard it is for him to write with that big old shadow of greatness looming over him. At the end he invited me to come over and he'd read to me and I promised I would. His name is Archbold, from some fine old family, which is interesting because now that we see her up close it's clear that Ashley Famous comes from somewhere south of quality. Arch, he said, just call me Arch. Sweet boy, but who knows how soon she will tire of him or what he will do then.

We think certain thoughts about handsome young men but we always go home to bed with our husbands, most of us, even so. But among our tennis foursome, I alone had been invited, even though it was by Arch and not his first-ever and only wife, at least so far. Whatever happens, he's entitled, the woman has been married four times.

In fact, Gloria was next to visit, and she wasn't even invited. Of course Gloria thinks of herself as a fellow professional, which gives her the right. She just bellied up to the door and introduced herself to Ashley Famous, writer to writer as it were, as though they were equals and Ms. Famous had to ask her in. In Schuylerton, maybe they are equals; in local matters Gloria has the edge, but otherwise, no. The prizes alone, money, passionate fans in droves, but it wasn't very kind of Ms. Famous to point it out.

Which—we finally got it out of Gloria, who is livid—she did. She told it like a sad story, but Gloria knew. Oh, Ashley Famous was dripping with self-pity, but Gloria knew.

She'd have to be drunk out of her mind or beaten senseless not to know. She says a little of both. Too much wine in strong sunlight bouncing off the river, it put her off her guard. She let herself imagine they were friends. Gloria is a giving person so she said kindly, "My contact at Valley TV would love to come talk to you, he's doing a show on writers living on the Hudson and I thought . . . "

Then wasn't she surprised. Gloria was knocking herself out to be helpful, and Ashley Famous rose right up and bit her in the ass.

"I don't like being famous," she said, sudden as a slap in the face.

"It's only local TV."

It was too late. This Ashley's voice went back to that deep place. Her face got all pink and she went on like an angry kindergarten teacher explaining to a stupid child. About that time Arch, who had been hovering, faded away like a painter's wet wash of a failing sky. "I don't like it at all," Ashley Famous said to his back, and there were tears standing in her eyes.

Gloria tried for a snappy comeback but all she managed was, "I just thought." Then she read that face and gave up.

"People keep writing books on me, they're making a whole movie about my life, they want me to narrate the Bible on PBS; they won't leave me alone! Everybody wants to send me presents and force me to take their prizes; they all want me to bless them or something, when all I want is to be left alone!"

Gloria was about to go there-there when Ashley Famous got all holy and condescending. "But you wouldn't understand."

Gloria blinked the way you do when a strobe light flashes and you have no idea where it's coming from.

"You wouldn't know," she said to Gloria. Unfortunately, that's true, but she didn't have to rub it in. "You would have no way of knowing how very, very hard it is to be as famous as me. The things people tell you, the things they ask you to do."

By the time she was finished laying out the tribulations of a literary icon, she had Gloria backing away on her hands and knees, anything to get out of there. She clamped the insides of her mouth until they bled so she didn't accidentally apologize for something she hadn't done, and when she could manage, she stood up. "Oh," she told Ashley Famous when she could bring herself to speak without screaming, "I would never give him your number without permission." Then she more or less tugged her forelock and left without ever once losing her temper and telling the truth, which was that she only said it to be nice.

Gloria says that behind all that sacred, holy stuff Ashley Famous is not a nice person, but of course Gloria is biased. People say mean things about Mother Teresa too.

Beth and I are here to tell you that Gloria is wrong. Ms. Famous is an inspiration, as we discover as soon as we and Ashley start spending quality time. I personally have been invited, and I take Beth along to ride post so Arch won't get in trouble for inviting me.

I just don't want Ashley to think there's anything funny going on between her husband and me and there isn't, attractive as he is. Even though she isn't expecting us she's glad to see us because naturally any friend of her Archie's is a friend of hers, but as it turns out, her man Arch just left for a reading in New York.

She waves us inside with an industrial-strength smile. It's bright enough to be seen from the back of any hall and Beth and I can't help thinking, *No wonder everybody loves her,* because this time it's shining for us.

Then we get inside and it's: *Hasn't she ever heard of Ikea?* I *mean* , Mariel barely scratched the surface here. It's all about vintage shag rugs in bad colors and milk crates stuffed with magazines and board-and-brick book-cases like kids make in graduate school, which makes me wonder whether all her taste is in her mouth or if she downplays the decor to make Archie feel at home. Jacket photos notwithstanding, Ashley Famous is no kid either, now that we see her up close. But she ushers us in, glowing as though she is completely unaware. Then dear God she says, "Things of this world are only things of this world so why bother," so we know she knows.

She sits us down and brings us steaming cups of Cambric tea, which our grandmothers remember vaguely and used to offer when we were small.

You don't exactly talk to Ashley Famous, you listen, which is how we find out why people fall down and worship her and follow her anywhere. It's a foregone conclusion, *voilà, tout suite*, when she starts going on in that thrilling voice. Actually, although it's a little embarrassing, we follow her upstairs into the loft. It's her meditation room, she says, and somehow the three of us end up sitting on that hard, hard floor in lotus position—or something like it for Beth and me—it's a little harder for Beth as certain parts of her have begun to spread. We sit facing the new sheetrock wall Arch put up for her, and we meditate, or Ashley Famous does, while Beth and I stare at the wall as instructed and try to empty our minds and see into the beyond, which is what she seems to expect. It's not easy to do when you're wondering if she's gone out of her mind and into the Pres-ence while you're still sitting there worried about how long you can be on this floor in a fixed position without screaming and offending her and whether if you got up and tried to leave, she'd know.

Can you really meditate with us watching?

Still, it is an honor to be hunched in a row like this, contemplating eter-nity. Imagine, contemplating. Us!

Just being here makes Beth and me feel special, and definitely close to the source—although of what—well, it's pretty ineffable. We're only beginners, after all. I guess we're expected to stare at that wall until we're cross-eyed, which if you do for long enough actually does move you to a higher plane unless that's all the blood leaving your head and pooling in your butt. Whatever it is, I could swear that *something* happened, so when Ashley Famous says, in hushed tones, "Can you feel it?" Beth and I both manage a breathy, "Yes," and for the moment and after we go limp and it stops hurting, we believe.

Then she kind of flows up while Beth and I creak and groan miserably and struggle to our feet, humiliated because we've failed. But, how glorious. Whatever we are suffering, Ashley Famous must be mysteriously transcending, because she says, "Wasn't that wonderful!" and rakes us with that white-light smile.

Ergo, voilà, mirabile, we are friends. We're invited back tomorrow, Ashley says she sees great promise in us, which is borderline divine. I'm sitting right down and reading every one of her books as soon as I get home.

When we come back on Wednesday Arch is there; I can't help hoping he'll come up into the loft with us because once I get the hang of this, maybe we can meet on some astral plane. Failing that, I'll have something good to look at while our minds are traveling out and beyond. But when she asks him, "Are you?" his face shuts up shop, so I know I'm right about them, although Beth doesn't pick up on it.

Then Arch goes off wherever he goes to write and we're back on that wretched floor maintaining fixed positions until I think I see paisley lights, unless I'm on the first step to the next level as Ashley promised and my life is about to change. I can't help it, I have to peek.

Surprise, Beth is peeking too and if you believe in that kind of thing, Ashley Famous looks pretty much transfixed, unless we're both giddy with hunger because she didn't give lunch before she sat us down to meditate. It's like seeing one of those intricate Chinese ivories with the 40-watt bulb inside, my God! She looks lit from within, but only for a second. In the next she yips and hits the floor like a felled log. Beth and I are gnawing our knuckles and reaching for our phones when she sits up with her eyes blazing and asks, "Did you see it? Were you there?"

We don't know what to say, exactly, so we don't.

"Well," she says in that breathy tone that enchants thousands, "there you are."

Who are we to say otherwise?

On the way home Beth says, "Did she just . . . "

"I don't know."

"Did we?"

It's amazing, I am thinking *not really* but I have to say, "I don't know!"

"I don't either," Beth says, "but wasn't it grand." Her voice drops so it's more a statement than a question, and we leave it there.

We get out of the car feeling somewhat exalted, and go back to our lives. I'd love to tell Richard, but there's no way to explain it so he'd understand. Instead Beth and I go around feeling special, *special*, whether because of the experience or because of all Schuylerton society we alone are designated friends of Ashley Famous, it's hard to say. We don't talk about it because this is precious and we owe it to Ashley not to tell. Also, it pisses certain people off. Mariel and Stephanie of course, but they were never part of the inner circle. Jeannie because she wasn't invited, and Gloria for sure.

To make it up to them we decide to give a party at my house, nothing fancy: champagne with Gloria's crudités, and the satays and teriyakis the chef from Kang's restaurant does on his row of hibachis, Jeannie's chocolate cheesecake, Japanese lanterns in the woods, and to double-atone for being best friends with her and leaving Jeannie and Gloria and the others outside the loop, I get Arch to make sure Ashley Famous comes.

We do these things so well that naturally she'll understand this is nothing special, we give beautiful parties all the time. Beth and I are looking out at the terrace just before the first guests come and everything is perfect: glowing hibachis, LED lights winking in the trees and Japanese lanterns glowing in the woods beyond; the peonies are out and I tell her, "Look hard, Beth, so you'll never forget what this party looks like. We're going to remember this night for the rest of our lives."

Ashley and Arch come in late, and look at her! My, isn't that the transformation? And don't our men, who had zero interest in the matter until the party, collect like mosquitoes around the bug zapper on a summer night? Where she came to church in a T-shirt and those tawdry flowered jeans, tonight she walks in barefoot in a beautiful diaphanous thing that I swear is by Issy Miyake, and a wreath of gold on her head with bachelors' buttons woven in. Her hair is flying and she looks like what she is: an ornament to the community, our star.

Instead of pleasing one and all with our own personal famous writer, we've alienated quite a few, because the only men who aren't glued to her are Bill Anthony, who foolishly wore the clerical collar, a turnoff for both of them, apparently, and the fourth Mr. Famous, who stalks the fringes looking every inch the poet, like Lord Byron under a cloud, but without the club foot.

Still it's a beautiful party, everyone has to agree. Beth and I knock ourselves out running around mingling, pulling outsiders from Hyde Park and Rhinebeck and Red Hook into the circle, mixing up couples with people they already knew; we are a storm, a flame of congeniality that seems to go out as soon as we turn our backs, because Ashley Famous is sitting on the steps to the fountain barefoot, holding forth, and that's where everyone is.

This seems like the time to let Richard know that the gauzy Ms. Famous and I are kindred, so I make my way through the throng and say "Ashley, dear!" Then she gives me the strangest look and does a one-two take. *Who **are** you* is quickly replaced by a manufactured smile and oddly, since Beth and I are, after all, giving the party—I mean does she not recognize us or what?—oddly she says, "How lovely, running into you here." And practically in the same breath Richard—my Richard!—shushes me: "Please, honey. Ashley is in the middle of a joke."

Not that anybody notices when I storm away. At my back I hear her trilling, "I think the two most interesting things in the world are sex and religion, don't you?"

Then, what is it the woman said to Bill Anthony that hooked him and brought all this down on us? Right.

Sometimes you. Just. Get. Tired.

What I hate most is that I'm trying not to feel wounded, but I'm hurt. Feeling perhaps a tad bit guilty, Richard puts an arm around me and tries to pull me back into the social mainstream, but I do what any woman would do. I float out of the mainstream and drift along in the backwaters, among dropped napkins and abandoned plates. One of the Japanese lanterns in the woods has caught fire—nothing serious, it's May, and too wet to burn long; Kang's chef is gone and the hibachis have burned out. As I bob along I hear Gloria grumble, "You'd think being famous would be enough," but I let it pass and drift on in the shallows until I fetch up against Arch, the lonely fourth husband, beached on the bank. I don't do much. When we collide I plant my fingers on that broad, strong wrist, warm in spite of the fact that the night just turned cool.

I want to draw his attention to the clump of men and ask him, *who's next* but in our circle we don't say the unspeakable and for all I know the poor boy has no idea that his time with Ms. Famous is growing short. I try, "Is she always like this?"

He turns, blinded by misconception and glowing with God knows what. "You mean, radiant?"

"Radiant, yes." I am too well bred to say, *Radiant, no. Voracious.*

"Ashley is . . . Well, Ashley."

He may be dazzled but he has not moved and my fingers are still on his warm, warm wrist, and I am thinking: *well, I'll show her!* I make them curl to make a bracelet for him, like a gift. "Would you like to take a walk?"

Look at our men, all gathering like cultists about to paint themselves blue and perform extreme acts. Look at my women friends, stewing in their own bitter juices. Look at me, bent on subversion, and look at Arch, grinning at me like a dirty boy. "Of course."

We push off from the ship of fools and head out along the driveway to Mill Road, and I have to wonder if she even saw us go; well, when her man comes home smirched and guilty, she will damn well know it. He recites yards of free verse as we walk, and I make appreciative noises and we both feel good enough about ourselves, going along in the moonlight. Then I think: Now, and nudge him until we're facing so I can take his hands. I tell him, "They aren't all like her."

Then, oh! Heedless boy; when he says, "There's nobody like her," he is glistening all over again. I'm about to despair when he says, as if to redeem it, "You know, there is one thing."

This could still go the other way so I leave my answer wide open. "Yes?" "Ashley isn't happy here." He frees one hand and we turn back.

"Oooooh. She isn't?" When he doesn't pick up on it I say, "That's too bad."

"When she's unhappy, it makes it hard for me."

"Unhappy. Hmmm . . . " I do this carefully, leaving a hole big enough for him to drive a forklift into, but he doesn't follow up, he just trudges along even after I prompt him with, "And?" One unkind word and we can start on her.

It's maddening, walking hand in hand with an attractive kid who is too stupid to know what's happened to him let alone what's possible here, and too obtuse to explain why.

The silence drags on until I am forced to say in tones controlled as tightly as I can squeeze them, "What. Ah. What's gone wrong?"

"It's hard to explain."

I hate this. "Is it something we did?"

"In a way. Sort of. Oh, this is embarrassing."

Right. He has been deputized. I try to make it easy for him. "What is?"

It appears that when you're the fourth Mr. Ashley Famous, nothing is easy for you. After a struggle he gets it out—well, part of it. "It's something you haven't done!"

Try playing twenty questions on a country road in the middle of the night. Make that forty questions. It takes too long, but I manage to ask them all.

As it turns out, Arch isn't embarrassed; where you or I would be humiliated, fishing on behalf of somebody who doesn't love you enough to stay by your side at parties, Arch says as though pointing out the obvious, "Your little party is nice and all, but Ashley. . . She's very upset." By this time he is strongly aware that I am done asking polite questions so he explains. "Usually when she comes to a new town people do something special, a concert, a dinner or a dance, something big, in her honor."

"Something big."

"Right. When Ashley Famous comes to town people get together and throw a great big party for her."

"Even though she hates parties."

"Oh, you know Ashley. She only says she does."

"At the club."

"Could it be black tie?" Even by moonlight there's no missing the grateful smile, and I still can't say whether it's triumph he's exuding, or relief. "She loves to dress up."

Oh, we'll give her a party all right, if that's what she expects, and it will be the biggest and most beautiful party ever to go down in the annals of the Schuylerton River Club. Before we're done it will rival the best efforts of the Vanderbilts and the first Roosevelts back in the day, a masterpiece of planning and execution, all in honor of our brand new local celebrity, *Welcome, Ashley, now you are one of us*, and naturally it will be black tie so the bitch can come in high drag without putting the rest of us in the shade, for we clean up nicely and put on our diamonds for events like this. Then the lovely Ashley Famous can float into the room in her most expensive designer-whatever, and I hope she has the good grace to blush at Bill Anthony's welcoming speech, after which she will truly be in our midst, surrounded by admirers, secure in the knowledge that where apparently we've been remiss without knowing it, we're pulling out all the stops, including picking out her name in dwarf roses on top of one of Tempest's most beautiful cakes. We will show Ashley Famous every way we know how that this whole beautiful, expensive evening is all about her. Before we're done, she will have drunk from champagne fountains and danced to the Tippy Little Orchestra and cracked lobsters in the driveway with the heel of her most elegant shoe; on her big night she will wine and dine and whirl around the dance floor at the center of attention in spite of her reclusive qualities, the cynosure of all eyes, and when that soft pink glow in the sky above the Hudson warns us that sunrise comes next we will by God do what you do for the GOH at any bacchanal; we'll chase our maiden up into the woods overlooking the River Club and push her backward over a slab of granite and cut out her heart.

If you've ever parented siblings or been one you know that no matter how smooth things may be on the surface, at least some of the time, even when siblings love each other, which isn't always, friction and intense rivalry are part of the package. Hence this pair. Thanks, Harlan, for giving this one its freedom. Like a girl saving herself for marriage, I was keeping it safe for your ultimate Dangerous Visions *volume. Until now...*

BABY BROTHER

Welcome to my hacienda. I want to thank you all for everything you've done for me so far, especially for coming all the way down here to Argentina. I am honored. Not everybody has such loyal friends, or should I say, such persistent followers.

I'm only sorry I can't rise to the occasion, but as you can see, standing up doesn't work for me any more. I save myself until it's time to usher my guests to the *porte-cochère* with fond farewells and thanks for coming, which I do as best I can—you have come so far; it is only civil. Ah, but in the old days I would have run behind your car, strewing flowers and shouting *olé* until you cleared the driveway and the double gates, waving even after you passed out of sight, but that was in the old days.

How sad that you find me so late in life, when even five or ten years ago we could have done this properly: deposed prince and loving loyalists; quarry, hunter—however you regard it. Now I am short of breath, as well as short-shrifted and shortsighted, and you—distinguished Jews— you are wearing thin too, strained and near exhaustion from the decades of pursuing.

The search has made you old, even as I have grown old waiting.

Look at you: your runover shoes, your tight mouths, the circles around the eyes, dust in the crevices that age has made around them. We have all been at this so long that we are near the end of our resources. We aren't any of us what we were; we must be who we are, and that's an end on it.

I must apologize for my appearance, laid waste as I am, and pillaged by the inexorable cohort of the grim reaper, but *c'est la vie*. Time has its ways, and in my ninety-something years I have gone a great many of them, with only a few more ways to go before . . .

But I am getting ahead of myself.

Friends, do not be disheartened to see me so, debilitated and in a *pensione* for the aged. I am still worthy of your attention. Unlike my brother, I am gifted with a fine bony structure, good for TV and perhaps, when they come, print photographers can still find a flattering angle. Nor should you be misled by my frailty. My mind is still as sharp as yours, and time, after all, as my brother used to say, time knows no undoing.

It is not what you have that makes the difference, he said to me, *it's what you don't get. And what you do with it.*

At least I think he did. As children we were so close that our senses became inextricably mingled—his hot breath in my mouth, my tears clogging his nostrils—so that when one sneezed, it was the other who asked pardon, while at other times one sinned and the other took the punishment, God he was hungry for it . . . But you know. Or should. Otherwise you would not have wandered for so long, or worked so hard, or traveled so far to find me.

Or am I second again, and you came thinking he lived and you'd finally found him?

How many times have I come out flattered, smiling and excited, to receive what turn out to be delegations seeking my brother. The smile fades, I droop and turn away with my shoulders sagging, like a puppy at the pound that springs forth with a fresh grin for every new owner, only to meet the knacker. I must not blame you, my friends, for coming so late, nor him, for being the big brother. Whatever has happened to us, God has done it.

Or I did. Let me explain this.

Are you comfortable? Are you enjoying your glasses of water? My apologies; I can no longer manage the slight emolument necessary to cause Estrellita to provide sweet cakes and maté with silver straws, or

Julio to bring his mandolin to score our deliberations. I am flat broke here. Disgrace drinks money like water.

Did I remember to thank you for coming? The way up these cliffs is hard, I know, and shards of glass top the walls around our *hacienda*. Did the razor wire hurt you? Your persistence flatters me. It's not every people that waits so long or searches so far or works so hard to rectify the past. Your peremptory entrance notwithstanding, I am glad to see you.

And you. I welcome you all, in spite of your expressions.

I particularly want to thank you, Dr. Weiskopf, for all your efforts—the TV documentary was most impressive, although I hated the actor you chose to play me, and the animated footage did not do either of us justice. The choice of Mahler was inspired. And the idea of employing music video! Thanks to your promotional acumen, every teenager in the West was enlisted in the search for us.

Which is how you happened to receive a certain phone call from one Estrellita Andujar, little Estrellita, who, even in my reduced circumstances has until now done my bidding... but we are all indeed close to the end—spent, to the last penny.

Meanwhile, Dr. Weiskopf, I am pleased to meet you at last, and fair or not, tasteful or cheaply exploitative, thank you for the publicity. I wish you had done it sooner.

As for you, Frau Rosenberg, I want to praise the likeness on the leaflets you caused to be dropped by air over every major city. I am flattered that you found it necessary to pull the lever and shout "bombs away" in every single instance.

Thank you, Herr Fenk, for the attractive likeness on the posters you circulated on three continents; you did indeed find somebody to blow the whistle, or, as they say on TV, finger me, and to you, Mr. Feigel, I am grateful for your tireless bloodhounding.

To be remembered thus! Friends, to be remembered at all! But you could not know what it is like to spend a lifetime in the shadows, ignored, invisible to history, nor can you even guess how it feels when the hand that reaches into the cradle picks up another. It is difficult indeed to be slighted by time and fate, one's Mama—to say nothing of the hands and pens of the world's historians.

You begin to understand why I am so glad to see you? We were made for each other. Together, we can make certain corrections in the record. That is, if you permit. It is a thrill to have you here, *this close*, ringing me with your grave and angry faces!

Perhaps you thought I would flee at your approach, but you see my hands are spread in welcome, and they are empty. I would never fight you, nor would I try to flee. My friends, my adversaries, if I can hardly walk, how can I run from you? If I could in fact totter, I would come careering into your grim embrace; look, I am smiling.

All my life I have been waiting. One way or another, in one city and another, asleep and awake, ill and well, unhappy and almost happy, from birth I have moved toward this confrontation.

You see, you and I are fated. Together we will complete the future. Yes, dear friends, you intent assembled Jews with your earnest and puzzled faces, if it is your function to seek, it is mine to be discovered.

Whatever you do with me, however the fatherland receives me, whether I am welcomed by a parade with banked flowers on the *autobahn*, by bells and banners and massed choirs singing the Hallelujah Chorus, or whether they stone me like a rabid cur through the streets of the capitol of the German Democratic Republic, I will at last complete the design that was limned in my brain from birth, according to certain blueprints etched in fire along every fiber of my body.

I am the instrument of your retribution.

Help, I don't mean now! Not yet!

Please, gentlemen. Madam! Remember, I am not him. I was never him! I was never him; I was only the means. Let me help you understand this. Are you sure you're comfortable? Very well. Listen.

Mama always made me wear Adolf's castoff underwear. The shirts. The vests. I slept every night of my childhood in Adolf's outgrown pajamas.

He also never let me play with his toys. He was used to getting his own way. Remember, he came first. Then I came, and he never forgave me. Were you a firstborn? Did you have a baby brother? Try and understand me! Anything I had, Adolf considered lost—the air we breathed, the food we ate, the smiles of our dear mother; with me in the house he would never again have all of anything.

Nor would I ever have anything unless he discarded it. This knowledge bonded us. *Mon semblable, mon frère*—he hated me. It is the way of big brothers.

He could never forgive me because he came first. I would never forgive him for making me second.

My first memory is of the two of us interlocked: hot baby flesh tangling, breath and blood mingling as we rolled and he overwhelmed me with flaming eyes and a mouth like a roaring furnace while I screamed in pain at his fury. Yang and yin we were, dark and light we grappled, closer than lovers, struggling in the intolerable embrace of brotherhood, shrieking mad with laughter.

When I was three he tried to murder me.

It is no wonder.

I woke to find him glaring into my crib; I looked up smiling, and then! He laid open my brow with a toy steam shovel.

See it through Adolf's eyes: shared thoughts, shared love, shared flesh, the intense need to do me harm; the certain knowledge that he would do even worse if he did not get rid of me.

My scream of shock and pain brought Mama, who discovered us— Adolf thunderous (my brother, myself) and me—poor Murray! with a great gash in my forehead and the blood and tears running. I needed her to hug and comfort me. *Mama!*

"Aha," he said. So smug. "Now Mama will beat me. Aha!" What was my brother then, a masochist? I've never known. I've never stopped wondering.

I cried, and Mama came! She swooped down like the wolf upon the fold, and just before she did he flashed me the prurient, vulpine grin of the soon-to-be punished: was that what he wanted? Adolf writhed in ecstasy, waiting for his beating, while I yearned to be comforted, wracked in a transport of weeping.

He wanted the beating.

Her passion frightened us—that good hausfrau with the son who would be a genius; then our mother—you will not believe it. She turned on me! She screamed, "Oh, Murray, how could you!"

I saw Adolf rip in two. Something interruptus.

With angry hands she fell on me, the victim, cursing me for causing all this trouble; I had brought it on myself, I Murray, the bloodied, was the offender; in my helplessness it was I, the victim who had brought it on! My fault. My fault! Mama hated me for it. But perhaps you can begin to see how these things come down . . .

I was desolated. She scooped him up and carried him out: "Oh there there you poor darling." Over her shoulder I saw Adolf's dark eyes gleaming with frustration; my brother!

He of the horrendous rages. In chorus we screamed the rage of the bereft—I, betrayed, he deprived of her firm hand.

Instead of beating Adolf, Mama smothered him with love. She made him sit up like a pet and take food from her mouth because she loved him too much. With me to punish, she could turn the fierce fire of her love on him. This was my fault, for being born.

Our mother! Sometimes she followed Adolf like a dog. She took candy from his hands and chewed it for him and handed it back with a besotted smile that grieved us both. She crouched on her hands and knees, watching him play. She would take the ball the second before he grasped it and throw it wherever he wanted it to go. She followed him to school, calling sweetly. When Adolph went in, humiliated by her attentions, she sobbed in the dooryard until the closing bell rang and he was restored to her. Then he would come home from school and tie my wrists to the back yard swing and think up ways to torture me. The pathology is clear.

You need not wonder why later he called it the Fatherland.

Enough. You get the idea. A domineering, loving mother, who, no matter what he did, would never cut Adolf loose, who would not punish him. No wonder he was warped. I would not have walked in his shoes for anything—I guess. Ah, but Mama, why not me?

Understand, he was not always a monster. In the beginning, he was nice.

As children, we were as one—Chang and Eng; love twinned us, while rivalry tore us apart. I used to wake in the night and hear us breathing: him, me. We tasted what each other ate; when I fell, he cried out. I felt his frustration when she whipped me for breaking the prized Boehm goose my brother smashed before her eyes in a doomed attempt to turn her anger on him because she didn't care enough to punish; she overloaded him with undiscriminating love.

I don't mean to shock you but that—need, that hunger for completion gripped us both; we writhed in a strange, pre-orgasmic flush that in her stupid love our mother frustrated, not once, but for all time. Perhaps it was this unceasing prurience that caused my brother's . . .

Sorry. Of course amateur psychology pushes your patience to its limits. Those who suffer the effects of pathology are too scarred to take an interest in remote causes.

Still, since you have come so far, and I have waited for so long, I beg you to bear with me. If we are going to accomplish this, I need your understanding. Listen. We were so close that what Adolf wanted, I wanted for him. Pressing against our mother, I felt his lust for pain; seized by her, I suffered his envy. Friends, we dreamed each other's dreams.

The dreams!

But you have lived those dreams. In black smoke and blood and memory you have spelled them out. Your dead have realized and magnified the worst of my brother's dreams, down to the last. Waking in a sweat, we screamed and screamed because we could not stop the future.

No wonder he was frightened.

We were burgeoning men: our parts, our hair, everything on us started growing; it was terrifying. Strange forces tore us to pieces: the need to be diverted from our course; the desire, verging on lust, for discovery, for punishment.

I fell in love. She had blond braids and her name was Anna. You'd think that since he was first in everybody else's eyes Adolf would be first in Anna's, but for a moment there, she loved me. Perhaps she was using me to get my brother's attention, but I was blinded by her blandishments—I forgot his envy; the danger, in love I was oblivious. He schemed. One night after Anna and I kissed goodbye at her gate, he fell on her and dragged her into the bushes. I was halfway home when I heard her screams. Then as my brother strained and failed to burst inside her I felt the anguish of his frustration. So there was this. Did he need to be punished before he could make love? Something writhed inside him— something, *interruptus*.

She pressed charges. Anna, who had been my dear, Anna, who was outraged by his hands and teeth and failing member, poor Anna testified that it was not Adolf but I who had done it, while in the town hall Mama sat by my brother's side and listened. When I was sentenced she reached for his hand, as if groping for a lover's.

It was almost too much! All my life I had suffered for his sins; all my life Mama had ignored me, until Anna nobody had ever even kissed me, and now there was this—the outrage, the overwhelming sadness of my betrayal and public humiliation.

I thought to catch his eye: if I felt his frustration, did he not share my suffering? But Adolf was fixed on Mama in a frenzy, trying to free his hand. Amazing! I was in pain and he felt nothing.

Alone in the dock, I grasped the implications. I laughed aloud. Accused as I was, unjustly censured, I came to the knowledge seconds before he did. I had what he wanted.

I heard him cry out. Then over the heads of the others we exchanged looks: *mon semblable, mon frere*, Murray is first in this!

That expression! Something, *interruptus*.

So it was that I, the younger brother; Murray the unwanted, overshadowed by the firstborn; I, Murray the unloved, came to accept the beatings, the lectures, the escalating tortures devised by our loving Mama and an angry society because I had something my big brother wanted. The punishment that my brother so needed *and would not have*. With the sly smile of the satisfied, I welcomed them.

Oh how he raged, how he writhed in an orgy of frustration! Reviled though I was for what he had done, despised and suffering, I could move on to that which Adolf could never know, exploding like a star— Completing sex. Again. Again. Again. It was a small thing, but it was everything. Did I forget to tell you that as a youth I was blond, and had blue eyes? I was better looking!

The tables turned, if one can believe in tables, or in turning.

We were eighteen. I woke in the night as I had so many years before, to find Adolf standing over my bed with his face charged with blood and his piggy black eyes burning. Did I mention that his eyes were small, or piggy? But you have fueled your endeavors on his likenesses.

As before, our breaths mingled.

I thought he had come to murder me. I rolled over to escape his blows, but he whispered: "Don't!"

"What are you doing?"

"Quiet. *Dummkopf!* I am running away."

Even before he did, I saw it; faster than thought, I grabbed his wrists. "Oh no you don't!"

Then he bent his head close to mine, twisting in his desperation and hissing at me with his teeth bared in a grin of entreaty, "Oh Murray, let me escape this—please. The love. It's torture!"

I bared my teeth in a silent scream because I saw what Adolf saw and—worse, in the flash of a second in which I considered—what would become of my brother if he didn't get away—what would happen to me if he did—I saw what he could not see: our past, the present, the future, God forgive me I saw the future and I permitted it. Forgive me, for I lacked the strength to take on the mantle he was trying with his last scrap of strength to shuck.

Grappling with him thus, rolling, flesh on flesh, I saw, no, felt as he did the voluptuous promise of evil, the sickly sweet seductions of unharnessed sin that summoned no matter how he resisted. Like him I twisted in the terror of foreknowledge, undulating in the sophisticated arousal of impending guilt; Jews, forgive me, in that second I lived the life he sought so fiercely to escape.

Yes, I felt the measure of his desperation, and still . . . Grave and passionate we fought, struggling silently in the last battle from which only one of us could emerge intact: Adolf tearing at my hands with gnashing teeth, I firm as stone, maintaining the grip I could not let him break, and wildly contorted as I was, slashing his knuckles with my teeth, I realized that I could do it; yes. I could still let him go and settle the mantle about my shoulders, accepting everything; I could become that which he was becoming.

More: I could do this and not only turn, but end it; I had the power. We both comprehended it; I could in fact save us all by becoming that which my brother was going to be; I could hurl it into a furnace or drop it from a cliff or bury it in the sea; I had the power to destroy this evil before it could mature and cause what it would do. Did. Had done. But I was weak. No, worse, I was selfish.

FRIENDS, JEWS, I WANTED MY LIFE.

I wanted to be first at something, just for once in my life. Is that such a terrible thing for a baby brother to want?

Hear me well.

It's the only thing baby brothers want.

He was hissing, all sweat and saliva: "Let go of me."

I did what I had to: pulling my brother to me in mingled love and hatred and terror, for the last time I felt what he felt just before I gnashed at his forehead, shouting as my throat cracked: "No!"

I kept on shouting then, my voice magnified by fear, and of course she came, Mama, well-intentioned idiot that she was, squashy with love and ever maternal in her flowered flannel nightgown; she came running into the room with her rosy face creamed for the night and her thick gray braid hanging down; Mama, the loving and unwitting villain. Our mother. Mother of us all. She did precisely what I knew she would. She sprang between us, shouting.

"Murray, stop it, stop! What are you doing to your brother? Idiot, **dummkopf**, you let go of him."

Which I did.

I will never forget his face as I let go and rolled off, or the cry that sundered him.

*In a flash Mama was on the bed, cradling his bloodied head on her bosom, doting, comforting, "Oh my darling, **liebchen**, sweetest."*

Panting, I awaited completion.

*Furious, she turned on me, fixing destiny. "**You!**"*

The implications made me tremble.

Then she smashed me with the back of her hand. And gave me what he wanted most of all, the mother's worst punishment: "Get out of my sight. Forever."

I slipped him the sly, sated smile of the victim. Victor. And the look on his face! I had won that one, and forever.

Voilà.

I was gone.

Naturally I suffered a certain *frisson* when Adolf rose to power, combined guilt and envy as he made that power felt: a rising mortification as the extent of it was known; he was first, still, but it was a monstrous first. While I . . .

I was ensconced here in Argentina before it began. I was that distinguished gentleman with the ineffable air of suffering whom you may have seen photographed at sidewalk cafes, the dapper dinner partner in the white suit who was so well known in the best circles in Buenos Aires, the graceful dancer and the charming houseguest who wore the sad smile, as if he harbored a secret, who moved among the citizens of the *beau monde* with the wistful, aristocratic air. I was the mysterious gentleman who so inflamed and pleased the ladies that they wept, the suave lover who was never alone and always satisfied; as he ravaged Europe I made my way through the golden, whispering succulent flesh of each new generation of young women—giddy, sated, drunken, glutted with love as my brother fed on blood.

But of course I did not understand that at first. Or would not look it in the face. He was running a country. He was having a good time. And I . . .

I was the exile, another remittance man, the homesick gentleman who draws the curtains in his chambers at midday to dream of espaliered plants and neat patterned walks in Austrian gardens, while outside, dense tropical breezes stir wild jungle blooms. I was the frustrated engineer, the erstwhile industrialist, the general manqué, who made the best of his circumstances by investing his stipend, and enjoyed a certain social standing only because he was new to the New World, and if I was ineffably sad . . .

Let us say that it was premonitory sadness, the first *susurrus* of encroaching guilt.

He was busy. I shouldn't be expected to keep track. So was I.

It was only as the continent plunged into war that I began to hear what he was doing. What he caused.

What I caused—however remotely. I did. I caused it. I brought him down on you.

I lost interest in my work. I still went to parties, but I found it hard to laugh. My hair grew thin. My muscle and fiber dwindled. I became gaunt and miserable. I could not sleep. It grew difficult to keep up appearances.

Using the funds I had amassed, I made as good a showing as I could. Elegant silk shirts hid my diminishing frame. The white suit concealed the worst. My smile covered a multitude of sins. His sins. You know the rest. You see me now.

You know why I am so glad you have come.

I have been waiting. How long I have been waiting!

The pain. Will it seem cheap if I beg you, "Do it"?

Please.

This came when the first two lines materialized in my head. The rest took longer.

DENNY

We are worried about Denny. We have reason to believe he may go all Columbine on us.

Experts warn parents to watch out for signs, and it hurts to say, but we've seen plenty. Day and night our son is like an LCD banner, signaling something we can't read. If he implodes and comes out shooting, the first thing to show up in the crosshairs will be us.

He was cute when he was little but now he's heavily encoded: black everything, hanging off him in tatters—Matrix coat in mid-August, T-shirt, jeans, bits of peeled sunburn and cuticle gnawed to shreds. Black lipstick and blue bruises around the eyes. That glare. Shake him and dirt flies out—grot and nail clippings, crushed rolling papers, inexplicable knots of hair. Stacks of secret writing that Denny covers as you come into the room, and no friends except that creepy kid who won't look you in the eye.

Shrinks list things to watch out for, and it isn't just to protect the innocent, sitting in class when the armed fury comes in and lays waste. They're warning us! Some lout killed his parents with a baseball bat not far from here, they were dead before the sleeping neighborhood rolled over and shut off the clock. In addition to knifings and axe murders, I read about deaths by assault weapon or repeating rifle, people executed by their own children on their way out of the house to massacre their peers.

It's awful going around scared, but there you are. Poor Steph and I are forever on the alert.

Our mutant enemy blunders around the house at night making messes and bumping into things, and, worse? We're the ones who apologize for being in the way. Back in our room, my wife throws herself down on the bed and sobs, "I've failed," but, listen! There may be an enemy within but in spite of the cycle of guilt and mutual recriminations, we know it isn't us.

I don't know what's up with Dad. He and Mom are getting all weird and creepy, lurking with their knuckles hooked under their chins like disturbed squirrels, jumping away with uh-oh looks and shifty eyes when I come in. It's not like they're avoiding me. Unless they are.

How did it get so bad? The tiptoeing and the shrinking, the nights when I go to bed in tears? I want to hug my boy and make it better, but it's like making overtures to a porcupine. Every gesture I try goes astray and if I get too close, I get hurt. What's a mother to do? He was a hard person when the doctor dragged him out kicking and screaming, and it's been downhill ever since. Maybe we were too old to be parents, unless we were too young. We had a baby because we were that age and it was expected, but nobody told us what it would be like. The event? The glories of childbirth thing is an atrocious myth. It was painful and scary and astounding. Stan and I spent the first months exhausted and terrified, but that's nothing compared to now. We love our son, but he's not very easy to like.

Denny's always been sweet with me—well, except at certain times, but God it's hard, and I've tried everything. We need to sit down and talk but my son is hooked up to his music like a patient to an IV and I don't even know what's going into his ears. If I ask him to pull out the ear-buds so we can have the conversation he gets all weird and hostile and slouches away with a look that frightens me.

Denny, if it's something I did, then I'm sorry. Isn't this punishment enough?

When you're warned about the enemy within, the first thing you do is blame yourself. It must be something you did, like failing to pay attention or hitting, which can make schoolyard assassins of kids. Hit Denny? I just wouldn't, although God knows there were times when I was close. The flip side of guilt is things you failed to do, but on that score Stephanie and I test clean. Believe me, we read all the books and covered all the bases—lessons, therapy, Ritalin or Prozac as indicated, contact lenses and braces, of course. Dermabrasion. Comedy camp. Implants to replace teeth trashed by playground bullies, a trigger parents are urged to report, which we dutifully did which made our son furious, I don't know why.

We brought home video games, tabletop soccer and a ping-pong table to help him win friends, but nobody ever comes over. Why, Steph and I spent last summer redoing his room. We've done everything for the kid, and what do we get back? Black polish on the fingernails, a show of teeth so sharp that I could swear he's filing them down to points. We try to give him everything he wants, and the hell of it is, he won't even tell us what he wants.

To this day my wife spends hours on the birthday bunny cake with shredded coconut fur and jelly bean eyes and a combed cotton ball for a tail. She does it with tears in her eyes because it pleased him once, and she has hopes. It does no good to remind her that he was two. Nobody's going to tell us that we don't love Denny, especially not him.

Take a letter off Denny and you get: DENY. Stan and Stephanie don't know it but in study hall I am making a tattoo. It hurts but it's easy to do. It isn't a heart, although I drew an arrow through it to represent Diane, from Spanish class. What I put, with a ballpoint and this safety pin? DENY.

Nobody told me what it would be like. One day you're a normal, perfectly healthy woman with a day job, a sense of who you are in life, the next . . .

You wake up the next morning like a slate that God erased. Your baby howls and everything you used to be is wiped away.

For thirty years of my life, Denny wasn't.

Then he was.

I was so scared. He was so small! Breakable! Like a Swiss watch I had been given to maintain with no idea when the maker would come back to check on me, just the knowledge that I was accountable. There was no clear list of instructions, either, just the expectation that I would take care of it. The machinery was complex and mysterious, but I could tell that it wasn't running right. You try, but what do you do when this precious object entrusted to you is congested with rage? Do I pick him up when he screeches, or should he learn to put himself to sleep? Should I feed him now or is he not hungry, should I change him even though I just did, and I ask you, who's supposed to be in charge? Which of us is supposed to have the upper hand? What if he gets so mad that he breaks?

Dear God, did I crack something in Denny while I wasn't looking, and is that why he grew up withdrawn and angry and sad?

It's like sharing the house with a wild animal. He slinks around like a night-blooming menace, glowering, thinking tainted thoughts. Denny hates me, I'm sure of it, and I don't know why. Still, we are coexisting here until he's old enough to get a life, so I try. I sign his report cards without comment because anything I say will lead to a fight, and the last thing we want here is to set him off. Although I don't much feel like it, I make a smile. I go, HELLO, DENNIS. HOW WAS SCHOOL? and he flinches like I slapped him in the face.

I come into a room and they go silent, you can tell they were talking about me. Then Dad gets all stiff and polite and goes: "Well, Dennis, how's school?" and I hackle. *Get out of my face.* How the fuck does he think school is? I'll tell you how school is. It sucks. I have eight guys lying in wait to beat the crap out of me for eight different reasons, Diane Caldwell being only one. Miss Gleeson in English made me come up in the front of the room and read my story that I wrote; I had to read it out loud which is why seven of the guys are out to get me and the eighth, I'm guessing it's about Diane; if I was sitting in the back and forced to listen to me reading this lame story, I'd beat the crap out of me too.

But Dad is all up in my face, "How was school?" and he won't lay back and let me walk away quiet until he gets an answer, so I go, "OK."

They want you to believe that when they put your new baby in your arms it's love at first sight, but instant mother love is another myth. I don't know who puts it out there, greedy grandmothers bent on posterity or men who want to see their spit and image popping out of you. You want to love your children, but the truth is you get used to them. You get used to being baffled and helpless and weepy, and you accommodate, over time. I went through the first year terrified. Was I giving him everything he needed or warping him for life? Now he's fifteen and the jury's out and it won't come back. You tell me, did I do it right?

God knows I tried. I tried so hard to do it right that I'm afraid I did everything wrong.

She plants fifteen candles on this year's cake. They bristle like armed cannons on a battleship. We knock ourselves out over presents chosen to change him for the better, whatever that means. Nice clothes. A leather bound book to write his thoughts in, along with a box so he can lock it away from us. Games, maybe we can bond over cribbage, or chess. After he blows out the candles she cuts off the bunny's head and presents it to Dennis with that heartbreaking tremulous smile.

Why, when we tried to give him everything, does he look like he wants to cry?

Over the years we tried everything. Tricycles and Christmas trees. Skateboards, sleds. Rollerblades. I used to throw the ball around with him when he was small! Now my son and I circle like boxers and my wife has to hold it in all night because she's scared to go out in the hall.

In school today I accidentally knocked off Diane's notebook when I accidentally went by her desk, which I did so could I pick it up, and when I handed it back we could talk, at least a

little bit. That was an assaholic thing to do, but it was cool. She thanked me with this look, but when I came out after, eight assholes were lying in wait for me, so does that mean she likes me and they know it, or what?

After I finally lost them I stayed back at the foundation to the new gym. Even though I knew the folks would be pissed off at me I stayed until I was good to go, which took a while. There are times when you just don't want people to see your face, you know? At home I have to hide what I am thinking or they'll ask.

I have to be in the right head so I can walk in strong and tough.

In China a kid killed his folks with a knife because, he said, they neglected him. When he woke them up complaining that he was unwell they exploded and sent him back to bed. What was he thinking, crouching in his room? *Neglect? I'll show you neglect.* Whatever he thought, whatever they did or failed to do to offend him, his father had thirty-seven gashes in his hide. His mother got almost twice that, now what does that tell you?

It tells you that no matter what you think you're doing, they're there to tell you that you did it wrong.

You go along doing what you always did under the illusion that it's OK, and nothing changes. Then menace creeps in like a cat when you aren't looking and goes to sleep on the hearth. Every once in a while it wakes up and licks its balls. It settles back down and watches through slits, regarding us with malevolent yellow eyes because unlike you, unlike Stephanie and me, it knows what's coming and it is content to wait.

There is a hidden clock set for an hour not known to us. Something big that we don't know about is counting down to detonation, and everything we see and hear tells us that it is Dennis. Our own flesh and blood!

Sometimes mothers have to be Geneva, the neutral party juggling warring factions, trying desperately to make peace. I try, but this is nothing like Switzerland. My house is an armed camp. Stan turns on the boy at the least provocation. Look at him with his jaw set in stone and his shoulders bunched, waiting for the shooting to start.

Why is he all the time going around ahem, Dennis, how are YOU today, like we are friends? Like we were ever friends, when I know the bastard never liked me, hates the sight of me, doesn't want to be caught walking with me anywhere that anybody from the office will see, and when we do go out somewhere big and anonymous, like a basketball game, he's always fake-smiling at me with that tight mouth and a mean little squint. At least thank God he's quit trying to talk baseball or make me play racket ball with him, or fucking tennis when he knows my hand-eye coordination sucks, and if I see a ball coming at me, I flinch. I don't know whether I hate sports more than sports hate me, but I'm fucking sick of it, and I'm good and sick of being locked in here with the two of them, like we are in jail together, doing life. If I was old enough I'd join the Army and get blown away in some foreign country that parents never go.

Everybody knows the joke about the eight hundred pound gorilla, when he talks you listen, or is it, he sits down wherever he wants? We need to be careful with Denny, because until we see the size and shape of the hatred, we can't begin to deal with it. In Canada, I just saw on TV, the cops are hunting for a kid who shot his parents when he asked for money and they didn't cough up. He emptied their wallets and took off.

Yes I am researching these things on the web.

High school junior knifes his dad after a fight over the family car, and this is only last year. Almost makes it to the border before his mother phones 911 and the cops catch up with him; there's a documentary on it scheduled for HBO.

On the web, everybody has a theory. There's the outsider theory, the video-game/TV-violence theory, the suspicion that shooters were abused at home, and then there's the chance that it's not something we failed to do, they destruct for no known reason because fate is arbitrary and vicious, and it's nothing anybody did.

One psychologist thinks they blow up because the adolescent's brain isn't fully developed until he's twenty-one. So how do we get through the next six years with our big son? I try to get on Denny's good side, but I can make a 360 around the kid and still not know which side that is, unless he's turning as I do, so I'll never see. Sometimes I walk into a room and find him hunched in a corner like a bag of feed that somebody dropped on the floor and I wonder, *How do I start the conversation?*

Do I say, "Who do you like for the World Series?" Or do I sit down creaking, so he and I are on the floor with our backs to the wall, sitting shoulder to shoulder, and go, *ahem?* When I think I have his attention I'll try this. It works on bad TV: "We need to talk."

Like that ever works.

When Stan does try to make nice, being Stanley, he says the wrong thing. Or Denny takes it wrong. One word and my firstborn clenches like a shaken fist. I love him, but, oh. It was OK when his dad outweighed him, but that was a while ago. Denny thinks that as he's bigger than Stan, he's probably smarter too. This is quite possible, but I wouldn't dare suggest it to Stan, who for reasons I can't fathom needs to be the personal best, no contenders, no argument.

They say every son needs to kill his father to become a man, but that's only in books. My men kill each other every single day. I'll admit it, Denny means well but he's a little abrasive. Like a bear cub that hasn't learned to sheath his claws.

I love them both, but my greatest fear is being pushed to the point where I have to pick one over the other. I just know it will happen sooner or later, and I will do anything to prevent it. The least little thing sets them off.

What I hate most is the questions. Can't do this without them asking, can't go out wearing that, can't even think about another piercing; she checks my underwear before it goes in the wash and she isn't only looking for blood. Like, do they think I keep snapshots of all the crap things that happen to me?

They are always around here, spying, prying; like, what ever happened to personal space? When I do go out they sneak around looking at my private things, when all I want from them, all I want in the world is to have friends and be happy and for once, just one time be not bothered, as in, totally left alone.

Just now a boy murdered his parents three counties over, we saw it on the TV nightly news. The cops got out an APB. So, what happens next? Will he throw his girlfriend into the car for a joyride or drive on to wipe out the contents of a college dorm?

We're told to stay on the lookout, but what, specifically, are we looking for? No parent wants to be the sneaky, underhanded snoop who reads diaries and tosses the kid's room as soon as he leaves the house. My wife and I were brought up to respect people's privacy, and besides. We're scared of what we might find. The papers say if you see a problem, reach out to your child. Easier if you know he won't bite your hand off.

If only he and his father would talk. *They have so much in common: quick tempers, those big, fierce heads, the Esterhazy slouch. If they tried I know they could work it out, but they sit at the supper table like rocks, and except for would you pass the whatever they are so stony that it makes me want to weep. Because it is expected Stan will say "how's school" in that routine, doesn't-want-an-answer way. Then Dennis says "OK" just to get Stan to leave him alone. Stan grunts and that's the end of that, and on weekends even that goes by. I hate the silence, but if they do get talking they'll fight so frankly it's a relief.*

I look at their hatchet faces and think; I'm so afraid.

They thought I was the one defacing lockers so I got detention, somebody that hates me used my personal hash, I don't care the way things are right now, detention is the safest place to be. They ran it across a whole bank of lockers outside the girls' bathroom and in a way it was kind of magnificent, scored into

the metal like the one on my arm: DENY, so I don't care what they do to me, and at home if they get all pissed off about me being late, I'm all, so what, and the hell with them.

I'm telling you, the situation is dangerous. Book says sit the kid down for a heart-to-heart and that would solve our problems, but what do you say when you've been warned that the least little thing will set him off? How do you walk free when your wife cries herself to sleep at night and you personally are hanging on like a squirrel in a hurricane, too stressed to know what to watch out for, or which is the least little thing?

Beware root causes, they tell us, *Signs of depression. Talk of death.* So, what if your kid won't talk? Do you count cabalists drawn on his hands and all over his school notebooks? Is the skull gouged in the bathroom windowsill with his fingernail a sign? *Listen to your children.* Well, you don't live here, you psychiatrists and grief counselors. That's easy for you to say.

I try to talk to them, to bring them together, to make it all right, but look what happened last night. I reached out to Denny but he shrugged me off. I called after him, "Are you all right?" He left the kitchen so fast that I don't know what went wrong with his face, only that it was skewed. Stan tried to get through in his own clumsy way, but Denny stalked away before he could clear his throat. Maybe if I put flowers and linens on the dining room table I could get him to stay. Instead of eating in the kitchen we'd sit down to candles, lemon slices in the ice water. Would we linger at dinner if I set the table nicely and pulled the dining room chairs close enough to touch?

Push comes to shove and this is intolerable. The waiting. The unfired shot.

Best-case scenario, I go looking for proof. It sounds ugly to say and it's vile to contemplate, but I'd love to shake out his clothes and watch needles or pills come rolling out, roofies or X or heroin, whatever gets authorities on his case because he's just too much for us and I can't do this alone. If

I found hard evidence in his diary, detailed lists of future crimes, I could do this. If I saw death threats or a hit list on his hard drive we could move in on him, get it all out and get this over with. Back him up against the wall and have it out with him, and I don't mean intervention, I mean ultimatums that he'll agree to and honor to the death because enough is enough, and I need to lay down the law. Better yet, I find his cache of firearms in the basement or loaded pistols under the bed or blood on the pillowcase, proof that he sleeps with a knife. It would be awful, but at least we'd have a place to start.

Then I could photocopy the evidence or turn the computer over to the authorities or march my son down to the river and stand over him while he deep-sixed every single piece of mail-order artillery he's probably charged on my Discover card and stockpiled over the years. Then I would force Dennis to his knees and not let him up until he apologized.

Then he would know that I am not afraid and we are not to be messed with, not now and not in any other life.

Better yet—sorry, Steph—I could take him and the evidence to the police station and turn the little bastard in.

Meanwhile the papers boil over with news of kids who kill their parents and forget what they did. What did they think they were doing, routing out vermin or swatting flies? Is this all we are to Denny, pests he can exterminate and forget? It isn't safe! Stephanie and I know what to be afraid of, but in the absence of proof, we don't know what to expect.

I hate when people expect you to go around smiling, like it's your fucking job. Yesterday Diane went backstage with Dick Fletcher at play practice and they stayed there the whole time. Mr. Hanraty yelled so they sent a kid back with the message not to bother them, they were busy running lines, yeah, right. It doesn't matter anyway, she can't see me for shit, and then I get home and Sunshine Stephanie wants to know did I have fun at play practice, yeah well, fuck you too.

I guess I said something that either hurt Denny's feelings or made him mad and I still don't know if it was asking whether he'd eaten or mentioning the ugly scrape on his chin, but he snarled and forgive me, I said, "If you're going to be like that, just go away," and he spat some insult I couldn't parse and stomped off to his room in such a rage that it shook the house.

This kid in England murdered his parents, just for the use of the family car; I read about it on the web. Took off on vacation with his girlfriend. Nice people: it's not like they beat him or some damn thing, they just said no. With every kid Denny's age a walking time bomb, what are we supposed to do? Should the wife and I arm ourselves so we'll feel safe coming out of our bedroom? Keep a gun in the bedside table or a shiv in the pocket of our robe? Probably. Every time I come out into the hall at night he's there and every time it takes me by surprise.

"Agh!"

He sounds outraged. "Dad!"

How did he get so big? I hate surprises. "What are you doing here?"

"Going to pee." *I'm coming to get you.*

"Go to your room!"

I don't have to see his face. I know that look. *And when I get you . . .* but he shouts, "What am I, supposed to piss on the rug?"

If I had the right words I would say them and zot! He'd disappear. Instead, I threaten. "I don't care what you do. Just go!"

He goes. Which of us wishes the other dead?

To prevent either, we need protection. The only question is whether to use Snuffy's Gun Shop, which means everyone on Broad Street would know, or buy on the Internet. But what if Dennis finds out because he gets off on hacking into my machine? What if he's waiting when the package comes? What if he's standing in the living room, locked and loaded, when Steph and I walk in the door? Smashes into our bedroom and blows us away?

Better forewarned, ergo forearmed.

Diane stuck her gum on my desk today, just left it in the corner when she went past, a perfect thumbprint, like a present for me, it's not like proof that she loves me, but my heart went up and stayed there until I saw her and fucking Dick Fletcher humping in the bushes outside the gym.

I love him, and I try so hard. Yesterday I made his favorite, blueberry waffles for dinner, with apple sausages, and he tramped through the kitchen without even looking and went on up to his room. How do you make it up to someone when you don't even know what you did?

You hate me? You hate your mother, and you want to sneak in some night and murder us in our bed? Well, not on my watch, buddy. Not on my watch.

At the sight of the neat pistol I bring home from Snuffy's, Stephanie bursts into tears. "You can't," she cries. "This is Denny."

"And this is to keep us safe." Although I stand a little taller, I do not tell her that I really mean: *empowered.*

She whips her head around. Tears fly. "But he's just a baby!"

Now, Dennis hasn't been a baby since that thing when he was three. He claimed the puppy wanted to swim, but I knew. We are cohabiting with danger, but to Stephanie, he's still her baby, which may be how things got so bad. When I'm not looking she indulges him, but I don't have proof. I suppose partly it's me, because the kid and I squared off the day she brought him home, mewling little rival for her love. Say his name and I bristle. There, it's out.

I'm embarrassed, but I'm not sorry. We know each other for who we are. I know he never liked me, but we've survived so far on mutual respect. What does this mean really, when push comes to shove?

When he comes in tonight I will be waiting. One false move out of the little bastard and I tell you, push will come to shove.

When he was small I could take him in my lap and hug him and forgive him, no matter what he did, and I hugged him like that with his head close to me and his legs hanging down, until one day he fought me with both fists, shouting, leave me alone, and when I asked him why he started crying and told me: I'm too big. I said, you're never too big, honey, but then I turned my back on the problem and now he is. On good days I can still call him—Denny? And when he comes into the room he stays long enough for me to ask him, Son, is there anything you want to talk about? when what I mean is, is there anything you're afraid to tell me. I stand there thinking if only I could hug you, but he backs away saying, Not really Mom, and just in case I don't get it, just before he slams the door he says firmly, No.

The paramedics leave me in the guidance counselor's office after the fight. I'm supposed to lie there until the bleeding stops. Then Miss Feely comes on to me all tremulous and wary, like, are you OK Dennis, you look like you're about to explode, and I'm so fucking depressed that it comes out and runs down my face so I'm fucking embarrassed too. Then she starts spitting questions and I can't tell if she's afraid I'm going to walk into school tomorrow and start firing or if she's afraid I'm going to destroy myself but I am grateful for the attention either way, and I dutifully shake my head no when she asks are there problems at home. Then she talks and I sit there waiting for it to end. I'm not convinced but by the time she's done at least I have a thing to do. I won't exactly bring home presents, but I'm going to, like, smile and be nice to Mom and Dad when I get there, because they are the only people left. Besides, I feel sorry for them. I have a shitty life but at least I'm not old, like them. We could probably be miserable together until I get big enough to go out on my own. Lame, right? But it's a plan.

This is how a mother's heart breaks. As the gun goes off and his arms fly wide, my only son reaches out to me and his voice rips me from top to bottom, so I will be like this, laid open, until I die. My Denny isn't mad, he isn't even reproachful; he is mystified. "Mom!"

A student writer who went on to do something completely different reported that his psychologist/psychiatrist parents took him for family summers at psychotherapy camp. Three of us, writers all, agreed that it was a terrific setup. Even if we all wrote about it, our stories would never be the same. I waited ten years to see whether the ex-student would come up with one. Not so much. Here's mine.

CAMP NOWHERE

"It had to be an island, didn't it?" I stick it to Mom. "Like, no escape."

"Don't be negative, Charlie, it's our best vacation ever."

"You always say that, and it never is." She has us trapped on a boat on some Great Lake in nether Minniesconsin, with no rescue in sight. I am stuck between nothing and nowhere, farther from the ocean than is safe. Cool people don't come here, not even on their way to someplace else. Landlocked even though we are floating, I've been jammed into the heart of Middle America like a slayer's stake. States that I don't even know the names of are crowding in. It's getting hard to breathe. I poke Mom, in case she isn't feeling guilty. "If I off myself, it's your fault."

"Don't be silly, it's beautiful!"

"It's fucking depressing."

"We're going to love it, you'll see."

"Yeah, right." This is nothing like L.A.

Mom's fingers bite my arm and I look where she is pointing. "This isn't for you," she says, and I'm like, *why are you whispering?* "This is for me and Dad."

I get it. He's up front staring moodily at the view.

Then the island looms up like a glacier that we're doomed to hit, and I groan.

My mom that I don't see much of except on these Quality Time forced marches, tries to pick me up single-handed, using only her voice. She wants to put me down in that good place shrinks claim is right inside our heads. "Oh Charlie, isn't it pretty?"

"Not really." But it is. Rustic cabins sit in the dirt like markers on a board game that I don't want to play. There's a log cabin lodge with long porches and chairs facing out to sea. Pine trees and shells line a beach that, although we are nowhere near the ocean, *looks* like sand. Trestle tables and a monstrous BBQ pit signal group stuff, you know, campfires with ghost stories and, yuk. Sing-alongs. Woodsy heaven, and I don't like the looks of it.

"Look, Charlie. Tennis courts. This is going to be fun."

At the Santa Monica Beach Club, at least you get to go home at the end. "Mom, it's a camp!"

"This is different," she says in that shaky soprano, like she has to sell herself as well as me.

"You know I hate camp."

This is ominous. She goes, "Oh, sweetie, this is different."

We are in yet another enclosed situation, the kind Mom picks for our annual stab at family bonding. She and Dad are such big deals at work that they have to pencil in two weeks in some high ticket resort so we don't get, like, alienated or some damn thing.

Platinum togetherness.

At home I play at the top on the hottest video games, plus I can do anything I want. I eat whatever, whenever, and if Blanca says do my homework or go hook up with my friends, I just blow her off. She knows damn well I don't have any, so I go, "Blanca, get over it," and she backs off. I do go out, just not like she wants.

I happen to work the dog parks, for, like, discretionary funds? Twilight is best. Little foofy dogs are easy, drop leftovers and they come right up to you. Then, WHAM. They're in the bag. You have to wait until the dog parents give up going, "Mikey, Mikeeeee," or whatever and leave. Then you sneak Foofy home. Some of the dogs I borrow are pissers but some are really cute. You can see how people get attached. What I do is keep their dog until I see them stapling up REWARD posters at the park. I wait another week. Then I turn up at their front door with Foofy and some story, and you have never seen people so glad. Never mind what I do with the money, it's not the point, although I do give Blanca some of it because she knows. More to the point is the licking and the jumping and the blissed-out looks on these fools' faces when I reunite them, the thanking and the hugging at the end, plus the begging me to stay in touch which I can not, repeat, *not* afford to do. I'm a hero, for a day at least. So, like, somebody notices. Besides Blanca, I mean. A blind asshole could see what's going on with me. So, so what?

You wouldn't think it'd be easy to hide a dog on the premises, but when the folks hit it bigtime and we moved uphill into the model home, Mom and Dad fixed up the pool house for me. They said I needed my own space. Like, they think I don't know they put me out there so I won't hear them fight? They don't get that living in the pool house cuts both ways. I could hide a giant panda under my bed, and they'd never know.

When I get back from these deliveries I hit the kitchen and pay off Blanca who, the minute she heard me going out, started to bake. We sit down with cappuccinos and hot brownies, and she gets all weepy because she's glad all over again because I got home safe, so it's like a party every time. Where, in Camp Nowhere, can I possibly get that rush?

This is not immediately apparent.

Sign on the dock reads: NO PETS ALLOWED, so that's out. Nobody in my demographic, as far as I can tell, which, given the nature of family vacation spots, is a little weird. So is the fact that Dad gloms on to the burly counselor in her gray camp shirt with a seal on the pocket, and OMG, a lanyard with a *whistle*, talking her ear off like he'd rather talk to her than us. Also weird? Going uphill, we run into campers coming down with tears streaming. They stumble along with stretched faces like comedy/tragedy masks, and the bad part? I can't tell which.

"Mom." I poke her. "Mom?"

Her face does things I can't make sense of. After eight squeaks where her voice craps out she goes, "You . . . You might . . . *You might as well know, this is therapy camp.*"

"Why, Mom? There's nothing the matter with me. MOM, THERE'S . . . "

Her soft hand stops my mouth. "I know," she says, like we are both grownups. "Charlie, I know."

"Then why."

"Hush," she says. "Don't." Then she touches my arm softly, which is truly frightening. She's begging. "Trust me."

Our cabin is, like, out of some horror movie where kids get mauled, usually while having sex: it has wooden flaps that drop over the windows, Walmart maple furniture with flowered seats, rag rugs and candle-looking bulbs in fake elk-horn lamps and up that staircase—you know, the one where creepy music starts because there's Something Awful at the top, crouched to spring?—upstairs in those bedrooms, *plaid bed-spreads.*

I'd like to say things pick up at dinner down at the lodge, but our first nights in these places are always the worst, even though it's when they serve the best food you're gonna get. They have family-style dishes of Jell-O salad and corn bread laid out on the checkered tablecloth. We sit down on the Ferguson family island, Mom and Dad and me. She makes us join hands, even though Dad's mind is somewhere else, and gives us this sad, hopeful smile. "Just us, just family. Aren't you glad?"

I think but do not say I am in no respect glad, because I am cornered in the area of No Escape. See, in a family resort you have to sit down at the same table with the same peeps every single night for two mortal weeks. Mom thinks that's the whole point. I think it's weird. Except for when Gramma comes and on Thanksgiving, we never do that at home, so when we do sit down, all we have in common is me.

My folks do talent management on Wilshire at Beverly, so dinner runs like a meeting, and on Mom's annual to-do list, the first item is always me. This is our pattern, and believe me, these vacations are patterned. They'll use up the dinner hour grilling me, and in these places we have to sit there for the whole hour to prove to the people that we're having fun. Every "So, Charlie" question is loaded. They're all, *What is your problem?* never, *Happy much?* Whether I am happy is beside the point. High rollers expect trophy kids, so, my bad. By dessert they've run out things to ask. I always promise to do better and we eat our pie. They finish their after-dinner decaf and we're done.

Food's OK, but one look at the personnel and I despair. Usually I can find somebody to hang out with: college kids who don't know I'm only in ninth grade, but these waitpeople look like they're older than my folks. They're all pasty and dismal in gray camp shirts, and instead of smiling when they bring stuff to the table, they come at you like they're fixing to medicate you or throw you down and give CPR.

In spite of which, Mom twirls her hand with this fraudy laugh, and for what? A bunch of mover and shaker moms like her, all waxed legs and flowered silk floaty things, matched up with aggressively ripped power dads in pastel jeans and polo shirts, totally the kind of people Gramma would say Measure Up, but it's like they all came here with an agenda, like Mom, plus a lot of them look too old to be here in spite of their ultra-white teeth and stretched, face-lifted grins.

There's only one bunch in the place that's having fun, lounging at the head table in red camp shirts that pretty much broadcast the fact that we are not all equal here. Unlike the waiting people, they have this glow, like an ad for joy. They laugh and talk like they couldn't possibly be related—weird, as this is supposed to be a family camp. Although it isn't on Mom's agenda, I point. "Wait. Who are they?"

"Oh, them? Nobody." Mom's voice is all trilly: la-la, but her fingers bite down. *Don't you dare follow up.* "Just psychiatrists."

Right. Therapy camp.

Then, oh the shame, everybody at each table has to get up and say who they are and why they're here. Mostly my eyes glaze over, people actually *say* gross things like "feelings of inadequacy," "helicopter parents," "sexual dysfunction," like they can't wait to start. One by one they let it all hang out, while the shrinks at the head table grin and cheer them on. I keep my speech short: "Charlie Ferguson. They made me come." Mom's is sad: "I'm Jane Ferguson, and I'm here in hopes." Dad's is not what you would call straightforward, like, he won't meet our eyes. "I'm Lionel Ferguson. Let's solve the problem."

There's a ping-pong tournament on the porch after, followed by the camp sing-along, because like Mom, we campers are on a schedule here.

A bugler plays "Taps," just like in military school, which didn't work out for me.

Then, accidentally, they wake me up in the middle of the night. I catch Mom fluffing her hair and hooking in earrings that glow in the dark, while Dad stares in the mirror, trying to make a happy face. Holy crap, they're going out! Where they were all boring and obvious at dinner, now they're all edgy and festive, like it's their first date.

I'm thinking maybe their problem is solved, but I can't say that. "So, what. Is this, like, a swingers' camp?"

Awesome. They both jump. "Don't be silly. It's the Late Show."

"And you have to sneak?"

Mom goes, "We're not sneaking. It's right here on the schedule. Now go back to bed." They're jiggling in the doorway, all shifty eyes and guilty grins.

I whine, "I wanna go," even though I don't.

"Sorry, it's not for kids. That's why it's so late." Then Mom says the wrong thing. "It's kind of X-rated."

And I do.

Mom fades out the door singing, "Don't think we're neglecting you. Look under the bed in our room, sweetie. We got you a Wii."

Does she not know I already have two? But I am thinking a lot of things, starting with that I just got *carte blanche* to go through their stuff. Plus, no way am I facing nature before I know what's out there. Tomorrow I explore. When I go, I have to go armed.

I toss their dressers and find about what you would expect. Camp gear from The Territory Ahead and Patagonia, store-folded with the pins still in. Underwear and cruise-type dinner clothes, not like they'll need them here. Self-help books on everything from getting it up (unopened) to getting ahead (dog-eared) but nothing about having fun. No, er. You know. Either one of them had their tubes tied or else they aren't having sex. Comics, my dad reads comics! Comics and, oh, cool! Utility belt with knife and halogen flashlight. I hide it in my room.

I never heard them come in.

Today my folks are all ragged and unsteady, like either they had their souls sandpapered last night or whatever they drank reamed their insides raw.

Breakfast is just *weird*. At the lodge last night we were, like, on our own little island? Today people come up to our table, mumbling and smiling like Mom and Dad are runners-up in a contest I don't know about. Behind Mom's back some lady goes all squashy on me, like a goldfish mouthing inside its bowl. I could swear she is is going, oh, you poor thing. This creeps me out but without coffee, which Mom says is bad for my ADD, it's a mystery I'm not feeling strong enough to penetrate. At home Blanca serves it black with enough sugar to float my boat. Another reason I hate these trips.

Gross. We have group calisthenics, followed by swimming. Then, gack! People line up outside the shrinks' cabins like they're going to confession. A squinty woman in a red shirt tweets and eight couples peel off and follow her and a guy shrink up the hill. For the rest of us? Schedule says: Downtime. No way am I going back to the cabin, Mom and Dad are in there. I guess they didn't solve their problem; I can hear them yelling from here.

Time to sneak uphill and check out the scene.

If you aren't used to nature it's creepy, crawling on stuff that you don't know what it is, but I need to find the trail to the X-rated Late Show. These woods creep me out. It's all the leaves and rocks and junk on the ground, and you never know what's moving underneath, it could be lizards or giant beetles or, ewww. Snakes! I find a forked stick. It makes me feel braver, just not enough.

They've, like, defeated nature by hacking a clearing out of the jungle, so there is a gym-sized clearing at the top. The campers are sitting around a raised platform, poking each other and giggling like kids at a puppet show. It looks like the set for some awful play up there, with two chairs and a table, a rocker and a ratty sofa with a guy on it. The show must have been really awful, because this great big guy is curled up in the ratty cushions, squirming like a snail trying to make it back into the shell.

The guy shrink sort of declaims, "And how does that make you feel?"

Then out of nowhere, wham! This humongous *grownup* breaks down on the sofa, thrashing and sobbing to break your heart. And, wow. People stand up and cheer! I creep out of the bushes to watch.

"Good, good," the shrink goes. "We want to feel your pain."

After a while the applause dies out, but the sobbing doesn't. The shrink hops onstage to uncurl his star from fetal position, because the show's over and it's time to move out. The red shirt is getting drenched by the big guy sobbing into it as he hauls himself up, "No more, please, no more!"

The shrink is thumping his patient's back the way a trainer works over his boxer, motivating him to fight another round.

Everybody goes, "It's good, it's all good," like it's the camp mantra and there's a prize for chanting. If it's all good, why is he still crying to break your heart?

"Catharsis is the first step to recovery. That's it for today."

Everybody leaves except the vic, who stands there sobbing even though the shrink wants to move him out. "It's right to get in touch with your feelings, Bradley, but enough is enough."

We wait.

"Come on, Bradley. Come on." The shrink starts backing downhill like a trainer holding up a biscuit to fool a dog. "All right then. You'll find me in the crying room. I'm only waiting til five."

So I'm alone at the top of nowhere with this lump of misery while lunchtime comes and goes. I creep up and poke his shoulder, like, *enough*. "You're gonna stop crying, right?"

He jumps. "Lady, lay off!"

"I'm not a . . . "

He turns and sees me. "Oh. You're a kid."

"Pretty much."

Now he is ugh-ugh-ing, trying to mute the sobs. "I thought you were that mean bitch."

I don't ask which one. "What the fuck happened?"

Ugh-ugh. "Psychodrama."

I know damn well what that is, but I play dumb. "What's that?"

"I really don't want to talk about it." Ugh-ugh. But I have unplugged him. He groans. "OK, OK." Ugh-ugh. "They took me back."

"Back where?"

That does it. "They brought my baby brother home when I was only five years old and I hated it, I hated them for getting one, and most of all I hated him. I hate him to this day. It was my *birthday* and they forgot, what kind of present is that?" Ugh-ugh. "But I thought I was over it until . . . " Ugh-ugh. "They made me go back there and feel guilty and awful *all over again*."

If I can't stop him, he'll sob out his whole story. "That sucks."

"You have no idea." He is one big Greek tragedy mask. "They lied to get me here. Now I'm their prisoner."

I am thinking, *Like Dad.* "Me too."

He doesn't exactly brighten, but he stops ugh-ugh-ing. "For all the good it'll do us. Do you want to hear my . . . "

"No!" I don't know what I want, exactly, but I'm starved. "Let's go eat."

"Frankly, I'm not ready to face . . . "

"No problem. I'll steal food."

We sit on the end of the dock gobbling apples and hot dog buns. Lame, but the only food left from lunch. We don't rightly talk, we stare out at the endless lake, and we are both thinking the same thing. We aren't ready to talk about it yet. I don't even know if he's smart enough to make a plan, so that has to wait. I don't have a story, and I sure as hell don't want to hear his, so instead I go, "If that's the early show, what's up with the late show?"

"Ugh." He uses Mom's exact words, except he is apologizing. "It's X-rated. Believe me, you don't want to know."

I do, but he doesn't want me to ask. "That sucks."

"Everything does." He sort of smiles, and once again we are on the same level. "Might as well go up there and get it over with."

I am too polite to ask. "This whole place sucks."

"Damn straight." He gets up groaning, because it's time to face whoever got him here. They'll make him say the mental anguish was good for him, that it was great, getting his soul torn down to the axles and his guts spread all over the floor of the shop like engine parts, oooh, yes, you bet it was, wonderful, losing it up there in front of everyone. Yeah, right, you bet it was. He throws me a look like a note tied to a rock. "But not for long."

So this Bradley Simpson and I aren't exactly bonded, but if one of us figures out how to get off this rotten island, we'll both go.

The second Ferguson family dinner is exceptionally awful, and not just the food. I have no idea what we're famous for, but tonight, we're stars. So many people buzz our table that Mom's usual second supper conversation, in which we dish the other campers and pick some to hang out with, gets derailed before it leaves the station. We are stranded with zero conversation, plus for reasons he won't talk about, Dad is sulking. What's up with that? Between flyovers, in which people accidentally bump our table on their way to the buffet, she and Dad exchange loaded glances. They know something I don't know, like what's going down at tonight's Late Show. So, fine. Tonight, I am prepared. After all, I know the way. Utility belt locked and loaded: flashlight, bug spray. Knife, in case, but in case of what?

In spite of the flashlight I get a little lost, ergo-therefore, I come late to the feast. I don't really want to know what happened before I arrived because those are my parents, Jane and Lionel Ferguson, up there on the stage.

A deaf person could track them by the sound. They aren't exactly tearing out each other's hearts and eating them up there, but the howling is fierce.

By the time I reach the clearing, it's done. At least I think it is, but oh, holy crap! That's *my mom* coming down off the stage, running flat-out; she is chasing my Dad. They're tear-stained and shaking and they look nothing like themselves. Dad comes charging toward the bushes where I am hiding, and I'm like, oh shit. Where he's usually all clipped and businesslike, my father is agonized and shaking, like something up there just laid him wide open and he hated what he saw, and Mom?

It's hard to explain.

The shrink on duty is small and wiry, but she's tough. She falls on Dad from behind and spins him around before he hits the bushes, which also means me. She twists his arm and muscles him toward the steps where Mom is waiting with people clustered around, all supportive and there-there. The shrink hustles Dad along, stoking his engine like a personal trainer. "Come on, Lionel, you can't quit now," and, "not now, when you're doing so well.

The rest of the, I guess it's the camp encounter group, is chanting, "You can do it," and, "Come on, come on"—well, everybody except poor Bradley Simpson, who's gnawing his knuckles like a corncob, agonizing because he's been through it and he's probably scared for Dad. I can't swear to it but I think Bradley sees me. He raises his ring fingers, like it's a sign. Light glints off somebody's glasses, and I see the bleachers set up in the underbrush behind the stage. I can't make out who's up there but I'm pretty sure they're all in red, so what's up with that?

The shrink on duty is all, "Seize the moment, Lionel."

Dad flinches like he's scared, and I'm scared for him too.

The shrink grabs Mom and Dad by the wrists. "Now, you two get up there and give back as good as you got, Lionel. It's your turn!"

Then she links Dad to Mom like a preacher and pushes them back up the steps and everybody cheers. I have to admit that for old people, like, they've got to be forty, my parents look pretty good up there. Dad gets his hair done in a place on Bedford Row and Mom goes to a spa and gets threads pulled tight under certain parts of her face. The outfits are perfect but they always are, no matter where my parents go. They stand there like a pair of life-sized lobby cards, and I don't know whether to be proud or mortified.

Mom takes his hand, like, *well, honey?* and they exchange a loaded look. Then that bitch the shrink goes, "Shall we begin?"

I would rather forget most of what my parents just said and did in the course of acting out their lives. What's amazing is that they get into it like a pair of old pros doing dinner theater at some crap club. It starts with them kvetching at each other about the usual, it could be any old fight except doing it for an audience amps up the performance. It adds an edge, and now even Dad is into it, waving his arms and making broad, showy faces like a pro. The performances get bigger and bigger. My folks are dishing out the same old crap, but now that they are into it, they start mugging like old troupers, because we are the audience and they are the show and I am glad nobody knows I'm here.

Spare me having to yack up the details. All you need to know is that, no surprise, Dad has been having an affair. The surprise is that where in our neighborhood affairs are a given, Mom let this one piss her off. Unless it's that this time, Dad proposed. He wants to divorce us and marry Melanie the script girl from the last *Batman*, who knew?

Once they have it out on the table, bloody and squirming, this Polly—the shrink gets down with them, like, "Call me Polly"—this Polly says, "Now, show us where it went wrong," and they do.

They reenact highlights of their courtship. Their careers. The wedding. Their careers. Me.

It all went wrong when Mom decided to have me, and this is the part I really don't want to talk about, so here's the short version, and don't make me spell it out for you.

In terms of who is the perp in this relationship, it turns out to be me.

These people that I look like, that *I thought I knew* start reenacting the messes I made in their perfect, over-landscaped lives, although like film school and the MBAs they got from U.S.C. to enhance the presentation, I was totally planned. My ostensible parents are all Greek tragedy now, like I showed up specifically to wreck their lives.

So Jane and Lionel, what were you thinking?

That you could hang me on the wall or buy license plates and roll me into the garage and say, "There?"

This is awful. I'm forced to watch them up there pacing behind the sofa, which represents, like, my crib? They take on about this forever, re-enacting me messing up their lives, especially their, er, their fucking sex lives. This devolves into nonstop recriminations and fighting, wherein they play out every bad moment from my first day home up 'til Blanca came, after which they step away from each other, all bleached out and shaking, and take a little bow. I'm shaking too, but at least it's over. Yeah, right.

The wiry shrink hops up onstage and they go, "Helloooo, Blanca" and she pretend-wrings her hands in her apron like a maid, which Blanca would never do. Then pretend Blanca picks up imaginary me in her arms and steps down, at which point my father and my mother that I thought might not like me but at least *cared*, fall down on the sofa and re-enact steamy sex. Then Dad says, "It's not the same," and I bleed for Mom until she comes up with the punchline. "It hasn't been right since he came."

And this? This is what kills me. *They are getting off on this.*

If I wasn't safe behind this bush, I'd be dead by now.

Then I wish I was. Up front, pretend Blanca hisses in this insidious voice, amped so it probably carries all the way down to the cabin where I believed they actually thought I was sleeping, "Well, Charlie, how does this make you feel?"

Every shred in me is shrinking, like I can fit my whole humiliated self back inside my testicles and roll away. Fat chance. The spotlight nails me right in the bushes, and at that exact same moment, two camp staffers grab me from behind. Polly, the psychiatric axe murderer hits the path waving her hand mike, bringing me on like a gameshow host: "Charlie Ferguson, come on down!"

No way. I struggle but the light follows as the shrinks drag me toward the stage and if it wasn't for Bradley Simpson's fist bump as they haul me past where he is sitting, I would despair. Then I'm up, somewhere between Mom and Dad. Beyond the light that blinds me the night is like a pit and as I whirl to escape the light I blink. At my back there are patches of red flashing behind trembling leaves.

The gray shirts make me face front. The head shrink pushes me to my knees. "Begin, Charlie."

The silence is awful. Everybody present is holding their breath.

"I said, begin!" I can't bear it much longer. Neither can she. "Now, Charlie. We want to feel your pain."

What I feel is the breeze stirring the bushes behind the platform, where unbeknownst to the audience the rows of hidden shrinks are going, in this low drone that cuts into me and splinters my backbone, shivering every nerve along the way, "We need to feel your pain."

You've gotta hand it to Bradley Simpson. Who else would have thought of yanking the cable that killed the lights? Who knew where it was? I was exposed and blinded up there in the spotlight until he did it.

We are all equals now. Everything is darkness and yelling, with Dad falling over Mom and rolling in the dark and the shrink getting kicked off the platform accidentally—Yay me, yaaay Maglite; she made a funny sound when she hit but nobody noticed because everybody was lunging here, there, as near to panic as it gets.

Everybody but Bradley Simpson, who moves really fast for a squashy guy that got too big for his clothes. "It's me," he says, but I know before he tells me, as he closes those fat fingers on my arms like an old friend.

While from wherever she's lying the shrink is going, "Wait, Charlie, wait for the light," in that weedy, penetrating voice. "Stay where you are, and let the people feel your pain" and behind me the drone from the hidden bleachers escalates like an order, "We need to feel your pain."

It is a definite fuck that shit moment, but instead of letting the bitch have it, I let Bradley Simpson help me down off the platform and lead me away in the dark. We are silent as creeping ninjas, while behind us I hear Mom and Dad going, "I told you it was a bad idea, Jane," and, "My bad, sweetheart, but if this works out, we solve our problem for once and all!"

I am too scared and distracted to parse this because behind us, camp personnel are marshaling to, I guess, give chase, although they try to make it sound like wheedling, "Stand down, Charlie Ferguson, we're here to help you" and "Sing out, we want to help you," and, "Where are you, Charlie? Signify."

"This way." Bradley drags me off the path and pushes me down. We lie there trying not to breathe as the mob trots down the trail and feet go thudding by, shrinks and campers and coming up last, oh God, I recognize their ankles, my mother, followed by Dad. For a long time we hear them crunching through the underbrush; we pick up the beams of flashlights going wild, the aftermath of the sweep going on below. We hear yelling, we hear threats and promises until finally they are out of sight and out of hearing, sweeping the lodge and turning out the cabins, I suppose. Then my awesome new friend Bradley goes, "There's always another way out. Let's go."

When it's safe to breathe I ask Bradley, "How did you know?"

"I didn't," he says, "but shrinks are all about escape routes, right?"

Turns out we slide down the raw backside of the hill without stopping, crashing into bushes and hurting ourselves on rocks along the way. We run into trees and double back where we have to, until finally we hit the bottom and the woods end. We come out in a place where we don't see or hear the others any more. It's a deserted beach. We drop on an empty strip of sand and lie there panting, and for the moment, at least, I think we're safe.

When I can speak I say to Bradley, "You were nice to do this."

He says, like we are kids together, "Dude, it's no big."

"You didn't have to."

"Yeah, I did. You helped when I was down."

"It was nothing."

"Like nothing it was nothing. You listened. You got me lunch. Are you OK?"

"Sure," I tell him, "I'm always OK," but when I try to sit up I get all weird and shaky, like my insides are all red and rough, like Dad's. "What *was* that back there?"

"Psychodrama," Bradley says.

"I saw hidden bleachers."

"Observation platform." He snaps forward to ask, "You don't know what's really going on?"

Even though it's too dark for him to see, I shake my head.

Never mind. Bradley gets it. He always gets it. "They get off on this."

"Who does?" I know the answer, but I need to hear him say it.

"The shrinks." My friend Bradley takes a little bit too long to follow up. "Your parents didn't tell you, did they."

This is so definitely not a question that I say, "You saw them. They don't tell me shit."

It's so quiet that I think I can hear their voices rising from somewhere a long way off. Sooner or later they'll give up on the cabins and start sweeping the island. Unless we can figure out how to dig our way to China, it looks like no escape. I am trying to resign myself to the whole nine yards here, writing speeches to give on the big stage at tomorrow night's Late Show, figuring out whether Mom will actually expect me to apologize.

I say what you say, when you have to get through a bad thing without dying of it. "It's OK. It's only two weeks."

"Then they really didn't tell you," Bradley says.

But I'm trying not to hear. "Hell, I can stand on my head for two weeks."

This is how Bradley brings me down. "It was never just two weeks."

"What . . . "

"Two weeks from now everybody goes home . . . except us."

"No way!"

"They keep people families want to get rid of. I told you. The shrinks get off on this."

"Oh crap. Ohhhh, crap!"

"They call it directed rehabilitation. It doesn't matter what they call it, we stay," Bradley says, and that's all he says.

I do not say the obvious. I don't need to. My best friend that I never had before today is on his hands and knees now, digging up the beach like a dog going after a bone, clawing up gobs of sand and seaweed in those big, flat hands and throwing them behind him and digging up more like there really is China under there, and it's only a matter of time.

Without knowing where this will end, I fall to and start digging too; what does he have buried here, food?

A bazooka that when they come out of the bushes or pounding along the sand and swoop down on us, shrinks, his wife, whoever, he'll blow them all away?

Whatever it is, I'm in. I'll go with it, right up to but not including wasting Mom and Dad. The folks may not like me, but they can't help it, and I can't say whose fault it is that I'm a pain and they are this desperate. Whatever it is, it won't be an issue any more.

When I get back to the house I'm cleaning out their earthquake emergency box that they don't think I know about, and getting Blanca. We'll start the backup car and drive to Albuquerque or someplace and she can take care of the apartment while I go to public school. We can make it on income from their slush fund, which I happen to know how to invest, another of those things they didn't want me learning online. We'll get to live our own lives someplace sunny and Blanca's cool. Unlike the parents, I'll give her weekends, and she can take the car.

This is not as crazy as it sounds. By the time the thundering hordes come to this spot on the beach, the lakefront tide will have wiped away the hole we made, where Bradley pulled out the inflatable raft and the air pump that popped it into shape, after which he buried the pump so they wouldn't know. The raft is gonna be a tight fit but we'll make it, Bradley and me. He apologizes for us having to leave on short notice, as there wasn't time to steal food, but this is a crisis situation, so what are you gonna do? I'm not complaining.

Whatever's going on back there is worse than maybe starving for as long as it takes before we find land and hey, Bradley's a certified grownup with a credit rating and all that this implies. Once we get to civilization, he has the power to rent and drive the getaway car, and from there? Does it matter, as long as we get away?

We don't talk. We don't need to. We wade out with the raft and when we get beyond the rocks I boost Bradley over the edge, helping him get on board, which, given how squashy he is, takes longer than it should. As soon as he can sit up without swamping the thing, he gives me a hand and I hop in. Then he picks up a paddle and I take the other paddle and I guess you would have to say we set sail.

By the time they hit the beach and the sounds of clamor and wild shouting come floating over the lake, we're so far out that they'll never know we were even there. Bradley and I are heading out, keeping our heads down, leaving behind the island and Camp Nowhere, with all the grief that this implies.

We don't have a plan, really, but right now we don't need one. It's enough to know that we've escaped.

A friend of mine who later became a nun got drunk with the youngest of the Trapp Family Singers after one of their concerts back in the day. She reported that while they toured as One Big Happy Family, the then-kids said they were prisoners of the enterprise, and pretty much hated it. So, OK, here's this.

THE BLIGHT FAMILY SINGERS

Tifney

Fat Myra Weingarten booked the Blight Family Singers without even asking where we were with elevator music, the stupid cow. This, like, weenie-bun *chorus* is headlining our Midwinter Bash. That's Dr. Weingarten to you and she has the power, for at Wingdale Junior College, she is the dean. She told us over the P.A., like that would prevent the protest rally that followed. We stormed her office during the harp intro to the Blight Family's biggest hit, they were going FAAAAAA la-la-la as Trig Masters, our leader, bunched his big shoulders and hit the door.

Myra, do you not *hear* them? What planet are you from? Did you never swim across a mosh pit or get so hammered and blissed out that you forgot what you did, you only remembered that it was awesome?

Have you even *looked* outside? Minnesota, in the winter from hell. Did your brain freeze? If we can't get loaded on Groundhog Day and roll naked in the snow, we'll die. We don't need much, just head-banging rock, a guy to hook up with and enough controlled substances to drink, smoke or snort or otherwise ingest so we can make it through winter, ergo the Bash. Listen. We held gazillion car washes and sold Whatever door to door to pay for booze, humongous speakers and a kick-ass band. Now look.

They're tuning up in the auditorium as we speak.

During the demonstration outside Dr. Weingarten's office, a few things came up:

A. The Blight Family Singers? Myra, who *are* you? The movie's on TV every mortal Christmas and it's awful, uplifting though it may be. So, what if the Blights ran away from this cult at Etheria, and what if evil Daddy Flagg's colonists chased them with guns and dogs? As they slide down the icy mountain, are they really going FAAA la-la-la?

As *if.*

B. The Blight children are not what you would call kids. You can see gross hairs in the guys' noses. *Tufts* sprouting out of their ears! The girls' boobs flop in the stupid dresses and go wall-eyed when they dance. And the *outfits*. Like their mom shopped at American Girl, Pioneer Days department, dress your girls like the doll they want, except that no way are these girls. The guys' shirts are tight, and not in a good way. The girls have pink wedges where their puffed sleeves ripped under the arms, because they grew or the dress shrank, and you can see they hate that there's fat popping out. So, do us all a favor and cancel, OK?

Right. This whole thing is the mother's idea. Do not be deceived by that syrupy smile.

C. Which is probably A: Fat Myra blew the whole party budget, thereby wrecking Bash. Our dean paid the Blights off in advance.

Do you believe she tried to shame us? "Think of Wingdale Junior College. The Blights will put us on the map. Now, disperse."

"What did she, think we'd apologize and go?"

Trig Masters started, "No way."

We all went, "No way."

I made Trig our leader because, OK, he's this year's Ice King and as of right now, he hasn't picked his Ice Queen to sit up there on the float with him which, the thrones are heated and he's gorgeous, both a definite plus. Look at him raising his fist, killer man. "No wayyyyy. . . ."

Then Marly Mason, whom I *do not like*, slithered up him like a snake up a tree, chanting, "Astro, Blazers, Full Frontal," and she got everybody shouting out their favorite bands.

Security came.

Fat Myra wasn't giving up. After it got quiet she tried to guilt us. "It's the least you can do. This poor, brave woman went through hell so her kids could walk free."

Well, they don't look too free to us, squirming in their dirndls and high-waters. So what if this Mother Blight like to died saving her spawn from the clutches of the infamous leader, the Most Reverend Jethro Flagg? She's the kind that's too smug to suffer, and besides, it's all *sooo* last-century, and have they not made money on it, bigtime? The escape story made the Blight Family fortune, plus! About the frostbite amputations. You have our condolences, but how long ago was that?

If she wants to save the ones they left behind in Etheria, fine, just don't do it on our dime. And look, if the damn fools that stayed back at the compound really think some heavenly craft is going to come down and float them up to Paradise, who are we to get in the way? Let them make soap and ranch elderberries and lie down and do Whatever with each other in one great big bed like their leader proclaims. If they think Daddy Flagg can get them to heaven that's their business, right? If they're stupid enough to drink the Kool-Aid, fine. Not our problem. It's theirs.

Besides. It's not like the Blights can't save everybody all by themselves. They're richer than dirt. Every school in America does the Blight Family musical. The movie alone! Residuals, music downloads, the DVD. That icky sound track is a platinum record now. Grandmother music, like, they buy it all the time. If you happened to be locked in an elevator with your grandmother and it was playing, you'd claw your ears off to make it stop, but she'd be humming along. Plus, grandmothers give it to you at Christmas a lot, because they think it's going to improve you or some damn thing, and they forgot they gave it to you for Christmas last year.

Dean Myra was banging on her chest like a grandmother, going, "Save the children."

Trig yelled, "Screw that, save us!"

I am very proud of Trig. We yelled right along with him until Security did its thing.

By the time the tear gas finally cleared, we were staring into the jaws of the trap Dean Weingarten set for us. I mean, she was like steel. "No matter what you people think, you will all be *very nice*. I don't have to tell you that Wingdale is in crisis. Think what would happen if the Blights set up housekeeping in our town! Tours. Special attractions. Jobs for every mother in Wingdale, important positions for every dad. Money, so they can buy you *things*."

We got really quiet then.

"The Blights are shopping for houses, and if they buy one here . . . "

Everybody breathed in.

Dr. Weingarten got taller. She breathed out for all of us. "Wingdale wins. Now. Clap. Cheer. Smile like crazy. Make them love Wingdale so much that they want to stay."

Clang.

Our big night and they're in there harmonizing like the Mormon Tabernacle choir, FA la-la-la, while we are pretending to be glad. I don't care how good this is for greater Wingdale, my man Trig and me (take *that*, Marly Mason) we're bummed.

Edwina Blight

Prosperity is an illusion, but I protect my darlings from harsh truths. I must, for if their smiles crumble for *one second*, the people will see it and we'll be done. We have to go out there tonight and no matter what the conditions, we have to shine like the stars we are and make them love us. If they don't, we'll never get another gig, but I spare my children the hard facts.

I've protected them all their lives. Believe me, it isn't easy. I have so many to watch, and they keep wandering off! There are my two big boys, Edward, who is Jethro's and my favorite, even though we fight. Then there are Ethan and the twins Edwin and Erna, from Willard Schott; Edna and Erness, Elton and Edgar, and little Earl—and face it—Mickey too, that is, Micah Blight, my husband ever since our leader joined us at the biggest group wedding in the history of Etheria. In spite of my feelings on the subject, the Most Reverend Jethro Flagg pronounced us, thus making Mickey, my primary instead, like it or not and thank you very much.

Most Reverend, hah! I could tell you a thing or two, but I won't. For good reason I fell out with Jethro, a.k.a. the charismatic and powerful Daddy Flagg. We fell out and I led my children over the snow to freedom, frostbite and complaining or no. To "children," add Mickey. He's fathered at least three of our nine, but he's one more responsibility. It's like having a large, extra child.

My children, my burden. If only they'd stayed little and sweet and loving to sing! But no, they grew. They started to complain. That's what got us into this hole.

Oh sweethearts, you don't want to sing in our concerts? You're quitting because they make fun of you at college? You want to try *acting?* Start a rock band? Study fashion design? All right, my darlings, enjoy! Canceling the concerts cut into our income, as did every public appearance and product endorsement my ungrateful children refused, not to mention the auditions and classes and demos I paid for because every one of the nine had illusions, and every one of them flopped. Everything comes at a cost.

Fall out of the public eye and you fall off the A-list, and that's only the beginning. They think we're touring to liberate the ones still locked in at Etheria, in Jethro's thrall.

They don't need to know we're singing our hearts out in the icy waste because we're broke.

It's not the first time I've protected them. What Jethro and I did together before we fell out, I kept from them. They don't know that during the Last Battle I found out certain things about our leader, or what came down when I confronted him. I keep the details of those sweet nights and the last, painful one locked inside my heart.

Good mothers are perfect, and my children don't need to know what grossness I endured with certain colonists to guarantee safe passage, or how truly dangerous Etheria was. My book's about the stockade with armed guards and the brave Blight family singing our way to freedom in the blinding snow, and the rest? Never mind. That's good enough for them.

I'm not about to tell my darlings what I had to do to launch our career, either, although they owe me, which, believe me, I do let them know. All they need to remember is that when we finished our first concert, everybody in the Bowl stood up and cheered, and my children loved it. They loved the money. They got off on the applause, and now?

Don't you want it all back?

That's how I put it when I made this booking. I do what's needed to take care of them, and if that means keeping a tight rein, listen. It's for their own good. Doesn't every mother do the same?

In return, I expect loyalty. I expect them to fall in line, and they do, except for Edward. He fought to stay behind with Jethro, but in the end I brought him to his knees. I am, after all, a mother, and mothers know how.

I dragged him out by the hair, "*That* will teach you to get in my way."

We fought every time he ran away and I brought him back. Of course I won; I always do, which is why the Blight Family Singers are back on the road. We stand as one. I can manage Edward, and the others?

They think we're on a gala comeback tour, by popular demand. They don't need to know that we can't go home because we don't have one. The bank's men were pounding a FORECLOSURE sign into the lawn at the Tupelo mansion as our tour bus rolled away. They took our lodge outside Denver and the Florida compound too. The hard truth is that all we have left is the clothes we stand up in and our old costumes, which the girls bitched about altering for our comeback tour. And although there are issues with the finance company, fifty per cent of the bus. Oh, and Mickey's vibraharp, but he mustn't know it's come down to that.

If they knew how bad things are, could they dance onstage laughing and singing, and could they face the public with those same bright, shiny Blight Family smiles?

Trust me, they don't need to know.

The town fathers in this wretched town don't need to know it either. They think we're poised to throw millions around Wingdale, which is how we got this gig. Pardon the vulgarity: if we can't get another booking on the strength of this one, we're screwed. In this business you do what you have to, to get what you want. I've put out that we're settling in Middle America, and the Wingdale Chamber of Commerce wants it to be here. If they won't accept this Midwinter Bash check as earnest money, where will we go?

Look. If my kids want to bitch about the road, outgrown costumes and close quarters on the bus, let them. They can vent all they want, but it won't change anything.

The Blight Family Singers are legendary, and I will damn well keep it that way. They're grumbling now, but when the lights come up and we go on and the thrill comes back . . .

When we march on stage and that first wave of applause breaks over the footlights and splashes us full in the face, it strikes me, like an electric shock. It's better than sex.

I come alive.

But, God! Are we not going to sing in the comfort and safety of this cheesy auditorium? The idiot stage manager just said "Showtime" and opened a door on deep snow. *Outside.* Have they *looked* outside? Why is that monstrous dean in her bearskin coat telling Mickey, and not me? Does she imagine that he's in charge because he is the man? Mickey blinks the way he does when he isn't getting it, poor fool. His chin goes all trembly. "Out there?"

The dean pushes the door wide and winter roars in. She slaps his shoulder and points. "Out there."

I shove him aside. "We can't sing in that!"

That face! "I can always stop payment on the check."

My God, is she serious? Are the school guards really armed? They herd us like prisoners through a trench in the snow. At the far end a ladder leads up to a crude platform, with curtains separating it from whatever lies beyond. I dig in. "We won't."

She bunches her shoulders and gives me a push. "Heaters onstage." It's like being wrangled by a grizzly bear.

The guards rattle guns. Snow fills our slippers and we trudge forward on icy feet. My family's bones rattle like wind chimes. I tell her, "We'll die!"

We clump at the bottom of the ladder, a little clot of misery. She points. "I *said*, there are heaters onstage."

Onstage. Then a wind carries in voices. There's a crowd massing somewhere beyond the velvet curtain that separates us from whatever waits. I hear movement out there, feet stamping, a beginning shout.

Audience!

I marshal my family. "We survived Etheria," I tell them. "We can certainly make it up on that stage. Brave smiles, everybody," I say as we start up the ladder. "Brave smiles."

Edward Blight

Look at her, preening in purple velvet like a budding diva. You'd think we were back in the Hollywood Bowl. It's fucking freezing out here.

If she thinks I'm going to stand up here grinning like a fool and sing until my corpse turns to solid ice, she's wrong. The Moment is close. I have seen certain signs. Mother is too old to know about mosh pits, but I'm waiting for the right spot. When I see it, I'll plunge. Then I can swim to freedom over the heads of all those brainless teenagers.

Waiting is hell. My blood chills and my brain stops cold. The past starts playing like an old movie inside my head.

"Your future is just around the corner and it will be wonderful," she told us, booking yet another performance in Paris, Venice, Prague, anywhere far away from home. School. Our friends.

OK, Mother. When? Nine childhoods lost to your agenda, months at rehearsals like forced marches, on a never-ending road trip with the bitch mother of all time rushing us back and forth between venues, and for what?

We're nothing but bit players in the story of Edwina Blight.

She dressed us like children for so long that it was obscene. It got old and so did we, with mandatory facelifts, as though us looking younger makes her young, but what's a little pain when Edwina's self-image is at stake? We're no better than extras, background for the never-ending story, expendable props to be moved around to decorate every scene our mother plays.

She is the star of her own life.

"Now do this. Do that," she said with that imperious wave and she was our mother, so we had no choice. She pushed us around for decades, and for what? We grew up, but what good did it do us? We still can't get away. I belong with my father and I can't get away.

"Children," she said last week, in that fake, motivational voice kindergarten teachers use. It worked when we were ten. "Pack. I've booked our gala comeback tour!"

Mother, I'm thirty years old!

"I can't." I stood my ground, but in private. We faced off under the wisteria at the bottom of the garden in Tupelo, where the others couldn't hear. They don't trust me anyway because I am Jethro's, so it was just as well.

"Do it for me, sweetheart." Her touch was soft and her tone was too sweet; I knew what went on between her and Jethro, and I hated her. "Do it for us."

You ran away from him, I didn't. I said, "I'm not going." I did not say, *I want to stay where he can find me.*

"But darling, we can't go on without your gorgeous soprano solo."

"I'm not a soprano any more. I have to stay here!"

"You can't stay here." Her eyelids peeled away from those wild blue globes; she was frantic. "He's after us."

My heart leapt up. I tried and failed to stare her down. "Is that so bad?" If he lifts me up, I won't have to do this. I'm sick of running, hiding, performing like a trick monkey and doing her bidding at every turn.

She shuddered. "*They're* after me."

I didn't say *Who?* Jethro hasn't exactly told me who *they* are, only that they're coming to take us, and it will be magnificent. I said, "Is that such an awful thing?"

"We can't stay here." She forced me onto the bus. "We can't stay here, Edward. We can't stay here!"

No apologies, no explanation. Now we're in this awful place. When the bus pulled into the Wingdale Motel 6 and she had us wedged into two units, she didn't rest. She sent poor Fa—I mean Mickey—out to buy a house, like she actually expects us to settle in this icy hole in the road.

Here, when all I want is to get Margaret and Sally and Felicia and take them home to Etheria, to meet the only real father I know. Mickey's OK, but he's nobody to me. If I can't make it back to Etheria in time, Daddy

Flagg will find me, he promised, but if I want to fly up with them at the time of the Great Upload, I have to live according to the Rule. Three women and no babies. Yet. Once I get my girls pregnant I'll take them home, and it will be wonderful, Father promises.

We don't see each other but we talk all the time.

I don't care what lovers' quarrel moved Edwina to yoke us kids like a chain gang and drag us out of Etheria, Father knows I fought her night and day. Nothing has been right between us since. Oh, I put on the costume, I sang, I kept on singing years after the critics said we were finished as an act; the venues got smaller and meaner, but I sang. I fell into line, but in my heart I belong to Daddy Flagg.

He's coming soon.

Through all our show-business success and all the trials intervening, I, at least, have stayed in touch. She doesn't know it, but he and I talk all the time, and I know when Father's coming and what he wants.

It's nothing like the poison you poured into our ears, Mother. He has great plans for us. You think you're free, Edwina, but thanks to me Jethro knows where you are right now, and what we've been doing every step of the way. He always knows, and when The Moment comes, if he wants you, whatever you're doing, he will find you! And if he doesn't want you, then fuck you.

As for the miraculous Great Upload? Where we fly up to Paradise? Light the field, prepare the straight way, and all you who believe will become luminous.

It's soon, and when I fly up I'll look back down at you standing there, Mother. I'll watch you get smaller and smaller until you're nothing more than a spot on the ground, and I'll *laugh*.

Unless—and I've tried to overlook certain signs but I can't ignore them—unless he wants you back.

Jethro Flagg

You're a hard woman, Edwina Ferris, I said to her after the fight, and she gave me that look. *Not Ferris, dear Daddy Flagg, remember? You married us, and that made it official. It's Blight.*

I never should have told her my intentions, about which of the flock I had chosen to go with me and which would stay behind and what would become of them.

She glared; her words split me like an axe. *It's Edwina Blight.*

When I came out of my yurt that night and flew over the snow to peel away the Etherian children curled around her and lift her out of her nest, I wanted to romance her until she forgot everything but our bodies and the stars overhead, but her family yurt was empty. My beloved, vindictive Edwina was gone. She decamped with her precious brood, every damn one of them. She took Edward, my boy! And that lame excuse for a husband that I gave her, Micah Blight. She didn't get that I chose him for her because he was so weak?

Mickey. What imbecile names himself after a mouse?

So this is my fault, I suppose, for not making Edwina my primary at the first group wedding, but I have many to love as per our masters' orders, and women are notoriously jealous. *They* want the cradles of Etheria filled to overflowing with citizens of the next world.

I have my own bed to fill. There's no time for exclusivity, Edwina's demand. I have bigger things on my mind. The mission, what is expected and which parts of it I must perform. I have to bring legions with me to the Great Upload, when *They* come and we rise. And the others? That's my job too.

I have work to do here, and through hell and high water, petty mutinies and federal incursions, no mere human can slow me down. And how do I know *They* will come for us? When *They* will come and whether *They* are who they say they are, which has never been clear?

Listen. I fell from a star, the blaze on my forehead is proof of that, don't ask. And when *They* come it is I, and I alone, who will decide which ones come with me to join the kingdom and who stays behind, and if I choose to humble my beautiful Edwina and destroy her instead of scooping her up? That's mine to say. My boy Edward yearns to make new citizens for the future, whereas she . . . Run, Edwina Ferris, if you're that intent on your precious freedom. Run wherever you want, you won't get far. I have my sources, and believe me, I keep track. Flaunt your fame and wait for me to bow down and worship, if that pleases you.

As if that worked out. Fame must have been fun while it lasted, but you haven't been famous for a while. Survival is the best revenge, and if, my dear, you're stuck in Wingdale, Minnesota with nothing but that bus and the clothes you stand up in, there's a reason.

Face it, you crossed the wrong man.

I know where you are and I know what you want, and I am here to tell you that you'll be sorry for walking out on the enterprise. You'll be sorry very soon.

Edwina Blight

In this cold, time stops. I see my whole life flash before my eyes, and it's over.

Jethro is blazing mad. Trying to keep me in Etheria, he told me about the mission. To make me see how important it was, he said an awful thing.

"I have instructions from the future."

"*For* the future?"

"No." He thought he was preaching to the converted, but he was wrong. "I have instructions from the future."

He described—what exactly? Etherians from the next century? Preternatural beings from Elsewhere? Not clear. I don't think he knows.

Whoever they are, he told me they were coming for us, he just didn't know when. And that when they take us, they want to . . . What? He wouldn't tell me. "Just be there."

"Why?"

"Just be there, it's important."

I hissed through bared teeth, "Then tell me why."

With one slip he revealed the endgame and drove me out of the kingdom. He said, "If you want to live."

Tifney

So, the concert? The first thing is, it started out bad. One minute Trig Masters, that I thought he and I were bonded, one minute Trig was hanging with me and in the next, he wasn't. He was down front in what should have been the mosh pit holding Marly Mason way up in his arms, like there was anything worth seeing up there, and he kept holding her, even though we could forget about the rock band. There was nothing to see but the bitch was up high and laughing at me, so take that, Trig Masters, you and I are done. Kids crowded in like bumper cars, squeezing me back and back until I squirted out of the mosh pit and onto the sidelines alone. There I was out in the cold and I was thinking, *OK Tifney, story of your life.*

Then I was either very lucky or it was fated and weird. This tall guy onstage made a lighthouse turn and stopped cold, and wow, he beamed brighter! *I think he saw me.* Then creaky old Mr. Blight started plinking away on, like, this mellophone thing and ta-DAAA, the Blight Family Singers concert began.

It was awful. The mother had this screechy soprano that ripped into us like a buzzsaw , yucky song after yucky song, with the chorus doing backup in crap harmony, even the guy I had my eye on, although unlike the others, he had this excruciated look. It was horrible, although I have to admit that I wasn't around to hear the whole thing because of what happened next and where I went afterward, not to mention what it was like out there when him and me got back from the bar.

I am, however, wiser now and changed forever by the experience, just so you know.

This Mother Blight was up there swaying in tight velvet, warbling "Whispering Hope" like she was giving the microphone a blowjob while the rest of them harmonized to break your heart, and we were all, like, ewwww. Nobody had thrown anything yet, but the kids in back had started to grumble and boo, and that guy that I had my eye on, I think he got it. She hit a high note and his face went all, SHEESH.

He didn't just get it, he got *us*, and everything changed.

He jumped UP like a seven-foot Laker making a hoop, and I could swear he was looking *right at me*. His fist shot up in the air and he howled, "BOO-RAH," and Mrs. Blight, she turned around in a purple fury, like, her glance would send him straight to hell.

Well, big lady, not so much. Instead of standing down or cowering like she expected, this tall, *cute guy* shoved aside the sisters in their ruffles and flounces and came down front and center. Then he jumped *high*. He shook that fist and yelled to crack icebergs, "BOO-RAH!" So we all knew that he was even more bummed by this experience than us. It knifed over our heads like a flying sword. "BOO-RAAAAAHHHH."

And all of us poor, pissed-off, frustrated Midwinter Bashsters, we raised our fists and yelled back at him, unless we were yelling with him, we gave out with the big "BOO-RAAAAHHHHH," and the next thing I knew, he spread his arms out and did a swan dive into the crowd. He landed where the mosh pit would be if this was a real old-fashioned rave and Dean Weingarten had ever heard of a mosh pit and hired a decent band, and he flew into that crowd grinning like he didn't care if they caught him or not.

Trig and his guys put up their arms and started passing him along, so he floated over their heads like a swan on a duck pond. Every kid out there was hooting and howling and passing this cute guy over their heads and it seemed like he was *steering*. Poor guy, he was OLD, my God he must have been at least *thirty*, but he was zooming over their heads laughing and howling like another kid.

Then the most amazing thing happened, he floated out of the mosh pit and pretty much landed on me.

Like it was intended. Like fate.

By that time Security was onstage with wands and shit, surrounding the Blight Family Singers, as we in the audience were more or less storming it, well all except me, because I was mesmerized by the one that had escaped.

He had black, black hair and thick black eyebrows and huge pale eyes and I was thinking, *I'm in love*, which I'm not—yet, although in spite of a couple of things, I'm close.

Wingdale Junior College was moving into high riot mode, and do you believe that Blight woman struck up with "Amazing Grace" as though the mutiny was nothing and all of us suffering out here loved her, and the chorus chimed in like none of this had happened and we could actually hear it over the yelling and sirens and all? A couple of other things also happened, not the least of which was me seeing Marly drag Trig off God knows where to do God knows what with him in the snow, and if you think I will ever forgive either of them . . .

Never mind.

I was *face to face* with this amazing guy. I said the nicest thing I could think of. "That was brave."

"I'm Edward," he said, like that explained it. He flipped his phone open, read a text message and clicked it shut with a nod, like, *There.* "Listen! He's on the way." He took my arm like we'd been dating all our lives. "Let's get out of here."

Which is how we ended up downing double shots at Schillinger's Bar, which I chose because it was within walking distance, and although I'd come to Bash with that jerk Trig Masters, no way was I going home in his car. "OK," I said and fell in next to him. "OK Edward," I said.

In the light at Schillinger's he looked not that old after all, but boy, he looked tired. Bud Schillinger gave me that look, like, I knew I would be carded so Edward pretended the two doubles he ordered were for him. We did the entrance interview, which bands we liked, whether we liked our parents and what was our favorite color and, this is weird, how I did in school: honor roll; it made him smile, but it's still embarrassing. He had to snort both doubles before he could get past that his mother ripped them out of Etheria to further her career, and wow, he hates the Blight Family Singers concerts more than he hates her, like, he says it's coming, and if she's not on board it serves her right. Then he thanked me for—what was it? Leaving my friends to bring him to Schillinger's so he could vent.

"It's not like they're *friends.*" I leaned in closer and wow, he was shivering! I touched his sleeve. "You don't have a coat."

Then he gave me the *weirdest look.* "I won't be here long."

"We just got here and you're leaving?"

"It's not like you think." How was I supposed to know that by *here*, he meant the planet? Accidentally my hand was still on his arm and he reached up and spread his fingers over mine; they were so *warm*. It was intense. I was waiting for him to explain but out of nowhere he said, "So meanwhile, are you seeing anybody?"

"Yes. No. Well, not any more." Oh, flirty girl, all fake-innocent. "Why?" Take *that*, Trig Masters.

He didn't exactly answer. "Did you ever think that there's someplace better than this?"

"What, Wingdale? Man, there's gotta be." *Man. I'm here in Schillinger's with a man.* Just thinking it excited me, so I wasn't rightly listening when he explained. Something about the Pre-kingdom with a leader designated by *Them*, which when I asked, he told me They knew better than us and if I came with him, we'd end up in a far, far better place. When he laid it out for me, his eyes were so bright that I knew that whatever he was seeing, it was real. I was thinking he was crazy, or I was crazy, or we weren't and something big was about to happen to both of us.

I made a silence for him to drop words into. It didn't happen right away. When he finally spoke, it was so sudden that I jumped.

"Did you ever hear of Etheria?"

"Yeah, sort of. Um. Not so much."

"It's wonderful." To hear him, you'd think it was downtown Oz. "It would have been so easy if we'd stayed, but Mother did this stupid, *stupid* thing." He almost choked on it. "They fought. She took us away. But it's OK. He stayed in touch."

"Who?"

"My father."

"That stringy old guy with the xylophone thing?"

"No, my real father." He looked so *proud*. "Jethro Flagg. He promised to come for me. For the Great Upload." He opened his phone. "It's tonight." He set it down on the table. He squared it on the table with a look, like he was expecting further instructions. Then he scanned me up, down, with those amazing eyes; he was, like, *assessing* me. "They aren't taking *everyone*."

"Because . . . "

"New society. *They* want the best." He nodded and Bud brought over a couple more doubles. I grabbed one; I needed it.

I made another silence and waited. It took him too long to go on so I pushed. "Who are *They*, that they're so important?"

"Jethro hasn't rightly said. Just that they have more brains and better technology so wherever they take us it will be better, and so will we . . . " He got all wrapped up in thinking about it.

"Yo, Edward." I fanned my fingers in front of his face. "Edward?"

Then he surprised me; he sighed. "I worry about the rest."

It was only a little creepy. "Which ones are those?"

The squint told me it pained him to say it out loud. "They aren't taking just anyone. We'll be fine, but the others . . . " He took my hands and sparks zapped between us for a long time. They exploded into words. "Oh Tifney, do you want kids?"

"Like, *now?*"

He shook his head. "When it's time."

"Maybe. Probably. Not yet, but maybe when I'm ready . . . " This conversation was spinning its wheels. Because he was so cute and anyplace was better than Wingdale I said, to please him, "Whenever that is."

His phone buzzed on the table. He didn't even look. He jumped up, tugging on my hand. "We have to go. We have to *go!*"

Just then the bar shook; the neon in the front window gave way to white glare bigger than a billion strobes going off all simultaneous. It filled the bar and bleached out all our faces. I froze until I heard Edward groan. "What," I asked him. "*What?*"

"Just *hurry!*"

By the time we got out in the street it was all dark again. He ran. I ran. We kept running even though it was slippery and we were pretty much blinded. I fell and he helped me up. He was so upset that I wanted to tell him we didn't have to hurry. Girls know these things. Whatever he thought was about to happen was already done.

When we got to the field it was empty. There was a big black patch where every speck of ice had melted. To look at the gouges in the terrain, you'd think something tremendous had landed, but it was gone and the ice surrounding had turned to water. Except for Dean Weingarten and the Blight people lurching around the stage bumping into things, everybody was gone. I didn't think that was so bad. I never liked them anyway. Whatever happened to them, my folks would be OK. They never come to these things.

I was OK but Edward crouched in the mud like a hunter looking for tracks. Then he fell on his knees and shouted at the sky. His voice was so full of pain that it tore me apart. He kept crying out the same thing over and over and over, "What happened, what happened?"

I heard thuds as two of the Blight people jumped down from the stage. Twins, maybe. They looked like Edward, but they looked more like each other. Edward was too forlorn and grieved to see them until they got all up in his face, one coming at him from one side and the other from the other. They did this, like, synchronized tap on the shoulder and said what they had come to say. This got his attention.

One said, "He came."

The other said, "She went."

"Mother left you a message."

"She said, 'This will teach you. Nobody gets in my way'."

I will spare you the hideous details of my broken leg, the steel plate, the cables, the screws, the three months on crutches and the five on a cane. I'll just say never run in the dark, especially with a despised piece of alien, uninvited furniture waiting for its chance. I told my daughter, "that damn thing CREPT out and GRABBED MY FOOT, IT HATES ME," and she said, "Why don't you write a Stephen King story about it?" So I did.

THE CHAISE

The object crouched in the Crandalls' back bedroom, angled into a corner but forever *present*, the uninvited guest. Nelda hated the thing. She was convinced that it had a mind of its own.

When she dragged it upstairs to the back bedroom Patrick protested, but even he had to admit there was no right place for his friend's castoff in their cheery, cluttered house. It was simply too big. At least Nelda didn't have to look at it in its dark corner, but she never forgot that it was there—a reminder of Ardis Vaill.

The French teacher's castoff was undeniably a presence. There was no getting around it, at least not without denting a shin or kicking her abandoned relic farther back into the dust underneath the attic stairs. From back to footrest it measured six feet, and it was all theirs, left to them by aggressively glamorous Ardis, who tossed her hair a lot and spoke her downtown Minneapolis English with a Parisian lilt.

It wasn't exactly a chaise longue, although it sprawled under the stairs in the same snotty, entitled way. She'd left behind a deck chair from the unimaginable Roaring Twenties. Sagging split bamboo crosshatched a rectangular iron frame in shades of tan, with an Art Deco border and an outline of the ocean liner it came from picked out in umber on the seat.

There would have been plenty of room for it on the first class promenade of the luxury liner where it started out, but that ship had drowned in World War Two, long before the Crandalls were born. Nelda could see bejeweled passengers swathed in laprobes, lounging on dozens of chairs just like this one, all parked like vintage Cadillac convertibles at a drive-in, facing the view.

The object was designed to impress. *Like its former owner,* Nelda thought bitterly. *It should have gone down with the Titanic.* She covered her mouth but failed to stifle the next thought: *and Ardis along with it.*

Everybody who saw the deck chair admired it, just not enough to take it home; whenever Patrick was out of earshot, she asked. Nice to look at, everyone agreed, but too big for their lives. Sorry, but Nelda, look! Split bamboo, a classic example of its kind: antique dealers would plotz. It would fetch a bundle at any flea market, consignment shop, on eBay, wherever she offered it, they told her.

As if. Patrick, who thought of Ardis as one of his best friends, was flattered and delighted by the gift. Nelda was not, but she had to admit that like Ardis, the unwelcome object had style.

Ardis, now, Ardis was resolutely charming even when she wasn't expecting you, as in the supermarket at dawn, sensuously outlining her upper lip with a fingertip even before she saw who was coming, self-consciously tossing that scrim of black hair. Patrick thought she was wonderful—attractive, funny, a talented gossip—but Nelda always knew that she was false.

Who else would make such a big production out of a simple thing like leaving town? Most people just pack up and go. Ardis, now, Ardis was downright ceremonial. Little parties, each with an agenda. Mimosas in the front yard on the last day, as her new man backed the U-Haul into her drive. Once Bartlett had jumped down, chiseled and looking buff for his age, she made a wide gesture that included them all. "My peonies are all yours—if you don't mind digging them up."

She took on like a diva at the taffrail of the Queen Mary as they pulled away, waving goodbye to Midvale and all the little people she was leaving behind: poor them.

Ardis had made such a point of divesting objects not wanted on the voyage, that Nelda knew old furniture wasn't all she was divesting, which, face it, was a bit of a relief—to Nelda, at least. The Crandalls and all the other friends Ardis had cultivated at the college were good enough as long as she was beached in Midvale, but after she had decided and long before she broke the news that she was leaving, she'd moved on.

"Old friends are best," Ardis insisted, hugging them all goodbye, but with Ardis, nothing was ever just that. The nice new friends waiting for Ardis in New York would be far too gorgeous and witty—face it, way too sophisticated—for her leftovers from this small town.

Nothing was ever just that, so when she invited the Crandalls to one of her little parties, it wasn't one. It was a pretext. She was bent on offloading anything not in keeping with her new life in Bartlett's PoMo floor-through on Riverside Drive. Before the yard sale and Goodwill, but after the antique and art dealers and consignment people had been, she called them.

Innocent social beings that they were, at the drop of an invitation late in a boring weekend, the Crandalls hurled themselves into the car. Patrick loved parties, although Nelda had her suspicions.

Of course she always had her suspicions. Her back hairs prickled whenever Ardis called, usually around suppertime—to gossip with Patrick, unless it was to scent-mark her prey. "She's going to crack your bones and suck out all the marrow," Nelda told him after one endless phone call. They always told each other everything.

Patrick grinned. "Have a little pity," he said in the early days. "She's new, and she's insecure."

Later, he was amused but pragmatic because she called often and never without keeping him on the phone. "She thinks I can help her get tenure." And a little flattered. "Hey, she knows where the power is." But he liked Ardis. She brought the best gossip, stinging one-liners about people Patrick didn't like; she knew how to make him laugh.

There was always a proximate cause. She always had a pretext, although the calls escalated when she was between men. At Midvale the pretext was her scholarly book: questions about her bibliography, foot-note, extraneous chapter, did you like this, Patrick? What about that? Should I do this in the preface, Patrick, is that chapter right? Unless it was the obligatory instant replay of some party or a meeting she and Patrick had just endured. Sameold, sameold. There had been murmuring and laughter as Nelda rattled cookware and their dinner faded to lukewarm, and now?

Well, she won't be rehashing French department meetings any more. Ardis sold a richly embroidered memoir and bonded with this man Bartlett over an editorial lunch. She was leaving them.

So this party would be the last goodbye.

Naturally it wasn't. *Ulterior*, Nelda thought. A rack of discarded outfits loomed behind Ardis when she came to the door; hung with clothes redolent of the owner, the thing crouched at her back like a molting mantis dominating the front hall. Nelda shrank at the sight.

Patrick had no idea. He greeted Ardis with a hug.

"Ardis, how nice."

"Oh, Nelda," Ardis said, noting the earrings and fresh makeup. "You shouldn't have gone to any trouble. It's just us."

Right.

She maneuvered so Nelda was facing the garment rack: heavy litter night on Seventh Avenue, for sure. "If you see anything you like, it's yours."

Nelda's smile was more of a feint. Never mind that the offer was condescending; wearing some old thing that Ardis Vaill had done God knows what in was much too creepy to contemplate.

Never mind that there was no place in their arrangements for the low-slung, unwieldy deck chair Ardis unloaded that sunny afternoon; who knew how badly this would end? As the Crandalls raised the first drink, she pointed grandly to the chaise sitting smugly amid dying plants on the barren floor, "I'm going to miss you guys. Sotheby's wanted it for the auction but I love you, so I earmarked this especially for you."

As if anybody from Sotheby's would come near anything Ardis had.

Patrick thanked her before Nelda could protest.

"Something," Ardis said with that heavily loaded smile, "to remember me by." Then, satisfied, she tossed her hair and passed the nuts.

Patrick was actually honored, grinning as she poured them another drink. Nelda had never liked the thing, it was too big and miserably uncomfortable, but she loved him so she pretended as, beaming, he thanked Ardis with one of those wonderful smiles and lugged the unwelcome object out to the car.

He didn't see the owner's expression as her castoff headed down the walk and out of her old life, nor did he see the sly grin she gave Nelda as he tried and failed to close the tailgate of their SUV over its protruding iron feet.

By the time he turned back to ask for something to secure it, Ardis was draped in the doorway, dangling a length of cord with the air of a medieval princess bestowing a chiffon scarf before the tournament. In the split second before Patrick turned and saw, she'd recalibrated the gloat, and the look she gave him was alarmingly sweet. She handed off the cord with her best camera-ready smile. "It's too bad," she said, "that we can't take *everything* we care about."

Nelda scowled. *What do you mean, we?*

Rapt, her only husband pressed Ardis's hands in yet another goodbye. She rewarded him with another little storm of what she obviously thought was her best feature: that color-enhanced, ostensibly enviable black hair. "Remember me," she told him, and started inside.

"Oh," Nelda called with a musical, fuck-you lilt. "We will."

"Promise to tell me when you're coming to the city. We'll have a party."

"Of course," Nelda trilled, although they both knew she wouldn't. Ardis was famous for unkept promises. More: the Crandalls seldom made it to Hartford, let alone New York. Still she said, for Patrick. "Of course we will."

Cheap at the price, she thought when the chaise slipped forward and grazed her cheek as Patrick started the car. *At least the phone calls will stop.*

Ardis Vaill left town but this was by no means the end.

After a slight lapse during which she and Bartlett found each other out and their love cooled, Ardis called. She still chose the most inconvenient time, although Nelda wondered whether any time would be convenient. The woman rose up out of the telephone like a genie, calling about which coffee table, Patrick, how should she open her next memoir, which books, Patrick, oh Patrick, I just called to say hello.

"Oh," she cried one night when Nelda relieved Patrick of the receiver without warning; his steak was getting cold. "How I *wish* you'd come down," Ardis was saying. Nelda heard that smoky voice curling up from the phone as she dropped it into the dock. "Do come, I need your best thoughts on this."

Ardis didn't mean *you*, she meant Patrick, and that was part of it, but it wasn't the only part of it.

There was the deck chair itself. Until they agreed on the back bedroom, the object had refused to stay put.

In the first weeks they tried it here in their big old house—in the living room, dining room; they tried it there—out in the glassed-in porch, exiled to the bay window among the plants, but in a house furnished with objects the owners had chosen together, there was no right place for an arrogant intruder too big and too pretentious to fit.

Nelda hated the thing.

It took her a little bit too long to realize that it hated her right back.

"Pat," she said after she kicked it into place under the attic stairs, "Ardis Vaill's deck chair bit me last night." OK, she kicked it and hit in the wrong place, nicking her shin on the rusting iron frame.

Patrick did *not* say "tetanus shot!"

"Oh," he said, "you hurt yourself; I'm sorry, let's see." They were in bed on a sunny Saturday, er, Afterward. Stroking her damaged shin with a loving there-there, he said absently, "It's not hers, honey. It's ours."

"Could we please just sell it, junk it, give it away?"

"How could we? Think how hurt she'd be!"

"It's not like she's coming back to visit the thing. She'll never know."

He muttered, so darkly that it was alarming, "Believe me, she'd know."

Maybe she did have the power.

Gone six months, without even a post card, and that Monday a copy of the memoir arrived by FedEx, Signature Requested. Patrick's. Even before he opened the package, Ardis. And called, "Oh, Patrick, what do you think?" She obsessed over every detail in the book until even Patrick dodged the phone. "Why do I feel so guilty?"

Fingers crept up Nelda's nape. "The woman has a gift."

That velvety, imperious telephone voice made Nelda want to shout, "Enough, Ardis. He's mine!" and the weirdness?

That she wanted Patrick, and he didn't even know. He still assumed they were work buddies. Old friends. Did he not notice that Ardis kept pressing him for a date—just you, Patrick, Nelda would be bored—to talk about her wretched book? That she and Bartlett were unraveling and . . .

The woman wouldn't take no. She persisted until Nelda heard sweet, obtuse Patrick promising that next time they made it down to the city, they'd certainly come. Did he not hear her angry hiss as she hung up on him? "Crap," he said. "I hope I didn't hurt her feelings."

Nelda hoped he had.

That night the deck chair made its next move. Did Patrick not see the link? Nelda had to admit she was distracted, moving too fast; now she had a fresh cut on her shin, as though the old bruise marked the bullseye for the thing's next shot. She kicked it hard, yelling, "Piece of shit."

Coming with a wet washcloth, Patrick said, "You have to be more careful."

No. The thought made her shiver. *You do.*

What did she mean? She wasn't sure. *Careful of Ardis*, she thought, but could not for the life of her spell out exactly what that meant.

The mark on her shin was shallow, no stitches needed, but Nelda took it as a direct attack by an item she'd wanted gone from the day it first came into their lives.

She couldn't shake the idea that Ardis had left behind a proxy, embedded in their household with orders to do her will. If only she could do it without hurting Patrick, Nelda would eliminate the thing. She wanted to drag it outside and throw it in the street. She wanted to see it sprawling on its back with its feet up and those sharp legs splayed; it would be like an invitation to vandals or scavengers. Let them have their way with it. But she had to wait her time. Eventually Patrick would forget about it in that sweet, Patrick way. Then she could get rid of the thing. It's not as if guests came in begging to see it. It's not as though he went in daily to visit the damn thing; he didn't want to settle into the brittle split bamboo and commune with his treasure. For the first time since they'd bought the house, she pushed the door to, a first step toward quarantining the thing.

Maybe it was her imagination, but the deck chair knew. It knew.

Never mind. All she had to do was wait. The trouble was, she couldn't wait. Ardis had taken to calling Patrick on his cell phone, and dammit, even though he had caller ID he picked up every time. Soon he was talking through all too many dinners, eating as he murmured to Ardis, cradled in his palm.

"Trouble with Bartlett," he explained yet again, covering the mouthpiece. "She's very upset."

He was apologetic, but still... Nelda wanted to be cool, but she couldn't hide her feelings. Complicated as her expression was, Patrick read it. He understood.

"Something's come up," he told Ardis. "Can I call you back?" She was still talking when his phone snapped shut.

Ardis Vaill might not see what passed between Patrick and Nelda Crandall, but the deck chair knew. Even though she'd lodged the thing where she wouldn't have to look at it; even though she'd all but closed the door on the thing, Nelda couldn't get past it. It was lurking in the back bedroom, her silent enemy, waiting its time.

The reckoning would come sooner than later, because Nelda couldn't leave it alone.

Unless it was Ardis.

Maybe Ardis couldn't leave it alone. Fear crawled up inside Nelda and took up residence. She couldn't tell Patrick the woman was conspiring against her, she was three states, several freeways or a plane ride away. She couldn't tell him what she wanted, but she knew. The deck chair had to go. She couldn't prove it, but she was certain that the thing had a mind of its own.

Nelda was a little giddier than she should be the next time Patrick dodged one of those phone calls. "Call you back in a couple." For the second time that week he snapped the phone shut, and Nelda grinned.

After dinner he said lazily, "I really should call her back," but he didn't. He seemed relieved. Delighted, Nelda laid on Irish coffee and another slice of cake, laughter and blandishments. And if that made her feel guilty and a little uneasy?

Well.

Still. She went upstairs after supper, troubled and compelled to check. Nelda couldn't shake the idea that while she wasn't looking, the deck chair inched out of its niche little by little, working its way farther into the room. She gave it a kick. When it resisted she put both hands on the woven arm with its carefully worked drinks holder and shoved like a lion tamer ordering the object back, back into its cage. *Take that!* As she did so, a length of knife-thin bamboo snapped and whipsawed a slash across her palm.

Never mind what she called it. Cursing, she went into the bathroom, patched herself up, came downstairs smiling. Any other response and she'd be giving too much importance to an inanimate object the real world had discarded a long time ago. Patrick had already half-forgotten, she told herself. Even Ardis could forget.

When he asked why the bandage, she didn't exactly answer. If she explained, she understood without being able to analyze the process, Ardis would know. "Nothing."

"Too many accidents. You need to be more careful."

"I do." *Ardis would know.*

Her man studied her, sober and judgmental. "I'm worried. This is your third this month."

Nelda swallowed hard and began. "Don't you think it's a little weird?" Then the thought completed itself. It lodged in her throat and she gagged because she couldn't make it go down. *The thing would know.* She gasped.

"Honey?"

"I'm sorry!" The hell of it was, she wasn't sure what she was apologizing for—or to.

"Oh, honey." He silenced her with a hug.

Nelda was a rational, highly intelligent adult with an irrational hatred for an inanimate object, and the worrisome part was that her hatred was edged with fear. Her hand mended and she tried to forget.

Let it go, she told herself, turning to her work, their friends, adding an hour a day at the gym, on the machines or on the indoor track. *It's only a thing.* But she was committed to getting strong—probably, she told herself, so she'd look better in her clothes. Unless it was to do battle with the thing. She shopped online, girding herself. She and Patrick would start going out more, maybe even to the city. In her new outfits, Nelda would be armed for any encounter. Confronting Ardis, she would damn well look her best.

Although she pretended to forget everything else, at some deeper level, Nelda was considering. How to get rid of the enemy. No. Who the enemy really was.

It would be hard to say when she concluded that the thing was doing the bidding of Ardis Vaill.

What she did know was the exact moment when she knew that offloading it wasn't enough. She had to destroy it. It was after the packet came from Ardis, a new manuscript in a Jiffy bag. Part Two of her memoir, Nelda knew. She'd put the Riverside Drive address sticker in the upper left-hand corner but she'd crossed out Bartlett's name. She'd framed it in red Sharpie so emphatically that the package was grooved. Scowling, Nelda turned it over.

GOT CUSTODY OF THE APARTMENT! Ardis had scrawled in red on the flap. Nelda knew what would follow. Phone calls and summonses. "Just you, Patrick. We really have to talk." Ardis was closing in for the kill.

Nelda stuffed the package in a grocery bag with the rest of that week's newspapers and took it to the recycling bin.

OK, she brought it on herself.

She did in fact consider, but only for a minute, resting the paper sack on the lip of the bin. Patrick would know that it was coming. Ardis would have emailed. No. She'd have phoned. At least she'd quit calling the house. She hunted him down during office hours now, and Nelda could only guess at what baggage she unloaded in those little threnodies of vanity and complaint, but no matter. No matter what new hook Ardis tried to sink, Patrick always slipped it in time to make it home by six, sitting at their kitchen table while Nelda cooked.

The manuscript wouldn't go away forever and Nelda knew it; Ardis would deluge Patrick with queries and backup copies until she heard from him, but even she must know that reading a manuscript took time. This might take weeks to play out. Let her wait.

Grinning, Nelda pushed it into the bin. It hit bottom with a satisfying thump.

As if temporizing ever worked.

Near midnight, Ardis struck, although not everybody would agree with Nelda that the freak hailstorm that ripped leaves off trees all over Midvale and slashed screens and ruined rugs and upholstery was the former French teacher's work. In spite of the season it was so hot out that Nelda had thrown open every window in the house. Patrick was out wrangling a visiting lecturer: dinner, an hour of boredom with question period and reception to follow, with instructions to go with the GOH from bar to bar after that, staying with him for as long it took, because the department chair wanted to make sure the eminent fool was back in his hotel room by four a.m. when the airport limo came.

This left Nelda alone to cope with sudden hail that turned into flying slush and then a deluge before she was fully awake. The racket jolted her into consciousness and sent her running from room to room ahead of the rain, closing windows in the dark: living room first, study, upstairs.

When she hit the back bedroom it never occurred to her that the deck chair would be anywhere other than in its usual place.

She ran for the window and pulled it shut as cold rain blew into the room, sheeting her eyes and misting her face. Window down. Fine. On to their bedroom.

Did the chaise drag itself out from under the attic stairs? Creep on iron toes? Crawl? Nelda had her suspicions, but she'd never know. She didn't even know it was out there, lying in wait. She was moving too fast to stop at the bite of the cold leading edge of the hated deck chair. She was running too fast to stop at all, which is why Patrick found her entangled with her nemesis, one foot hung up in the torn split bamboo and the other ankle swelling rapidly.

"Are you all right?"

She was sobbing, furious. "No!"

"Thank God I got home in time to hear the crash!" Once he'd administered port and aspirin, once he'd put her to bed with an ice pack on the ankle, which didn't look too bad, and Band-Aids applied to the bamboo cuts with enough sympathy to ease the insult and take away the sting; once she'd stopped sobbing with pain and rage, Patrick kissed her and said, "Is there anything more I can do for you?"

Not her fault pain and too much port left her angry and incoherent. She thinks she said, "Get rid of it."

"What?"

Through clenched teeth and lips drawn so tight that they'd gone white, she managed, "Kill the wretched thing."

"Shh," he murmured into her hair. "Don't. You're just upset. You'll feel better about it in the morning." He kissed her lightly on the forehead and turned out the light.

Nelda didn't. The ankle bothered her, but not as much as a visit to the local E.R. She drew up her knees under the covers and thought. She wanted Patrick to drag the thing out in the back yard and set fire to it, but she knew better than to raise it with him today. He'd just come in smiling, bringing coffee. There was a rose on her breakfast tray.

When she brought it up later, he looked surprised—and a little hurt. As though he, Patrick, and not the chaise, was the object of her rage. Nelda fumed, but they were still in love. They knew each other so well that she didn't press.

She was entirely too smart to press Patrick on this, even as she knew never to say a word against Ardis, or warn him that his ex-colleague was trying to lure him into her arms with an unfinished manuscript. She'd cross that chicken when it hit the doorstep again.

And it would, Nelda knew. Whatever it took. When she understood that this copy had misfired Ardis would FedEx, receipt requested, or send a messenger, and if those vanished before Patrick could read and admire, she'd probably hand-carry the next copy, unless (here, Nelda found herself gnawing her knuckles in rage and frustration) unless she lured him into Manhattan and held him captive in her satiny stronghold while she read the entire thing to him aloud. It was too much to contemplate. Just. Too. Much.

The next copy of that half-baked memoir hit the kitchen table the day before Nelda went upstairs to the back bedroom with a box of matches and an axe.

"Look." Patrick put down the FedEx pack where the platter would go. "Ardis is writing another book."

Did he notice that her voice broke when she said, "Great"?

For whatever reasons—distress call from Ardis? Amorphous but distinctly threatening vibe?—for whatever reasons, Patrick came home from work early the next day. He turned up unexpectedly and found her with the axe raised over the deck chair, shaking with rage and uncertainty.

"What are you doing? What are you *doing?*"

The ship design was torn but still legible; a corner of the split bamboo was slightly scorched, but it hadn't caught. Trembling, she looked up. "What I have to."

"Stop!" He fell on her and she dropped the axe. Sweating and desperate, they grappled, Nelda incoherent and frothing, Patrick shouting. "Nelda, this is crazy," although he could not have said why she was so angry or why this mattered so much.

Just before they tipped and fell backward into the rickety instrument of destruction he finally pinned her, asking through locked teeth, "Why, Nelda, why?"

How could she tell him? She couldn't, she could only wail, "Patrick, what are you doing? What are you doing to me?"

As he locked his arms around her and they fell he cried, "I love you and I'm saving you from yourself!" at which a shudder went through the wreckage beneath them and in a last spasm of vengeance, the chaise punished Nelda with its iron footrest, bashing her sharply across the face.

Everything changed when he saw the blood, both in the room and somewhere miles away, although Patrick still didn't understand that there were conflicting interests here or what they were, and Nelda was unconscious and would not know until the next day. Once the cut in her face was stitched up, as soon as she'd been sedated and settled in a hospital bed for the night, he was going home. Then he'd go up to the back bedroom; he would pick up the axe she had dropped during the struggle and finish the job. Dragging the ruined deck chair outside, he would decide he needed to wait to set it alight. He wanted Nelda to be watching when he crumpled Ardis Vaill's unread manuscript, lit the match and torched the thing.

*I was asked to write a story set in the most exotic place I knew for **Haunted Legends**, edited by Ellen Datlow and Nick Mamatas. New York was taken so I chose Fatehpur Sikri. Once you see it, you never forget it.*

AKBAR

Even when you've dreamed of the trip for years India is hard, and not only for people who come here, as the poor could tell you. For Sara Kendall, teetering on a ridge in the Rajasthani desert, it's becoming impossible. The air is dry. Red dust blows across her ankles. She is stalled on the incline outside the red sandstone gate to a fortress, or city, she isn't sure which, only that she is reluctant to go in. Parched, unaccountably exhausted, she knows Terry has delivered her to this place for a reason.

Like a ringmaster, her husband makes a wide gesture and says in a *ta-DA* voice. "Fatehpur Sikri, the famous ghost city."

She whispers, "Who died?"

"I guess you could say the city did." His nervous laugh frightens her. "This is your present. Aren't you excited?"

What do you want? Sara wonders, but does not say. *What do you expect from this?* Because it's their tenth anniversary, she tries to please him, saying, "The domes are wonderful." They are. They rise in stages, like ornaments on Rajput warriors' helmets, but anxiety betrays her.

Terry catches that telltale tremor in her voice and pounces. "All that money, all this way and you don't like it!"

The trip she thought would go so well is going very badly. With her mouth dry and her belly clenching Sara snaps, "We just got here. How am I supposed to know whether I like it?"

Things have been strange between them ever since he brought her to the subcontinent, and Sara can't for the life of her tell whether this is delayed jet lag working in her, or an early symptom of extreme xenophobia. It's just so odd! Their first night in Bombay was glorious, they ate superb Indian food in a rooftop restaurant high above the glittering harbor. At sunset they looked out through plate glass, marveling at the way the changing light played on layers of smoke that rose from a thousand cooking fires in the city far below.

Then in the elevator going down to their room Terry said weirdly, "You know, there's a lot riding on this trip."

News from the front: *Terry has an agenda.* "What . . . "

For whatever reasons, he wouldn't answer. "Wait 'til you see!"

"See what?"

His face went through a lot of complicated maneuvers, none of which worked out. When he used that evasive, infuriating singsong tone, he sounded exactly like her father. "You'll see."

This made her step away from him, squinting. Married ten years and nothing between them is clear. She and Terry have always had a strange relationship, half needy adoration, half power struggle. "Are you playing me?"

"Relax," he said with a laugh that made Sara wonder if there was such a thing as too joyful. "Live the legend."

What legend? She rummaged for what little she knew but all she could find were dimly remembered names: Brahma, Vishnu, Shiva, Ganesh, oh God, did she have it right, did she even have the right religion? She'd resisted doing homework for this trip, and she'd rather die than ask Terry. This was not her country; she was not herself. She was too disrupted and ignorant to ask questions.

On the night train to New Delhi Sara grappled with mystery and dislocation, compounded by the unbidden knowledge that in a country this far from home you are always the foreigner, and nothing is what you think.

She was upset by the weirdness (Terry's) followed by the being sick (hers). It was sudden and apparently endless. Dying inside, she looked down the hole at rushing tracks and faced death at dawn, armed with a tin cup and leaky faucet. It went on for hours. Outside, odd trees and desert rushed by under astounding blue skies sliced by wheeling vultures; she saw great stretches of nothing between villages and train stations overflowing with people. Unshelled in New Delhi, she was struck by the noise. It was nothing like ordinary American street racket. It was as if she could hear the entire country breathing, groaning, tossing in its sleep, and she had the idea that nobody slept for long. She was overpowered by the feeling that all the people on the teeming subcontinent were all talking, and all at once, unless they were wailing in despair, or singing, and the worst part was that she did not know which, only that she had no right to question.

There was as well Terry's expectation that she would walk into the unknown gladly and face the world of strangers smiling.

She didn't feel safe until sliding glass doors closed behind them, sealing them into their hotel. After a night and a long day sleeping, after dinner in a four star hotel restaurant, she felt strong enough to confront him. "What, Terry?" She needed to look into the man she thought she knew, and find out why they were here. "What do you mean, there's a lot riding on this?"

But Terry, that old master of bait-and-switch, lifted her with his voice. "Look." His gesture took in the marbled interior and the tiers of marble balustrades, where guests prowled the balcony shops with no beggars and no vendors to hound them, no disorderly street life to break the carefully polished surface of the experience.

"Terry, I need to know . . . "

He opened a small velvet bag and her voice trailed off. Something fell into her hand. It was a ring. "I had this made for you today. Blue topaz."

"Oh." The stone caught the light. "Oh!"

"Happy anniversary."

Ten years. There were still those questions. Enclosed, poised at the bottom of a four-story waterfall in the hotel's marble atrium, she told herself they could wait. If the trip would just end here, they could wait forever. She and Terry would eat and play inside the vast hotel, riding out at dusk to see monuments through sealed car windows, marveling at the sights as they zipped by and heading home before anything too bad could happen, they . . .

"We'd better crash. Car's coming at four a.m."

"Car?" *I can't.*

Terry's tone said, *you will.* "Girl." He diverted her with another velvet bag. Blue topaz earrings spilled into her hand like promises. "This is India!"

They headed out at first light—before the heat, too early for most of the city's millions. The streets were as empty as they'd ever be. As long as they were contained, Sara was OK: air conditioning on full, Ravi Singh nodding deferentially as he handed her into the car. Once they cleared the city the fierce, dignified Sikh driver turned into something else. He plunged through traffic like a warrior preparing to die in battle. He drove as if fixed on flaming out in holy martyrdom—next stop, heaven. Sara gasped as he swerved into the path of an oncoming semi to avoid the cow that had plopped down to rest on the tarmac. Shaken, she had to wonder what it all meant to him, how much hair he had—a lifetime's worth, twined under that yellow turban—do Sikhs expect God to grab them by the hair and yank them up to heaven, or did she make up that part?

Which god? She didn't know. Driving, Ravi Singh presented a massive profile so stony that she was afraid to ask him.

Riding along in silence, she had time to wonder.

It was her fault she wasn't clear where Terry was taking her. She'd been tied up at work; she let him research this trip and he did all the planning. She told him she wanted to be surprised, but she was afraid. India was too big, too strange. People could be born here and spin out their whole lives in a place this rich and complicated without knowing it. They could read and study, travel the length and breadth of their country and still not know any more than a fish knows about the ocean, so preparing, she'd just packed and walked out the door.

Now she was beggared by her ignorance. With Ravi closed and locked for the day, she touched her mate's arm. "About this legend we're living. Which one, Terry? Which one?" He never snored, so she knew he was pretending. They rode for hours. She slept until the car stopped.

Ravi pulled the hand brake and got out to open the door for them. Heat rushed in. "From here, you walk. Where shall I wait?"

Terry answered, "Jami Masjid. That's big mosque to you," he told her condescendingly.

Anger flared. *Don't pretend to know places you've never seen.* If thoughts could kill. No. She could say it out loud and he wouldn't hear her. They spilled out on the scorching road like two peas dropped on a griddle. Because this was her last chance, Sara turned to Ravi. "There is a legend?"

He touched joined hands to his forehead. "Salim Chisti."

"Who?"

Damn Terry, why did he look so smug? He tapped the guidebook. "It's all in here."

She grimaced. "I was asking Mr. Singh."

The driver said dutifully, "The emperor Akbar built this city to give thanks. It has been empty for many years."

"Thanks for what?"

Terry pre-empted. "We have that, Sara. It's in the book."

"Sunset," the Sikh said, as if the timing was a given.

She comes to herself with a start. The light has changed. What are they doing here?

Want.

Startled, she whirls. *Who spoke?* Terry tugs on her hand, oblivious. There's nobody else around, no one in line for tickets. There are no guides clamoring, nobody begging, nobody selling curios or street food or—God!—water. Their car is gone, Ravi is gone, and the road that brought them to the ghost city is empty. For the first time since they landed on the teeming subcontinent they are alone. "Where is everybody?"

"Inside, I suppose." Even Terry sounds uncertain. "Unless it's some kind of holiday."

After the bustle and outcry, it's so eerily silent that Sara shudders. "Are we safe?" She is asking more than one question here, although Terry won't notice.

"Sara, it's a national monument! Don't you think these places are protected?"

"How am I supposed to know! I don't even know why we're here!"

He wants.

What? She turns to Terry. "Did you say something?"

"I said, this is it." His tone speaks of more than the city. At the top of the ramp, the gate waits like an open mouth. He pulls her through the vaulted gate and out into the sun-blasted courtyard. "Downtown Oz."

They always want.

Troubled, she turns to look at the ancient city. It is magnificent. Amazing. Deserted. Above the archway, outlining onion domes and minarets, fortress walls and the turrets, that wild blue sky is empty except for the white sun pasted overhead, blazing. What is it, noon? Later? "Oh." Blinded in spite of the hat, Ray-Bans, everything she marshaled to protect her, Sara gulps scalding air. "Oh!"

"It's . . . " Terry is trying to pick her up with his voice and put her down somewhere she never intended to be. "It's like . . . "

Reflexively, she tilts her water bottle. "It's hot."

"I don't know what it's like, it's just so beautiful."

She drinks and feels better. "It is."

"Like the emperor's wet dream, it's . . . " Then Terry goes that one step too far. "Oh Sara, let's bring the kids some day."

Dazzled by the light, momentarily seduced into dreaming, Sara comes back to herself with a jolt. "You pick the worst times to bring things up," she snaps, and in all the times he's raised it, this is as far the discussion ever goes.

Sara Kendall grew up motherless, and for a scary reason. Not going there. Not being that person. Not dying that way, not like her mother, not ever.

She survives by keeping her elbows close to her sides. Given the pressure of her job, one extra person in her life is her limit and Terry knows it. "Now," she says tersely, "About this legend."

"The emperor Akbar made a pledge," he says so fast that she knows he is hiding something. "Sikri means thanks, he got what he wanted and that's why he built the city." Terry says all that and throws in a short history of the Moghul emperors, but doesn't say what Akbar was giving thanks for. Like a pitchman for some product he isn't ready to unveil, he retreats into the guidebook. "Says here it took years to build the fortress and the palaces, everything up here had to be hauled to the top of the ridge except the sandstone they carved out right here. I mean everything: marble and malachite, all the metal and rugs and furniture, tools and fuel, everything they needed. Bearers brought clothes and jewelry and weapons for the hundreds, everything it takes to run an empire, and when it was done all of Akbar's people came up, and there were hundreds—warriors and courtiers, wives and concubines, the slaves, then there were the animals . . . "

The heat is making her dizzy but Terry drones on like an amateur hypnotist until she cries, "Oh, Terry. Don't go all tour guide on me."

Listen.

She shivers. *Oh, don't!*

"The emperor's elephants," he finishes anyway. "The place where Ravi let us out at the elephant ramp," he adds in a scholarly tone that makes her want to smack him. "You may not care about this stuff but we're talking about the greatest of the Moghul emperors. Look at the place! Akbar thought of everything."

"It's been a while since Akbar," Sara says. When he pitched this trip to her on a cool night in Providence, Terry never told her how hot it would be, or that she would be too limp and dehydrated and disoriented to enjoy it. She shuffles uneasily, stirring the red dust that blows across the courtyard, clinging to the hairs on her bare arms, caking in her nostrils. "If he thought of everything, why is it so quiet?"

"It was amazing, it was beautiful, for a while. He had a system, but all those people, all those animals." Terry sighs. "A few years up here and they just plain ran out of water."

She sighs. "The city died."

"Pretty much. It's just tourists now." He says in a loaded tone, "And pilgrims."

This drops into her head, uninvited. **Pilgrims, yes**. This makes her twitch like a horse trying to shake off a fly. "What pilgrims?"

Instead of answering, Terry leads her out of the covered walkway, into the open. The light is blinding. White sunlight brings every outline into sharp relief—the cornices, domes and turrets, passages and intricately carved screens of red sandstone that set the margins of the emperor's ghost city. The great courtyard is alarmingly still. Nothing moves; there are none of the expected tourists dutifully shuffling through the shady corridors or striking poses for point-and-shoots or digital cameras; there are no guides-for-hire struggling to be first, no hopeful little hangers-on smiling their hardest and no vendors, and if she thought she could buy food or another bottle of water, it won't be here in the deserted city.

The silence is profoundly troubling. She touches his arm. "Terry, where is everybody?"

"What do you care? The place is ours!" With that creepy laugh, he locks her fingers in his. He leads her into another passageway screened by lacy red sandstone.

When he finally lets go she steps back, studying the man who brought her to this strange place: familiar face, dark hair blowing, same Terry, and yet she is thinking, *Do I know you?* They stand for a moment, looking out through stone fretwork at the surrounding desert.

"All ours," Terry says.

Her mouth is dry; her skin is dry. Even her eyeballs are drying out. "It is," she says, because he is waiting.

She doesn't know what the problem is yet, but there is a problem: Terry's urgency, the bizarre sense that the stones or something trapped within the stones is speaking. She is listening hard, but Terry's voice drowns out whatever she thought was speaking. "It says here that Akbar had five thousand concubines." He points. "I think that's the zenana, but you know, of all those wives . . . " He considers. Decides it isn't time yet and doesn't finish.

He wants.

Alarmed, she looks here, there, *What do you mean, he wants? I give him everything he wants.* She'd like to face this figure. She wants to argue. If she could catch someone following, some helpful soul keeping pace behind one of the intricate sandstone screens, some living human whispering things only she can hear, she would feel better. At this point she'd even take an enemy bent on her destruction. A person. *That,* she thinks, *I could handle.* But there is only Terry.

She puts it to him. "What do you want, Terry?"

He is running on ahead and doesn't hear.

Weird, she thinks. *This is so weird*, in spite of which she finishes, "Some kind of sacrifice?"

More. Words float into her head—a warning. **They always want more.**

"What?"

Typical Terry: he deflects questions with information. "See that platform in the water? That's where Akbar sat when he was holding court. You had to go over the little bridges to talk to him. Studying the book, he turns her around. Sometimes, he sat up there, on that platform? And played games. See the squares, this is his game-board, and the squares?" He turns her so they are side by side like a pair of dancers looking at the courtyard, where Akbar's design is laid out in stone. "He moved people around like living chess pieces."

Like the objects of his desires.

Terry finishes, "And he always won."

What? It isn't the wind she hears, and it is not a voice, exactly, but something bent on being acknowledged. Warning:

Like you.

Like me? If this is a warning, what should she be afraid of? Their major issue is dead and he knows it. They agreed on that years ago, so what is this? Intent on his agenda, Terry keeps the book between them, reading entries on everything they pass like a teacher who cares more about the sound of his own voice than anything his listener has to say. She'd put the question, but he uses the book as a shield against questions.

As they go along for what seems like miles the sky overhead bleaches to the color of melting lead; she is exhausted and dying of thirst and yet Terry pulls her along on a string of words, relentlessly reading. "The emperor brought craftsmen from all over the known world to build his city and the architecture is rich and varied, showing design elements drawn from every known religious building."

"Don't," she cries as he launches into yet another long passage. "Just don't!" For the first time in a marriage she assumed was built on love, Sara hates him for this. She bats words away with her hands; there is no way to explain without hurting him. *How can I listen with you yapping?*

"And this," he says, reading instead of looking, "is the Diwan-i-Khas, the hall where Akbar held audiences. He sat up there, at the top of that pillar, behind all those screens, so he could hear but not be seen, because he was the power here. When he spoke, none of the subjects waiting down here could see him but every one of them could hear every word when he passed judgment. See?" Terry points.

For once Sara does as told. She follows his finger up the stone column that supports Akbar's screened pedestal. From down here the thing looks like an inverted sno-cone or an upside-down wet dream of a wedding cake ornamented with what could be dangling... *Oh, good grief.* "He had audiences here?"

Oddly, Terry says, "Down here we could hear him speak, but we couldn't see him deciding."

We. "Deciding what?"

Whatever he wanted.

Thank God you're back. Frightened, alone in a strange country, Sara can't even guess which god she is thanking.

"Oh, all the important things."

The next thing she knows Terry is climbing, scrambling up worn stairs to the balcony. "Where are you going, Terry?" She sees him running along above her. She calls, "What are you doing?" With a wave, he crosses one of the six bridges that lead to the emperor's platform and disappears into the central pod.

They always get what they want.

This makes Sara groan. Anxious and disrupted, she tries again to make him answer. "Terry, what are you *doing?*"

After much too long his voice comes from above and the bastard, bastard is reading aloud from the guidebook, sitting up there in the pod:

"According to the legend, it says here, Akbar's wives couldn't give him a male heir. Then travelers came to him telling stories of a great Sufi saint and so he came here on a pilgrimage. He came to sit at the feet of Shaikh Salim Chisti, and tell him of his great need, and then the saint..."

"Is that what you want?"

"...prophesied that he would have a son, but the mother must be a Christian."

Words pour out of her like vomit. "You son of a bitch, is that all you want from me?"

Then the air changes and something huge thunders in.

SO MANY WIVES, SO MANY WOMEN, SO MANY DIED AND NOT ONE SON TO CARRY ON MY RULE.

Deafened, she thinks, *This can't be Terry talking.* "Terry! Did you hear that? Terry?"

SALIM CHISTI GAVE ME THE MIRACLE . . .

The voice is so big that it shakes her to the spine. "Terry!"

MIRIAM.

"What's that, Terry, what *is* it?"

But as if none of this has happened, her husband goes on reading smoothly, untouched and voluble as a talking head on NPR informing her: "Akbar searched until he found her and she bore him a son, the future Emperor Jehangir, and in gratitude, the emperor transferred his capital to the ridge at Sikri and built his new and splendid city here."

"Dammit, listen!"

Above her, hidden, Terry goes on as though he neither hears nor cares. Then when she is at her most vulnerable, he stops short. "No, you listen." Then he cries, "Sara, I want a kid."

"Terry, please!"

Just then heavy words roll out of nowhere, unbidden, piling up like stones closing an emperor's tomb. **IT IS BITTER, BUT EVERY MAN NEEDS A SON TO BURY HIM, AND SHE** . . .

As it speaks something in the audience hall changes. Terrified, frantic, Sara understands that her friend, her ghost, her familiar is receding. Her friend's last words come out in a dying fall. **Now you know.**

She calls out in a thin voice, "Miriam? Miriam, don't go!" but Miriam is nowhere now. It is as if she had never been.

She is alone with the men.

DO NOT ASK ME WHICH IS TRUTH AND WHICH IS LEGEND. GO.

Stone grates against stone, as though some huge trap is closing.

Shuddering, Sara calls, "Akbar?"

But there is only Terry, scrambling out of the stone pod above her head and over the walkway to the balcony where she can see him. If she lives until she dies, and she will, if she thinks about this every day until she is an old, old woman, Sara will never figure out who or what was speaking.

What she will do, standing there in the bare, beautiful audience hall in the emperor's ghost city at the top of a dry ridge in the Rajasthani Desert in northern India, waiting for her husband to scramble downstairs and come running toward her with his arms spread, is come to a decision.

He hurries back to her, grinning. "Well, what do you think?"

Sighing, she dissembles. "Let's don't do this right now, let's just enjoy what we have here."

When they step outside, orange-gold light staggers her. The sky is streaked with sunset. What happened in there? How long has it been? She doesn't know. Swallowing sand, she clutches at her water bottle and finds it empty.

Terry takes no notice. He just hurries her along the ridge to the tomb of Salim Chisti. A sign in English tells them to take off their shoes before they enter the tomb, but Terry ignores it. Even though there's nobody around, Sara slips out of her sandals. The marble underfoot holds the heat of the day but drained and thirsty as she is, Sara is comforted by the long shadows. Terry looks up from the guidebook. "It says the Sheikh is buried here."

Stunned by exhaustion, frantic and raging, she rips the book out of his hands and hurls it out into the plaza. At the center of the tomb, Sara looks down at the spot, wondering. She thinks to pray but has no idea what she would say or who she would be telling. They stand under the marble canopy, and the world stops. It is as if they are in a vacuum. Terry takes her hand as if they have a done deal and her heart turns over. Then they turn to leave, shuffling out of the shadows and into the fading daylight.

Then in a sudden, terrifying rush, all India comes back, roaring in on them: tourists, beggars, guides, musicians and vendors jostling for space in the courtyard of the giant mosque, the smell of red dust and food cooking and a large crowd gathering in a space that will never be big enough for them, accompanied by the ambient noise she recognizes from her nights in its cities—the voice of India. She recognizes the noise, but after the silent hours she wandered here the sound is hyped and amplified. It's as if the great, rich, incomprehensible civilization is flexing like a tiger waking up from deep, preternatural sleep.

When they come out of the marble tomb Terry stretches dreamily and rubs his eyes the way he does when he realizes it's Sunday and hits the snooze button again.

For the first time today Sara runs ahead, wide-eyed, alert and jangling. At the edge of the ridge, she sees a crowd gathering at the foot of the monumental gate to the mosque for some event—listed, she supposes, in Terry's stupid guidebook. Outside the city walls, she knows, Ravi Singh is waiting with the car but for whatever reasons she is not done here. Instead she elbows her way closer, to see what the crowd is waiting for. There are figures standing on the top of the heavily ornamented gate, poised above—what? Sara thinks the people on top of that are fixed on something in the courtyard, but she can't see what's at the bottom.

Then somebody grabs her arm and she turns. It's a kid in a T-shirt and cut-offs—fourteen? Sixteen? What do you want? She doesn't know. At the gate something happens and a shout goes up.

"Only forty rupees and you can see," the boy tells her, pointing to the massive gate. "See me jump into the pretty water."

She gulps sand. "Water?"

"Only forty rupees."

"When?"

"Now!" The boy breaks for the gate, but he isn't fast enough.

Sara grabs the tail of his shirt and darts after him, running where he runs no matter how he tries to shake her off, climbing where he climbs, sobbing as she scrambles up the stones behind him.

"Ma'am. Ma'am!" The boy turns on her, trying his best to get free, but excited and mystified, compelled, she clings tighter. He almost escapes when the torn T-shirt starts to give way but Sara adjusts her grip, locking strong fingers around his ankle.

He can't go up. She won't let go.

They are at a little impasse here on the rocks. "Please."

Wild-eyed, he gasps, "What do you want?"

"I don't know!"

Below them, reduced by perspective, Terry runs in circles, begging her to come down.

Hanging on to the rock with one hand, the boy gropes in his pocket and throws money, shaking his head: *NO*. "Take it back!"

Shivering, she absorbs their position on the rocks, the distance to the top, the fact that she can't see the water below, can't tell how big the surface is or how deep it is; she does not know where this child will land, or what she thinks she is doing, only that there will be water.

"A thousand rupees if you take me with you."

You might as well know that I've always been a literary split personality, self-labled as transgenred. There is nothing speculative or fantastic about this one, but I did make it all up and it's one of my favorites. It appeared in The Yale Review.

MISSING SAM

"**I** had a brother who died." Most people hide some central grief that they think defines them. Hers is Sam. She's been this way ever since she was twelve years old. Elise has been grieving for so long that she forgets what she was like before.

Peter squeezes her hand. "I know."

How well he understands her. For years she thought of herself as happy, even though missing Sam was a condition of her life. When you're still young you have to think you're OK and everything is fine. How else could you go on? Elise took her marriage to Al Carney and those weekend parties in Al's Doghouse as outward and physical signs. Handsome couple, two little boys, everybody happy at home in the solid brick house she grew up in. Mahogany paneled bar above the three-car garage. Initialed silver cups for Elise and Al and six of their nearest and dearest, how could it not be fun? Instead she was what passes for happy, even before it went sour. Was she only ever acting the part? Before Peter, she had no idea.

Points of reflected sunlight glitter on the water; they're entering the Grand Canal but she has to ask, "Have you ever done anything you were ashamed of?"

Her new man says, "Don't, honey. Not today."

It is much too late for a first visit to Venice but here they are, two nice old people on their honeymoon. You probably think it's incongruous, all that touching in public, and at their age. Don't they know they look foolish? Listen. It's not their fault that they came so late to love that their faces no longer match what they are feeling. They had to wait for their spouses to die.

They don't mean to upset you, this is all so new and surprising that they forget. Besides, they try. Peter hides his comb-over with a natty Panama and keeps his well-cut jacket buttoned to spare you the paunch. Bridling like a kid in love, Elise diverts your eye with gaudy poppies splashed across her expensive silk. She has nice jewelry. Careful hair on top, curled and frosted to take your mind off the fact that underneath she's built like a little tank. Beautiful shoes. Everything's in the right place, mind you, that is, everything that money can contrive, but before Elise Fenton met Peter Barnes and was really happy for the first time since Sam died, she ate.

You may think it's offensive, two old people rubbing in a gondola like randy teenagers, and out in the open where you have to see. Don't they know their place? At that age, they must be beyond all that, or they should be. Well, they aren't. Don't for a moment tell yourself they're too old even to think about it, because they do. They think about it all the time. Never mind that they're headed for the back door of life. If you reminded them, they wouldn't care. Right here in broad daylight, Elise's fingers curl in her new husband's palm, scratching the hollow of his curved hand. She traces Peter's lifeline with her index finger, their signal for sex. They think the code is specific to them, although everybody who's ever been in a relationship knows it. Remember, these people come from a different time, when you married young for the sex because nice girls didn't do what you wanted and you wanted to be a nice girl, just like the others. Except for their unhappy first marriages and that one time in the doghouse when Elise almost, these two have never slept with anybody else.

You may even think they're too old for romance but Elise and Peter don't. They're more in love than couples in a movie even though they look nothing like stars and their meeting wasn't anything like that. It was simple and prosaic, one of those things you pay for instead of having it happen to you, the way it does on the screen. They met on a Lindblad Tour.

No wonder it took so long. The probability of finding your life partner on a tour of the Galapagos is slim, especially given the delays: more than four decades wasted on sad marriages.

It was her first cruise.

Elise met Peter when the lights went down for the professor's after-dinner lecture. In the darkened dining room the academic droned usefully while slides of giant turtles reflected on obedient, upturned faces. She didn't have time to waste trapped inside. She was wearing her purple silk that night, even though the regulars turned out in Patagonia fleeces and heavy boots. Peter followed her out. On deck, Elise and Peter got talking, partly because you can say anything in the dark. Seven times around the first class deck made a mile, if you believed the sign. By the time they finished at the taffrail, Elise had told Peter all about the brother she'd lost and they were holding hands. In another moment his hand was sliding around her waist and they were facing. Except for her children, she hadn't been touched that way since the last time with Al. Surprising what feelings his hands brought, and after so long. The rest would follow, no question about it, and a first for them—a new partner, with everything enhanced by the roll of the ship.

Shipboard romance. It was a marvel. *This is so beautiful. I'm so lucky.* The novelty overturned her. Elise didn't recognize what she felt as being happy, quite. She had no past experience she could take out and compare. She wanted to sum it all up but these were the only words that came. "How did this happen?"

"I don't know," he said. Prosaic Peter, fixed on the black ocean boiling in their wake.

"Was it fate?" For Elise, it felt more like getting out of jail. It made her giddy and exalted. "Do you think there's a design for everybody and we just don't get to see it until it's time?"

Before he retired, Peter was a civil engineer. He is not as well fixed as Elise, who controls Daddy's business and the Fenton portfolio. The kids kick in to send him on these trips. "I don't know."

She told herself it was words that failed him, not his imagination. "Whatever it is, I'm glad."

"Me too."

"Oh Peter, this is so wonderful."

He said in that sweet, flat voice, "I thought I would never get over losing Mae. But you know."

Sam caught in her throat like a fishbone, impossible to dislodge. It made her voice odd. "I do."

"Is something wrong?"

"I'm fine."

"I miss her every day."

"I see."

When Al moved out on Elise she was glad, but she couldn't tell Peter, at least not right away. Her new man would be nice about it, but he'd take note: *That makes two.* She's not exactly tainted, but it marks her as a bad risk. Losing a person you love is a terrible accident; add a rotten marriage and it begins to look like something you did. When you are grieving it takes everything you have to dress nicely in the mornings and smile and dissemble. When there is only one thing wrong in your life you can hide it; you can even talk about the grief you cherish, if you talk in code. Two miseries make one too many to put over on the world. Money is no protection. Daddy had plenty and they lost Sam anyway. Even though she had plenty, Al turned out to be a rat. Too soon to tell him. Instead she said, "I'm sorry."

"The cruises help." Before Mae died Peter used to spend hours just getting her through the day. The cancer took its time and at the end he quit his job because somebody had to get poor Mae up in the mornings and dress her and try to make her eat. It made him feel guilty, bathing a woman he never really liked, but he couldn't tell Elise and so he said, "I'm surprised this is your first."

What could she tell him without showing herself up as a patsy and a fool? What could she tell him about her life? "I had a lot to do."

This was no lie. She did. She had to help the children grow up. She had to outlive Al and she had to get angry enough to move on. What strikes her now is that at the time, she actually believed she was doing fine. Amazing, the things you do just to continue.

In Venice today, Peter nuzzles her ear. "Is there something you'd rather be doing?"

His hand is gentle but the skin is rough and cracked. The contact makes her blush. Elise wants to tell him everything. Instead she lets him think what he wants to, leaning in to whisper, "There is."

He scrambles forward to whisper to the gondolier, making his point with crumpled dollar bills when language fails him. A slicker traveler would be offended by the laughter. To outsiders, their progress looks comic. Even Peter and Elise are laughing as they get out of the gondola and run for the hotel, breathless and ungainly. Peter is happy and excited. He can't believe his luck, and Elise? She has a lot of material to process, and she can't tell him.

When Sam died Daddy never said anything directly but he started taking her to the office with him. It was understood that Elise would run the business when he got old and had to retire. On his days off Daddy walked her through the family portfolio, laying out all the details he didn't want to bother Mother with, because you didn't in those days. He never made a big thing of it, it just happened, and even though she never went to business school Elise knew as much about the market as any man. Daddy was cautious about his investments; he didn't have to tell her that it paid to be careful about what you bought and when you sold. She grew up cautious about everything, because when you have lost somebody who means everything to you, you have to be careful. You have no idea what else you're going to lose.

Mother scolded Elise for saying she could hardly wait to grow up so she could marry Sam. She turned so red it was embarrassing. Elise was five at the time, how was she supposed to know? She loved him *so much*. She can still hear Sam's laugh when she told him what Mother said. *That's not nice,*

Elise. It's not nice! By the time she followed him into junior high he was so handsome that all the big girls were talking about him. It made her proud because he was her big brother, and jealous too. He was always nice to her, but it was the big girls who got to follow him into the closet at Jane McNally's parties and come out laughing, with their hair messed and their lipstick smudged. Almost fifty years later she sees the way Sam's hair fell over his eyes, pale brown that chlorine had turned to straw by August every year. She thinks she remembers her mother coming back at the end of the last day he spent in the pool, "If you don't get out of the water you'll shrivel up like a prune." In the night sometimes she can see the way he looked as he laughed and swam away.

See, her handsome big brother sat around in a wet bathing suit all day the last summer before she turned thirteen. It looked like rain but Mother was going to a meeting so she had to drop them off at the club where they could eat anything they wanted and sign for everything. Elise couldn't go in the water because she was having a period and Sam made so much fun of her that everybody knew and she cried. It didn't help that it was practically her first. To make up for it he got out at noon and sat with her while they had club sandwiches and lemonade. By that time the weather was bad and the big girls had gone home so she didn't have to chew her knuckles waiting for Sam to talk to her. He even signed for ice cream and swam from the shallow end to the deep end and back with the cone over his head and chocolate ice cream dripping down his right arm.

"Statue of Liberty," he said and she applauded. It was wonderful.

For once she was the only kid watching. It started to rain so he came out and played poker with her. It wasn't real poker, they had to use book matches for chips, and by that time it was raining hard so they sat under the painted metal awning watching big drops slice into the pool. When it slacked off Sam did cannonballs off the high board just to make her laugh. Elise was so happy because they were having fun and Mother wasn't coming back for them until five. Later she read in the newspapers that was how you got polio, but she didn't find out in time. If she had, she could have warned Sam and maybe he'd be OK now. That night he started a fever and by morning he was in the hospital. A week later he was gone. The family never got over it. He was only fourteen when he died, which she acknowledges may be just as well. If he'd lived poor Sam would be a quadriplegic now, older than Elise—fifty-some years on crutches, unless he lived on, trapped in a motorized wheelchair or worse yet, atrophying in the iron lung where the hospital had him the day he died. They wouldn't let her go see Sam in the hospital, they told her it would be bad for him. The best thing she could do for him was go to church before school every day and let the doctors do their job. When they came home from the hospital early, she thought it meant Sam was getting better. Mother was crying and Daddy wouldn't look at her. They told her to pray for his soul.

She and Daddy got up the next morning anyway. They washed their faces and got dressed and went about their business because you have to. It's what you do. Mother was outraged. She stood in the hall in her blue bathrobe with her hair loose and her face shaking. *Samuel, how can you, don't you know what's happened to us?* He put a Navy pinstriped arm around Elise and did not answer. *I'm only going to the office, dear. We'll be back at five.*

By the time Elise met Al Carney she already had more than enough to do. Managing the investment firm, the family portfolio and the foundation, her mother's continued care; after Sam died, Mother Fenton simply quit and when Daddy fell over at fifty her mind went out and never came back. Elise had to wait until Mother was settled and she had to wait until Daddy was so far in the past that she could finally think of the family money as hers. She didn't need any more grief. Then Al proposed. If it was for the money, she didn't want to know. He was new in town so as far as she knew, her backstory was closed. He had brown eyes and gold, curly hair and he laughed easily, life of the party she supposed. Elise didn't know it but her somber smile put people off, that and her strong business head. With Al she felt frivolous. When they walked into parties together, people treated her differently. He laughed and it made her laugh. Her girlfriends looked at them together and thought, *nice couple.*

They said, *Elise looks almost pretty. It must be love.*

She thought happy ever after was about to begin, but of course it never is.

But, you know what? When it didn't, Elise was surprised. Maybe it was her fault for missing Sam. The thing is, people failed her all the time, but he didn't betray her and he never changed. Grief like hers is somehow comforting because it is familiar, like your best friend or the Teddy you had. It made her resentful. Al Carney had no right to walk around happy and careless when her brother was buried in the cemetery overlooking the bay. He had no right to be such a shit.

For Al, happy turned out to be about girlfriends, but Elise didn't find out until they had their first baby. She was going through his suits before she sent them to the cleaners and a note fell out. He said it was an accident; he said it was her fault because he was so scared she'd die in childbirth that he needed her, worst way. He needed her and the doctors wouldn't let him touch her because it might hurt the baby, do you know what that does to a man? He said he never meant to sleep with Cheryl and he would never do it again; he said it was nothing, you know, just one of those things you do without thinking and live to regret.

For Elise, one of those things was one too many. She should have known there would be a lot more of those things. The baby was a boy. He didn't look anything like her brother, he looked like Al, but she named him Sam. Later she had the apartment above the garage paneled and plumbed to make up for the things she said right after she found out.

"He was a rat," Peter said when she finally told him about the infidelities. By then they were traveling together. They were in a floating classroom touring the Greek Isles. While other people tramped through ruins, they stayed on board the ship. Peter told the Greek guide and the professor that Elise was under the weather but she was always fine by dinner when they came in blushing and sat at the Captain's table. They always danced afterwards. The dining room had a tiny dance floor and even though the wrong body parts bumped when they moved close, Elise wore chiffon and imagined Fred Astaire.

"Is that the worst thing you can say?"

Peter didn't enlarge, he didn't come up with worse words for Al and what Al did to her, he just said, "You married a rat."

She let him pull her off the floor. "I did but I didn't know it at the time."

So Peter knows about Al and she told him about Al's girlfriends, and she told him about the day long after, when she finally understood that the real problem with Al was not that he was lazy and unfaithful, it was that he was a drunk. She told him about everything but the parties in Al's Doghouse, which she kept secret not because she did anything she was ashamed of but because no matter what she tells him, he will have no idea what it was like. She can't understand it herself, at least not well enough to explain.

They'd have plenty of time once they were married, she told herself. The right words would come to both of them. She needs to hear something from Peter, but what? Wasn't it enough that he'd bought her a ring? By that time she'd given him a pair of sapphire cufflinks and he'd given her a sapphire ring with little diamond baguettes. He'd dipped into his retirement fund to do it, but she didn't have to know. From the beginning Peter was committed to paying his own way.

In the motorized launch passing the Doge's palace, Elise and Peter lean close; light bounces off the water and strikes their faces; Elise doesn't know where it comes from but she hears the distinctive sound Venice makes, the meeting of stone and water in a subtle, pervasive boom. Her throat and chest are flushed and parts of her are still shaking. They have just come from the hotel where they ran their hands over each other's sagging faces with fresh delight. Never mind that you think it's unseemly, it's the sex. She can't speak for Peter but for Elise, the intensity is astonishing, because new. But even in the middle of this sun-shot morning in Venice she listens for the overtone: the hum she's heard all her adult life. She is joyful, but marked—happy today but comforted by the fact that even though she has Peter now, she has Sam too, the refrain in the minor that makes the composition so rich.

"Oh, Peter, this is so . . . "

"Yep." It's all her new husband can find to say but his thigh presses hers as though this is high school and she is his first.

When things are too perfect Elise is like most of us. She needs to shoot herself in the foot. "Peter, there are things . . . "

Bless him, Peter always knows what to say. As they scramble up the stone steps he turns to her with a sweet, bland look in those polar blue eyes. "Whatever you think you did, don't worry," he says as though they've already had the conversation. "Nobody's perfect."

"I suppose not." Trembling, she waits for more, but his confession is so far off the mark that it by no means releases her.

"There were times when I wanted to murder Mae."

Look at yourself in the mirror for long enough and you forget what you look like. Elise has been looking in the mirror all her life. If she could see herself as you see her, she'd be surprised. Of course she recognizes the signs of age—lines around the mouth, the sagging jaw, who doesn't?— but she still thinks of herself as an attractive, sexual being. If she saw what you see, she'd probably be surprised. As a girl she developed a sense of what she looked like, even though that's changed. Her jawline's gone soft and her body has solidified. Take away the expensive silk outfits, the jewelry and the frosted curls and you might mistake her for a big, friendly guy—smiling now, although the smile is relatively new. She's been through a lot. It accounts for the swift, stern look that can level you. Finance makes a woman decisive. She has to be tough. When did the transition begin from sweet, pliable girl to what she is now, was it right after Sam died, when Daddy sat her behind his desk? He handed her the pen from his black and gold desk set and they practiced signing her name. He didn't have to say, *now you'll have to be the man.* It accounts for the way she walks into rooms.

Surprising that Al Carney mistook her for pretty, given the long face and preoccupied glare. She was young enough to blush when he drew her out on the terrace at one of those club dances. They kissed and she giggled like a girl. Al came to town from Galveston or somewhere, some Gulf state that gave him an easy accent with a lot of vowels and the charm of a playboy from a time when people like that actually functioned in the world. He was seriously working on dashing: a little Clark

Gable, a lot of Errol Flynn. If he'd lived here all his life like all the other families who came to the club, he'd know what the others had known ever since they were boys. Poor Elise had a brother who died. Cross her and she scowled like it was your fault.

After the first kiss Al Carney held her at arm's length and took her in with a look that made her insides flutter. "You know, you're really a very pretty girl."

For the moment, standing in the slanting yellow light from the ballroom, she was.

When she couldn't speak he let compliments rush in to fill the space. "Why aren't you already taken?"

There were too many answers to that question. "Oh," she said. "Oh, you know."

He was new in town. He didn't know. "We'll change that," he said with what she would come to think of as his trademark grin.

Amazing: stern and lonely Elise was pretty now, pretty enough to start seeing the handsome out-of-towner even though you could tell from a block away that they were a bad match: laughing, curly-haired party animal from Tulane and Elise, steely chairman of the Fenton Corp., who was working hard to hide the steel. Boys she'd grown up with knew, all right. Elise was smart, maybe too smart, so dance with her, but not too close and whatever you do, don't cross her. But when she was out with Al she changed from formidable to fluffy; her stride shortened and her voice went soft. She leaned into the curve of his arm as if she belonged, and Al? He didn't know. Did he know about the money? Even after it ended years later, everybody had suspicions, but not even Elise could be sure.

Listen. Even a woman set apart by an early loss can dream of being swept off her feet. She's entitled, same as you. Besides, Elise was sick of being alone. She was almost thirty and most of her friends were married at twenty-two. At some deep level she may have been uneasy, but her misgivings were outweighed by the thrill of being just like everybody else for once. "My fiancé," she said at parties, flashing the ring. "My husband," Elise said at the club, flaunting Al, and like the diamond on her finger, he sparkled for them. This was in the pre-Assassination Sixties, before society as the town knew it began to unwind. All the first marriages still held. In their tight circle women and their mothers gave engagement parties—breakfasts, coffees, pretty lunch parties by the club pool. In this sweet, hermetically sealed society, girls she had grown up playing bridge with—girls like Sally and Marsha, Carol and Patty—had wedding showers at the pretty houses their new husbands had bought for them.

Al used to pick her up at the end of those evenings with her tissue-filled boxes of satin underwear and vermeil ashtrays, useless booty that meant so much because she'd been a bridesmaid in half a dozen weddings and she wanted—what. Parity. The state in life. "Oh, Al. Look what they gave me."

"Nice," he said without looking at the contents. "Nice."

She didn't know why it made her sigh. He was flirting with her brides-maids, married women all, and all old friends of hers, which she hoped meant it was silly and innocent, because married women never. . . "If only we could go to an island somewhere, where no people were."

"This is wonderful," she says to Peter. His means are modest, but they are sitting on the balcony of a hotel overlooking a canal at dusk. The unique sound of the submerged city echoes in the canyons the villas make—background music for Elise who is not so much intent on telling her story as on reaching into Peter and pulling out the best of him to examine so she'll know what, exactly and how much she can give back. "It's like being the only two people in the world."

He turns a lovely, uncomplicated smile on her. "Yep, it is."

"I'm just so glad it's you." She doesn't have to add, *and not Al.*

"You were telling me about the alligators."

"I was." She's been trailing the story like bait, hoping to draw some like confidence out of him.

There's no logic to it, but you can be romantic and canny at the same time. Elise knew it would be bad for Al to move into the Fenton offices as long as she was in charge but she was entirely too prudent to step aside. After they closed the doghouse she helped him invest in an alligator ranching scheme some company in Louisiana guaranteed would net him millions; later she helped Al front for a herd of vicuna to feed his alligators so he'd get both revenue from manufacturers of high end alligator boots and bags and as a byproduct, profits from companies that made vicuna coats. If Elise saw these people coming, she was kind enough to keep from saying so to Al. It was an expensive dream but for a few months, it did the job. Later she found him a place in Marsha's father's insurance firm, and that kept him well enough until he got involved in a tri-state real estate scheme that put him on the road much of the time. Elise would have told you it was just as well.

The details about the alligators have Peter laughing. Pragmatic Peter would never be foolish enough to believe the investment was lost because the water in the alligator pens overheated and his cash crop boiled to death. "Why, when you knew it was a bum deal?"

She shrugs. "Some things are just cheap at the price."

The worst part of having a secret is the need to burden someone else with it, but Elise can't shake the sick confessional urge.

It won't do anybody any good to tell Peter about the doghouse and she can't really talk about it without betraying herself but she and this nice man who married her are lovers for life, and how can she not tell the love of her life? If she can find the right way to tell it maybe Peter will laugh as if it's just another thing like the alligators and she'd be over it but, oh.

There are things you can say in a fight that are absorbed and forgotten and there are the ones you hold back because they are unforgivable, the telling of some ruinous truth. Maybe Elise should have handled it differently but when she confronted Al with the fact that he fucked Cheryl when she was nine months pregnant, she forgot she was supposed to be a fluffy wife. She raked him with contempt.

"It was just so hard," boyish Al said with his back to the wall, craven Al, trying to turn it back on her: "I missed you, and besides. We never have any fun."

"Fun. Fun!" Awful words fell out of her mouth.

Al cried out as if he'd been gored. "Honey!" Everything between them changed.

For the first time they both knew what she really thought of him. Her shiny new husband wheeled so she wouldn't see his face.

"Oh, Al. Al!" She ran after him with her arms out. "I didn't mean it!" She caught him at the front door.

"I can't stay, not with you so . . . " He didn't finish. Instead he stopped messing with the knob. He was waiting for her to beg.

In scenes like this people always embarrass themselves. Elise doesn't remember what she said but she can't forget that she was kneeling, sobbing into his thighs. "Please don't. You can't go."

He lingered. "I have to."

He was waiting to see what she would do. With her baby upstairs and his father leaving Elise said, "I love you more than anything."

Al waited three beats too long. "I love you too."

The next morning she hired a contractor to remake the rooms above the three-car garage. She went for the best instead of the lowest estimate. She paid an architect to make up the plans. Because it's hot in the city where she grew up she bought central air conditioning and ordered furniture from a company that supplied men's clubs. When it was done she had her handsome husband come out to the garage with her and she stood back so he could go first up the newly enclosed stairs. He stopped, staring at the new Gothic arch set into the wall at the top. The paneled door was strapped in polished brass, like an expensive steamer trunk.

"What's this?"

"It's for you."

"Yow."

"Go ahead, open it."

"Oh. Oh, babe." With its Gothic paneling and brass-fitted mahogany bar, the garage apartment gleamed like a rich boy's fraternity house. She and Al could put infidelity behind them and have fun here. Maybe, she thought, they could get back to being what they were, one of those things you tell yourself when you've spent too much on something you think you want. With the beveled mirror and brass fittings, glass shelves stocked with full decanters and the twin port wine leather sofas, it looked like a set waiting to be occupied. Al picked up the silver cocktail shaker and studied the monogram. "For me? You did this for me?"

"I'm sorry I've been so busy with the baby."

For the first time since the fight her handsome big boy tried on a smile she liked. "Looks like I'm out of the doghouse."

A steely part of Elise that she managed not to show him clicked: *That one.* "I'm so glad you like it," she said, and arched when he slid his hand down her belly, because Al had been punctilious but indifferent ever since the baby came.

"Oh my," Al said, "we're going to have some good times here."

"I hope so."

Forgive her for gritting her teeth when he spooned out a big dose of that old Al charm. It's not his fault that he sounded like a lounge lizard out of some bad old movie, "Come on, honey. Let's try out this nice new couch."

Everybody wants to be in a movie at least some of the time.

They had live-in help to keep the baby Sam and Elise was back at work, yes, in charge and capable as ever, but as she'd only ever made love on her back in their bed and she found sliding around on the sofa exciting, she giggled and shrieked like a girl. Success.

The place was a success.

Al had a local woodworker carve a sign with the legend incised and picked out in gilt: **Al's Doghouse**. He tacked it into the paneling above the door and pulled her inside to see. She was shocked by the gash the nail had made in the stained oak.

"Don't you like it?"

Better not to speak.

Al didn't really need an answer. For the first time in too long he was looking at her like something he wanted instead of something he had to do. "Let's have a party."

"I guess we need one," she said. Shopping, she would have to go shopping for something new because she was a little thicker now, babies did that to you.

It was the summer after the assassination, the orgy of mourning started in November right after little Sam was born. Like her brother's death it was one of those things that changed you so you could never go back to being what you were before. The difference was, this marked everybody, not just Elise. It was OK to cry publicly for JFK because this was the kind of grief you could share, so what if it stood for a lot of other things?

The assassination was awful but summer had come after all, and with it the sense that the grief had to be purged. Who wouldn't want to have a little fun?

Everybody came. Couples she'd known since first grade, along with the ones who'd married people from out of town, spouses who always looked a little brighter because they weren't quite comfortable in this crowd. At first the parties were loud, messy nights with too many people packed in so tight that nobody knew who was groping who, and everybody getting loaded on Old Fashioneds, which were Al's specialty, heavy on the bourbon with lots of sugar so it was easy going down. Al loved Old Fashioneds and it made him especially loving to her. With his expression blurred and his bright curls stuck to his forehead he looked like a Cupid on an old fashioned Valentine. Those evenings were exciting, with lots of people dancing close. Some couple was always fighting and if you looked out the window you might see one of your friends running into the moonlight with her husband close on her heels begging to be forgiven, unless it was the other way around.

Jammed. These parties were always jammed and too many guests made messes it took too long to clean up afterward. A lot of these people were no fun after all, so Elise and Al began to pick and choose. The discussions brought them closer because it was fun, deciding who would stay and who would go. The keepers were the ones that stayed up with you after everybody else went home. They settled on perky Sally and Ben; Elise's grade-school friend Timmy and Marsha, with her lipsticky heart-shaped mouth. Loyal Patsy and Dave, who could be funny even though he looked like Eeyore. The Doghousers. Al had eight silver Old Fashioned cups monogrammed. "For us Doghousers," he said, presenting them on the first night the eight of them met. Although the cups were put away for the big parties so nobody would have hurt feelings, the insiders always knew exactly who they were. They were the ones who sat back and ate Al's nachos and gossiped by candlelight, tumbling in the deep leather sofas like children worn out by a long day playing tag. This was the hour when the silver cups came out of the freezer with neatly sugared rims. It was the time of night when Al got out the champagne and made Mimosa chasers because it was pretty much morning by then.

Alone in the hotel room after dinner in Venice, Elise finally begins the story she's been reluctant to tell. Peter is in the silk bathrobe she bought him this afternoon and Elise looks sweet but improbable in an embroidered peignoir she had made for her honeymoon. "You look around one night and there are only six people in the room. Two of your friends who aren't married to each other are gone. You don't want to look in the bedrooms even though the apartment has two, listen, they could be drunk and lying down in separate rooms. You can't afford to know for sure. You just try to distract the leftovers—her husband, his wife—by talking about something else. Remember, this was the Sixties."

Peter says drily, "In the Sixties I was building bridges in Vietnam."

"I'm sorry."

He surprises her with a laugh. "Sounds like I was better off."

"Oh, it wasn't Al, you know? That was sneaking out, I mean, it was two of our nearest and dearest, it was . . . " She sighs. "If I told you their names it wouldn't mean anything to you. It's just, when people you think you *knew* . . . " Funny, she thinks, sexy and exciting, six of them sitting there on the sofas in the candlelight and *in the very next room* . . . On that doghouse night she flashed back to Jane McNally's makeout parties in junior high, Elise in the solemn circle on the rug, squirming on her bare heels and wondering what was going on behind the closet door. She had that same feeling, sexual. Unsure.

Peter prods her. "But it wasn't Al."

"First it wasn't," she says. "Then one night it was."

"Rat."

"It wasn't like that. We kept it so dark in the doghouse that I didn't exactly notice, I know you don't believe it but Timmy brought in our very first pot and we were already pretty drunk."

"You would never get drunk."

"You don't know me that well," she says because he's hit the truth dead on. She never got drunk, even though Al did. It was easier to pretend. Drunks didn't have to know. "When I missed him I went downstairs and back into the house.

"The next morning he was in our bed just like before. I didn't say anything but he saw me looking at him and he said, *Whatever you're thinking, you're wrong.* I had to trust him, you know?"

"Because he'd promised?"

"Because I just did."

It was Marsha he was fucking, Elise knew because without knowing, women always know. It was also Marsha who started the game the first night, when she sneaked off with Dave. As if to call her friend's attention to the fact that something amazing was about to happen, she squeezed Elise's hand as she skipped out of the darkened room. The next day Marsha confided that being with another man made sex with her husband so much better that it blew her mind; she kept it secret from Carol and Patsy ("Patsy, Dave and I were just *talking*"). She told Elise because Elise was, after all, her nearest and dearest friend. It wasn't the kind of thing you're grateful to be told. First it was Marsha and then it was Timmy who disappeared—he went off with Patsy, surprise, and Elise and Al discussed all this with grave promises that they would never, ever.

They also agreed there was no need to quit having parties in the doghouse because the most important thing about fitting into a society is having a place where you can be comfortable with the people you love best. By that time they were bonded. They went as a group to restaurants and shows, and they sat together at all the games. Al bought warmup jackets for the eight of them so even in a crowd you'd know. The women had matching sweaters and embroidered flares, and later Al bought engraved gold bangles for the women and matching tie clips for the men, which they wore out to big parties and dances at the club. Part of the game was wearing them outside the doghouse and the other part was the secret, superior feeling they got because friends came and friends went but in any gathering, the Doghousers were the nearest and dearest, bonded, tight.

So late on weekend nights in the doghouse there were comings and goings and there were assignations on football weekends out of state but after Cheryl, Al had made a promise and Elise believed.

Weren't parties in the doghouse proof that she believed? For the others, there were silences, tears and recriminations but their marriage was, well, their marriage. It was the only marriage Elise had and she'd built this playpen for her handsome man to keep him happy, hadn't she? Didn't gossiping about Marsha and Dave and Patsy and all bring them closer? *Not us*, Elise thought even though her mother had told her a dog that will bring a bone will carry a bone. *Not us.*

Until the night she fled the doghouse because Al disappeared, Elise was content to let it flow.

She did, in fact, let it flow that next week. After all, Sunday morning he was back in their bed, but her belly was tight and her throat closed and whether or not Al was telling the truth he had slipped out *right there in front of her* and she couldn't just let it play.

That Saturday night they gave the party anyway. Then Al slipped away again. This time she looked around in the dimness to see who else had disappeared. There were seven of them left, sunk deep in the leather sofas, including Marsha—where did she go? Then there were six. Patsy and Timmy drifted away and there were four people left, even-steven and then, as though they were completing the final figure in an intricate dance, Sally turned to Ben. Elise had a choice here. Rise up like an avenging angel or go with the flow. She was a smart woman, tough in business but oh, my. Amazed, she felt her body changing and she yawned and stretched with her arms above her head, sliding backward into sad Dave's arms which clamped around her hard and fast, mashing her breasts. "Not here," she murmured and Dave followed her down and across the yard to the house where her baby slept; as they reached the back steps where she'd played with Sam, grief came out of nowhere, simply rolled down on her like a barrel full of nails and she coughed: "Not anywhere!"

She and Al didn't have to discuss it.

Monday, contractors ripped out the paneling and dismantled the bar. She and Al had another baby, almost as though in some oddly transactional way she needed to prove she wasn't mad. There was the alligator ranching scheme and then, perhaps because her father had done Marsha's father favors, there was the job in Marsha's father's firm which was oddly satisfying to Elise because she and Al kept ending up at the same table in business meetings where Marsha couldn't go. Marsha was remarried now to somebody she assured them was twice the man Timmy ever was. Al lost his job when he started laughing at meetings, probably because he was drunk. Next he got into the real estate venture, which he managed to mismanage. At the end there were no funds left in his account. Even though he and Elise both knew where the money he'd lost had come from, they both pretended it hadn't. He asked her for a loan. In the realm of diminishing returns Elise smelled bourbon on his breath—it was ten in the morning—and with that look that could level strong men, she cut him loose.

Strong woman, bringing up two boys without a man at her side. Seeing them through college and into lives of their own. Smart woman, look at how well she's done with the firm. Kind woman, sending money to Al after he came out of the drying out program she paid for and started fresh in a new town. Sad woman, when he ended all their miseries by driving his car off a bridge in the next state with the new Mrs. Al firmly belted into the shotgun seat. Free woman, once she buried him and settled his debts. Pretty woman? Not for a long time. Not until she met Peter on the Lindblad tour.

You can look in the mirror every day of your life, you can see all the marks time made and still not know yourself, any more than you can truly recognize the changes time has made in you. You woke up this morning and you were still the same person you've always been; if you haven't changed, then maybe your face has changed with time, but only a little bit. It isn't so bad. You can look at a man you're in love with who really loves you and see only the best of him. It is important. Like grief, this kind of love is a condition of life. Elise wants more. If she could only figure out what that was! Elise Fenton, who took her maiden name back, soldiered on through the post-Al years without once noticing what grief has made of her: a solid, capable, resolute woman who hasn't had a joyful day since she was twelve years old. The wonder is that in spite of all this she's found one man who loves her whether or not she lost a brother once and then lost her handsome husband, along with some fifty years of adult life.

Now she's told Peter about the doghouse, if not all about it, and it makes her voice light. She is walking into this marriage with a take me or leave me air. "You're not horrified that we did all those things?"

He blinks. "You didn't do anything."

Afraid to test his limits, she hints. "What if I had?"

"If you had, you'd tell me," sweet, pragmatic Peter says.

Why is she angry at him for not picking up on it and forgiving her? What does she need from this man who's trying so hard to give her everything? She has to get a rise out of him. She does!

"Would you be horrified if I told you I'd almost." Stop.

Don't.

"Peter, would you love me anyway?"

Peter, whose vocabulary is, she sees, limited, blinks and after a struggle says blindly, "You'll always be beautiful to me."

Not a truth, exactly, but a necessary truth of love. Looking past Peter, Elise sees herself in the mirror but from across the room this time, and as she is: stout woman in her sixties with a sagging face and a body to match, every angle slanting under the mauve peignoir, and when she pulls back she will see Peter's comb-over, thin and inadequate, curly from the shower. The satin bathrobe highlights his paunch, and without the glasses his face is ludicrous because they found each other late in life, and with death sniffing at their heels they rush forward because what happens in lives is not as important as how she uses it. "Oh, Peter."

"I'm sorry about your brother."

He's only trying to please her but this is so far off the mark that she gasps: "Oh!"

"Ellie, Ellie, I didn't mean to make you cry."

"I'm not crying about that." In seconds she's crying so hard that she can't stop, but choked as she is, she needs to explain herself, insisting: "Really, I'm not crying for Sam."

Several things went through my mind: that in a way, trees hold hands underground, entwining roots; ancient relatives sometimes come to visit and outstay their welcome; that sometimes you can look at a very old person and not know whether they're dead or not. Ergo, "Aunt Lizzie," written for Portents, *Al Sarrantonio's newest anthology of "stories of quiet horror."*

AUNT LIZZIE

"**S**mile, girls, she's coming! Aren't you glad?" Mom wasn't all that glad. She just washed the cake. Accidentally she slid the whole top layer into the sink instead of the tin.

Taddy yelled, "Mom!"

Then she noticed and went, *eeek*. "Oh good grief, I just . . . Your great-great Aunt Lizzie is coming, and . . . " For a minute there, Mom lost it. "It's just . . . I didn't know it was today."

She is making a birthday cake for this Aunt Lizzie that we don't know who she is. We didn't even know we *had* one until Thursday, when they phoned up from the home. Dad asked why was Mom freaking but when she told him, he did not go there-there. He got all pissed off, which is not one of my words.

"Please, Derek. She doesn't have anyplace to go."

Oh good grief. Our father yelled at her. "How about there?" He was pointing at the spiked fence next door; the yard is so weedy that you can hardly see the broken stones, but we knew.

Mom shouted, "Because she isn't dead!" and began to cry.

That night he brought presents to make up and we had waffles for supper. They were what Mom calls trying to put a good face on it, like with the soggy cake.

"Quick, Sylvie, a dishtowel." Mom got all la-la-la like she was happy, but we didn't believe. "What a silly thing to do!" She kept fanning the bubbles, trying to make them go away. The edges started to crumble and she went shitshitshit, even though me and Taddy are not allowed.

It was getting so nervous out that I said, "How long is she staying?"

The edges of Mom's face crumbled too. "I don't know."

Then Taddy went shitshitshit because they are sticking Aunt Lizzie in her room.

Mom harshed at her, "That's not your word," and even she could see that this was not going well. She dried the cake anyway, like if she got the soap off and larded on enough frosting, if we could just sing Happy Birthday loud enough, maybe Aunt Lizzie wouldn't know. "Now, she's ninety today, so I want you girls to help her blow the candles out."

"Awwww, Mom." My little sister is a whiner, which sometimes works.

I'd rather growl. "Why can't she blow out her own damn candles?"

She didn't even bother to say don't, Sylvie, damn is not your word, she said, "Because she's too old! First we sing and then we have the party, ice cream and cake, and then we'll show her to her room, and then I want you to give her a nice big birthday hug, and then . . . And then . . ." Her voice floated away.

"But Mo-ommm . . ." Taddy had every right to whine. Her room was jammed floor to ceiling with Aunt Lizzie's stuff. Crates and boxes started coming in batches last Monday. They started shipping them from the home before they ever phoned, and Mom had to unpack everything and set it up. When she was done you could hardly get in the door. The special furniture had levers and cranks on it, and they sent medicine bottles and oxygen tanks and droppers and tubes full of—well, you didn't want to know. Aunt Lizzie was definitely moving in, and nobody would tell us when she was moving out. Too bad, Taddypoo; you might as well stop going, "Mooommmm."

"Don't whine." Mom smooshed the wet cake on a plate and bubbles flew up. "Just don't!"

I thought, *good thing there's another layer.* I tried to hand her the other tin but our mom was thinking about something else, so I stood there holding it, duh, duh, duh.

"And when she gets here, smile like you're glad to see her."

Taddy yowled like a pissed-off cat. "But I'm not!"

Mom banged the mixer on the counter, WHAM. "Then pretend!"

I didn't care either way since it wasn't me scrunched up on the RollA-Way, but Taddy and her stinky stuffed animals are crapping up my room and I honestly do not care that crap is not my word, but what could I do? Her bed is standing on its head in the basement for as long as it takes, Mom says, but she doesn't say what *IT* is, or how long.

At least I tried. "So, when's she going home?"

Poor Mom, she wailed, "She doesn't have a home!" She even scared herself, so she changed her tune. "Now, listen because this is important. We have to be very, very careful with her."

My turn. "Why?"

"Because she's. Um. Agh. Unsteady."

"Like she could break?"

"Like she could get mad at you and cut us out of the will." A long, long sigh blew out of her. "It's just, this is important. You don't want to make her mad."

"Why?"

"Because you don't!"

I hate my baby sister but sometimes I just love her. "Then why did you invite her?"

"I didn't!" Poor Mom.

"Then why..."

It's not like she answered. "And be nice and keep smiling no matter what, and whatever she says to you, you do what she says because..."

"Why?"

"Because..." There was no rest of the sentence.

Thank God Dad showed up before she despaired; he came in mock-whining, to make her laugh. "Why, Helen. Whyyyyy..."

"Because, Derek, because!" And *zot*, Mom laughed, but even I knew. "Look, honey. Can you believe I washed the cake?"

He hugged her, but she hung on a little bit too long.

So we all clustered while Mom stirred a whole nother box of confectioner's sugar and another pound of butter and extra chocolate into the frosting so this Aunt Lizzie wouldn't know about the soap. Dad licked the frosting knife as soon as she slapped the layers together, and it held. I guess he decided we were OK because he stuck it back in the frosting and drifted away. When she was finished slamming icing on the cake, Mom gave us each a spoon. We forgot for a while and the afternoon was sweet. Taddy and me were going along, la, la, la, we so were busy scraping that the big event went by us while we were getting the last bits.

We didn't even know it had happened until Dad came running in. "Helen. She's here!"

We ran to the window just in time to see the big black car moosh the hedge and crunch over the border onto the grass in front of our house. He almost hit the marble bench! Then the driver that Mom's relatives paid to take Aunt Lizzie away from wherever she had been staying got out of the car. He stood back and squinted, like: *this can't be the house.*

There was something about that car, the black uniform, the way he tilted the cap and the way that he was standing, well, one look and my heart sank. He was trying to smile nicely in case we were watching, but it was like somebody had started painting a great big happy clown face on him and gave up in the middle and took off before we found out they'd botched the job.

"Sylvie, Taddy." Mom was trying to sound happy and excited. She scrabbled behind her on the hall table and came up with two bunches of snapdragons and shoved them into our arms. "Take these flowers out to Aunt Lizzie. Say happy birthday and welcome to our home!" Then she shoved us out the door. She tried to push it shut so she could hide from Aunt Lizzie but it bounced back, which is how I heard.

Behind us, Dad was muttering, "You could have refused."

"Derek, it's a lot of money." Mom forgot to keep her voice down; she was practically yelling, "What was I supposed to do?"

The next things she and Dad said to each other after were lost to us, because she gave the door another kick and it stayed shut.

After that Taddy and I waited and waited.

It was taking him forever to get Aunt Lizzie out of the car. He stuck his head in and we heard him going mumble mumble mumble, all polite because somebody was paying him a bundle to leave her here and he probably had orders not to bring her back. From inside the car this dry voice was going, it sounded like, wa wa wa, which came out all pissed-off and cranky, even though we couldn't make out the words. Whatever the driver and our Aunt Lizzie were saying to each other took a long, long time. Then we heard a clank and a tinkle, and this sort of cart thingy with a tank hooked to it landed on the gravel, and the driver stepped back from it, like: *there.* Then he leaned inside the car and started to pull. The next thing we saw was two stringy arms and two bleached Popsicle sticks poking up out of a pair of humongous black gumdrops which, actually they were her shoes. It was the bottom half of Aunt Lizzie, plus her skinny old hands, which the guy tugged and tugged on until the rest of her came out. She was hooked up to the cart by tubes taped onto her face, so whatever was in the tank was going up her nose, but she took so long to stand up that we couldn't make sense of the arrangement until she was lurching toward us, bent over that cart like it was the bones that held her up.

It was awful. She had no hair, just a couple of tufts sticking out of her naked head, although she'd screwed on a pair of perky white earrings to take our minds off it. It wouldn't matter what they did to that stuff on the top of her head, no way would it come off looking like hair. She had on a fur neckpiece even though it was hot outside, a gang of squirrels or some-thing hooked in a circle, biting each other's tails, and underneath she was wearing a great big white dress with violets on it that fit like she used to be fat, and that wasn't the worst part. White, papery skin hung down off her in places, like her body had forgotten too. The driver hustled her along by the armpits like he could hardly wait to get her into the house. The two of them were mumble-mumble and wa-wa-wa-ing, and after about a year they finally got close enough so we could hear Aunt Lizzie begging, "Please, I need to sit down," and him pleading, "Mrs. Ansible, *please.*"

"*Miss* Ansible."

"Come on, lady. We're almost to the door!"

"I can't go another step," she said, and then she saw us. Then she did the scariest thing. Instead of harshing, she smiled the sweetest, shakiest old-lady smile. Her whole naked head lit up, like she was really glad and we felt guilty because we weren't. "Oh, girls! Ansible girls."

"Hello Aunt Lizzie."

She plopped down on the marble bench in our front yard in spite of the driver and dug in her heels. "Thank God I'm here!"

Taddy was all, "Hellooo, Aunt Lizzie!" Big showoff. Little fraud.

Nobody said anything for way too long. When she'd been sitting there for so long that we thought the driver was going to cry, Aunt Lizzie held up her hand. It wavered like one of those frondy things growing in the bottom of a fish tank. She couldn't hold it still. Then she said the weirdest thing: "Do you see this hand?"

We did, even though it flapped like toilet paper in a wind. It was dead white, and you could see right through to the veins. They were blue, like there was water instead of blood rushing along inside.

"This is the tie that binds us," she said anyway, not that we knew what she meant. "Ansible blood." Now, our name is Patterson, so that was confusing, but this Aunt Lizzie lit up the bench and our whole front walk with that gi-normous, silvery smile, like whatever she was saying was probably true. She patted the seat like we should join her, but no way were we going that close.

"Ansible generations all connected, like a vine." Her voice kept coming out like she couldn't control it. "Oh children, I'm so glad."

We forgot everything we'd been told. We forgot to tell her we were glad, although Mom said it was important—something about the money, I guess, which we were supposed to get all of at the end. We forgot to give her the flowers but I think we remembered to smile.

What we couldn't quite do was answer when she asked us, "Aren't you?"

We didn't even know if we liked her. How could we possibly be glad?

"Family," Aunt Lizzie said like we were actually having a conversation.

Nobody said anything except the driver, who sort of tugged at her, going, "Ma'am?"

"And some are here and some have gone where you can't see, but we're all part of the same thing." Then she settled herself on the bench with her pocketbook in her lap, smiling like a passenger waiting for the train to go somewhere we didn't know about.

"Ma'am!"

Aunt Lizzie turned to us and beamed. You'd think Taddy and me had just now showed up at the station to get on the train with her, like we were a couple of old friends coming along on the ride.

"This is the Patterson house, right?" The driver was desperate to leave and she wouldn't move. How could she even be smiling, old and miserable as she was? But she sat there beaming, like we were her best friends and everything was fine. Listen, if that's where time takes you I'm getting off the train right now.

"Right," I said, although Mom's middle name was Ansible.

"OK, Ma'am. Let's get you inside."

Aunt Lizzie stayed planted, nodding and smiling while the driver stood there with his sad mouth open, waiting for this to end. Then Mom rapped on the picture window and he parked the cart thingy next to Aunt Lizzie and ran for his car. She was flapping her hand at him with a dollar in it like she wanted to give him a tip but I don't think he cared about her or the money, all he cared about was escaping. Who wouldn't want to get away?

"Nice girls," Aunt Lizzie said, "Ansible girls, and I'm here to tell you there's nobody like the Ansible girls."

We weren't, really, at least I hope not. We tried like hell to get her moving, although hell is not one of my words. "Um, Aunt Lizzie? Want to come inside?" At least there would be cake.

"Not yet."

I said, "Come on, Aunt Lizzie. It isn't far," in the voice you use on a dog when you've run out of biscuits but you have to make them come. "We're really close." I pointed. "It's right over there!"

Unfortunately she was looking the wrong way, at the spiked fence and marble slabs and all. Dad got our house cheap because it's, like, adjacent to the property. What with the weeds and all, you can hardly see the graves. "Not yet." Aunt Lizzie sounded cranky and distracted, like her train was coming in any minute and she hadn't packed. "Not yet."

"No no, Aunt Lizzie. Over here!" I tugged her sleeve even though I was scared to touch her, but she didn't budge. "You have to come in!"

"I can't." She patted the bench. "Sit down."

So we sat, Taddy as far down the bench as she could get and me in the middle, next to this old, old relative, listening to the tank attached to Aunt Lizzie's walker wheezing as she breathed in and out. For a long time she said nothing. It was kind of like sitting next to a parade balloon that all the air was running out and the empty skin was going to collapse and smother you. At least she didn't smell bad, if you don't count the perfume.

We looked at the house but nobody came. It was like Mom and Dad were waiting on us, but we were afraid to touch her and we didn't want to make her mad so we waited and she waited, although I don't know what for.

If you do something for long enough, after a while you get used to it, which is what Taddy and me did. We sat there looking at the spiked fence and the broken tombstones next door, and I guess Aunt Lizzie did too, sitting there with her hands on her knees, open, like she was waiting for something to fall in. After a long time her eyes teared up and her papery mouth opened and words came out. "Oh Helena, oh, Maud."

I don't know who Maud is but Helena is our grandmother's name.

When we couldn't think of anything to say Aunt Lizzie got talking, like she was trying to pay us back for waiting with her. The perfume was *Trailing Arbutus*, she told us, her favorite, favorite ever since she was a little girl. She used to buy it at the five and ten cent store way back when you could get practically everything for a dime. Then she put dabs on Taddy and me at the bend of the elbow, where, she said, it counts when you're trying to attract a man because, she said, you are family, and you ought to know. So Aunt Lizzie talked and Taddy and I listened because Mom had told us, *Whatever you do, don't make her mad.*

"Cherry phosphate at the counter," she hummed, "with cute boys behind the counter, making egg creams. I did the Charleston back when it was new. Have you girls ever had an egg cream?"

We shook our heads, and while we waited for Mom to figure out that we were stuck out here, Aunt Lizzie talked on. First it was boring. Then it wasn't. She knew a lot of nasty things about the Ansibles and a couple of cool things about our mom.

"Did you know that Helen was fat when she was little? Your mother got all A's in school, but she ate her own snot, now ask me how I know."

When we giggled she said, "And your grandmother started flirting in grade school, but when she kissed boys it turned their mouths blue because her other bad habit was drinking Parker's ink. Good thing it was Washable Blue."

I looked at Taddy and Taddy looked at me: Woo Whooo!

"Helen was stolid until she lost the weight but her mother was a baggage, if you want to know the truth. Sweet Helena, who would have guessed her future when she was a pretty little thing lying in her crib?" The way she talked it sounded like we really were all connected, all these girls dancing in a long, long line. "My sister Edna named her Helena. What was she thinking, Helen of Troy? Look at all the trouble it brought down! God knows what Helena did or who she did it with, all those nights when Edna and I thought she was reading in bed, she used to turn on the light and slip out the bedroom window, going down to the corner to do God knows what with all those boys . . . "

When Aunt Lizzie first started talking it was creepy; then it got funny, then she started talking about stuff we were supposed to be too young to know about, like where babies came from and how nobody knew how to keep it from happening, at least not back then, and we weren't about to make it stop. She told us that even though she was overweight and not pretty our Mom was *boy crazy*, she used to carve their initials into her fingernails, so, wow! It turns out there are amazing scandals in Mom's family that Taddy and me never knew about, which is kind of, sort of the whole thing.

Aunt Lizzie said, "Your grandmother had a habit of running away." She said Helena, that baggage, that baggage, gave up on Mom; she dyed her hair and ran away with a sailor, leaving the great-aunts to raise Helen all by themselves, "You can imagine the scandal it caused. In fact, this family is built on scandal." Then she dumped the biggest news.

"Now, listen close and don't tell your mother I told. Your grandmother and your great-grandmother and her mother, who was my mother, all had children by different men, so none of us know who our fathers are."

I looked at Taddy to see if she was getting it, and she looked at me and it turns out we didn't, quite, but that wasn't really the biggest news. The biggest news was this.

"Remember, we can't name the men on the family tree but Ansible women are all joined by the blood..." Aunt Lizzie was talking so fast that there was no room for questions, "Family, like a living vine; there are branches that pull you down and others that hold each other up, into eternity, and nobody living can tell you which is which."

No wonder Mom didn't want to have her stay over! Taddy and me were scared but excited, wondering what other awful things Aunt Lizzie would say, so we sat and listened for a long, long time; we sat there even though Mom and Dad were both tapping on the window because it was late. Cake or no cake, I guess they didn't come out because they were scared of making her mad.

The shadows were thick by the time Aunt Lizzie's stories trailed off. Out of nowhere she said in this small, sad voice, "Hold my hand?"

It was too creepy to think about. I told her, "No. We have to go in."

After a long, long time she got up. She just got up all of a sudden if you can say that about something that takes that long. I put the walker in front of her and she smiled that smile and said something that made no sense. "I'd love to," she said to somebody we could not see; she was sweet and polite, like she was sorry to be missing a party, "but another time."

It was so late that Mom said we'd have cake after dinner, which she spent a lot of time making, except it was nothing Aunt Lizzie could eat. She went, "Chicken. You know I hate chicken!" and "You know I can't chew that, not with my bad teeth!" It was good the cake held up. It was not so good when Aunt Lizzie took one look and misted all over, like Mom had punched her in the heart. "That's cruel, Helena. You know I'm not supposed to eat sweets."

"I'm not Helena!" To make up for snapping at her, Mom brought Saltines and coffee for her to have while we were eating the cake.

"Are you trying to murder me? Coffee is out of the question and I can't eat those things, they're loaded with salt!" at which time our mother blew up.

Then Aunt Lizzie took us out on the bench and fed us nasty stories about the family that went down sweeter than the cake we never got to have because Mom got so pissed off that she picked up the platter and smashed it on the dining room floor.

They got her to bed, finally, and for a while things went OK, although it turned out Aunt Lizzie wouldn't eat anything Mom brought to the table, no matter what she cooked, and every time she stood up to go to the bathroom, which was often, she farted, not to mention how long she spent in there getting ready for bed or after she got in bed how loud she turned on the TV, which we had to get used to because whether or not she was in there she kept it running day and night. Pretty soon I was sick to death of Taddy and Taddy was sick of me and Fletcher nipped Taddy when she tried to pet him, plus Mom and Dad were fighting even though not one of us could tell you what it was about. Thank God in the daytime, we were at school.

It went on like that for it seemed like a million years, but we got used to Aunt Lizzie, well, everybody but Mom and Dad, we heard him rr-rrr-rrring and her yelling practically every night, "We have to. She's run out of places to go!"

At least me and Taddy and Fletcher didn't mind. She liked to pet him, and every night we'd go out after supper and sit on the bench while she fed him parts of her dinner because she got Mom off her back by pretending to eat and sneaking the leftovers into her lizard skin purse. We sat on the bench while Aunt Lizzie trained Fletcher; she taught him to sit up and hold it, and then she taught him to count, he learned all kinds of stuff just to get the meat. Every night she thanked us for bringing her out and gave us each a five, which was only a little gicky because of being in that purse with all that mangled food. It was like sitting with her in the station, waiting for her train to come.

We slid into summer, and every night after dinner we helped Aunt Lizzie outside with her tank of air and sat with her on the bench so Mom and Dad could have a minute to themselves. It was OK, she knew great stories plus me and Taddy were saving up for cool things at the mall, so the money was good. Every night we learned new stuff about the Ansibles, the aunt who kept the newspaper boy captive in her attic and what she did with the cop who came to rescue him and all the stuff she did to stay out of jail, plus everything about the twin Ansible girls who had sets of twin babies the same week, none of which looked alike, and that, Aunt Lizzie told us, was before DNA. So she told us about DNA testing and a lot of other things that Mom would say were X-rated, like exactly who in that great big family did what to who including which parts went into which places, but when she asked us about Mom now that she was finally married, Taddy and I just sat there and blinked until she started on somebody else. We sat out there every night until it got dark, and if Mom came out and said in that fake nice tone, "What are you girls up to?" Aunt Lizzie would tell her, "Nothing, dear. Just waiting for our flight," as if a monster jetliner would be landing in our yard any minute now, and she'd climb on board and it would take her away.

She was waiting, OK, we just didn't know for what.

I knew Mom was wishing the grim reaper would come down and take her instead, but it wasn't happening, although Mom and Dad brought it up in the middle of every fight, and the fights were getting worse. Even with black-flies and mosquitoes, it was better outside. Inside the house, everything was horrible; Aunt Lizzie kept dropping things or banging them with her walker and every time something bad happened Mom would yell at Taddy and me and then she'd start to cry. The bathroom was like a giant spider web of long black stockings and wet underwear that Aunt Lizzie washed out by hand in the middle of the night; plus every time you came around a corner Mom and Dad were fighting about, well, it wouldn't take a brain surgeon to figure out Guess Who. My birthday came and went, and either Mom was completely over baking or so upset that she forgot to make me a cake.

At least Aunt Lizzie remembered, she gave me ten dollars, sitting right there on the bench and then she said in this sweet, sad little voice, "Tell your mother I'm sorry about the cake."

I thanked her and she took my hand, which had stopped scaring me. Her fingers were long and so light on my wrist that they could have been hollow, but strong at the same time. I guess Aunt Lizzie had run out of Ansible scandals. She didn't have anything to say. After a while I said, "Should we go in?"

She looked at the churchyard fence, which only looked like it was moving closer and said what she'd said the night she got here. "Not yet," Aunt Lizzie said. "Not yet."

It was weird. Taddy and I were so used to her by that time that we hadn't really noticed that she was talking less and less.

We were used to sitting on the bench with her, kicking the dirt underneath our feet and staring at the fence next door until it was too dark to see the spikes; we sat there sucking candy that Aunt Lizzie had gotten somewhere and handed off to us the way she gave her leftovers to Fletcher, to keep us quiet and happy on the bench. Taddy and me, I don't know what we were expecting, but we knew she was expecting something, and from the look on her face when we sat down with her that last night, she thought it was coming soon and maybe, OK maybe we thought she would tell some amazing new secret about Mom or hand over the heaps of money and all the candy she had in the lizard purse.

Just when we'd gotten used to her not talking, she said, "You know, all those people over there are holding hands somehow, the family of man all holding hands somehow, underneath the earth," which creeped me out because she was pointing at the graveyard on the other side of the fence.

My voice came out high and thin and nervous although I was trying to sound firm, "OK Aunt Lizzie, time to go in."

"Not yet," Aunt Lizzie said in that stony, upsetting way.

For the first time in practically forever Taddy whined, "But Aunt Lizzie, I'm bored."

"Not yet," she said and she was begging. "Not yet."

Then when the sun went down for good and it was really dark I got up. "Ready or not, Aunt Lizzie. I'm going in."

"No!"

"I'm sorry, I'm going."

"You don't understand."

"It's really late."

"This is when it happens," Aunt Lizzie said and her voice floated up like a great gas balloon taking us three up with it, "when we all join hands with them because there are enough of them to reach each other and reach us and keep on reaching back and forward and all the way around the world, look, look at us all!" She pointed at the moon, which was not normal, it was not normal how she did it, and neither was what she was working so hard to say. "Up there. Here. Down there. All these families. We are all together, all holding hands . . . "

Later Dad would say she was disconnected and raving, but Taddy and me, we knew. We were too scared to tell him or Mom exactly what happened, like if we said anything it would come true, but what happened, was this.

Aunt Lizzie was still talking and looking at the moon and smiling that quivery smile of hers, it was so bright that it lit up the yard; she was sitting there shining when something quiet started happening at our feet. Whatever it was, it was gnarly and strange and impossible to miss, but our great-great-aunt was too excited and distracted to see. She hardly noticed the hand coming out of the dirt underneath the bench and I don't know if she even felt the great fingers closing on her ankle or whether she minded that whoever or whatever was pulling hard, dragging her into the ground but what she probably did notice, for which me and Taddy will forever feel guilty, was what we did when at the last minute she threw up her arms screaming, "Girls, oh, girls! Come take my hands!" Taddy and me shuddered and backed away.

See, we didn't know if she wanted us to pull her out of the ground or push her down in, but we were so scared that we just let it happen, with me yelling at Aunt Lizzie, even though it is not one of my words, "Fuck no!"

"Girls!"

Then we screamed and ran like hell for the house and if I've spent my whole life since then feeling guilty, it's OK, because right before we slammed the door, I heard Aunt Lizzie calling out to us as she sank into the dirt, "Come back, let's hold hands together, all of us, to the ends of the earth."

*Ellen Datlow came back from a talk by a forensics expert with inside information about a mysterious black dog. Apparently, he roamed hospital halls until he settled down at the doornot of the dead, but of the patient who was next to die. Later this animal or one like him helped find and save earthquake victims before death took them. This story appeared online at **scifi.com**, where Ellen edited SciFiction.*

SONG OF THE BLACK DOG

"The black dog is not like any other," the forensics officer says. It is a little incantation.

In the journalists' skybox high above the civic auditorium, Bill Siefert strains to see the distant stage, the speaker and at her back, the beast he is here to deconstruct. That's the way he thinks of it. Siefert hates anything he doesn't understand. If it doesn't make sense, disassemble it. He's always been uncomfortable with the idea of supernatural powers, but this is not his stated reason for sneaking into the press box. He thinks he's here to crack the black dog program and show the people its inner workings. If the wonder dog is just a dog, then the police are money-grubbing charlatans and the expose will move him from unemployed to famous.

He'll be all over CNN. Networks will come calling. *Silence the black dog,* he thinks, and wonders where that came from. Stop mizzling and get the story. He needs a job. He needs the attention. He needs the power. He needs to be more than who he is, and before any of this and all of this Bill Siefert needs to figure out why this morning, on a perfectly ordinary day, he woke up screaming.

Get the story, he tells himself and does not know what about this makes him so uneasy. Cell phone for instant screen shots. Notebook, digicorder, nice smile. Seat in the booth. Fake press pass to get him backstage. Piece of cake.

With the black dog, nothing spins out the way you expect.

"The black dog can cut through the welter of visual and olfactory stimuli in a disaster situation and find those most in need of rescue," the forensics officer says matter-of-factly, as though this is a given. She is sleek in the black uniform. Persuasive. It is disturbing. "He is only the first," she says, and then she says portentously, "His descendants will save thousands."

Cut to the chase. Startled, Bill shakes himself. *Did I speak? Who?*

The speaker glitters in a cone of light, but the wonder dog—if there is one—is nowhere present. Peering into the shadows behind her, Bill looks for the darker shadow signifying a living creature, reflected light pinpointed in the eyes. The darkness gives back only darkness. Nothing to see, he tells himself, and wonders why this comes as a relief. No dog. Another wasted day like so many days in what is shaping up to be a wasted life.

With the black dog, the future is open to question.

In the next second he shivers, transfixed. He can't even guess what just happened, but all the furniture in his head has shifted.

It sees me.

Given that the stage is far, far below this is unlikely, but the sense that he is being watched is so acute that all of Bill Siefert's bones begin to itch. No, he tells himself. No way. He swallows hard but his throat closes. It's just a dog.

Far below, she continues, "Of course the prototype is a genetic fluke, but one that can be exploited for the good of all."

Yeah, he thinks bitterly. Yeah, right.

There are a thousand people in the auditorium: city officials and guests, all in some variation on black tie, velvet, opera length pearls. The gentry have come out for this press conference—the unveiling of the superdog. A thought flies across Bill's mind: *If there is a dog.* Shifting on his haunches, sweating for no apparent reason, he thinks: *what if I kidnap the thing?* Down, boy. Focus. First in his class in Communications Studies, but a tad bit A.D.D. No wonder he can't keep a job.

The woman who discovered and trained the black dog continues thoughtfully. "We're not certain exactly which combination of phero-mones alerts the black dog, but we do recognize his singular power. He can rush into a burning building or dig his way into earthquake debris and go like an arrow to the victim most in need."

Fine, Bill thinks, your basic St. Bernard. It helps to picture him bounding over the snow with that keg of rum and the pink tongue flap-ping. Pant pant pant. Hello, I am here to save you. He tries to laugh but his belly is jittering and when he tries to swallow, the spit won't go down. There is something terribly the matter here, and nobody sees it but him.

"The black dog is unique," she says. "He has no interest in the quick or the dead."

Unaccountably, Siefert feels twin points of light like paired lasers, fixed on him. The eyes—why can he not see the eyes? It leaves him jittery and unsettled.

What the forensics officer says next will overturn him.

"His peculiar skill is like no other." Severe in black, with her own offbeat elegance, the tall, bony woman creates a silence so profound that even the mayor gets nervous.

Then she says into the hush: "He can identify the dying."

The journalists mutter among themselves. From the orchestra seats far below comes a muffled cry.

"He has the uncanny ability to smell impending death." In case they still don't get it, she finishes: "The black dog knows who's next to die."

Everything inside Siefert's head skids to a stop. He wants to silence the other journalists, stop them breathing if he has to, so he can hear what comes next. He has to know! He leans forward with his mouth open and his tongue out like a dog hanging out a car window, gulping the words like rushing air. If he could, he would find a way to stop his heart to create the silence he needs to grasp her meaning. Stop the pounding of his blood so he can hear.

"Understand," she says, "he can predict the exact moment."

The audience gasps.

The speaker smooths her varnished hair with a proud, confident smile. She is in the home stretch now. Explain. Make the pitch. Walk away with an extra million in public funding. "This makes him particularly useful in triage situations, like earthquake and building collapses, when the living and the dead are trapped under tons of rubble and for us, there is no telling which is which. Of course we have instruments to detect body mass as well as warmth and motion and the sound of breathing, but we have no time to waste excavating cadavers and no way of knowing who to rescue first. Only the black dog knows which of the victims is poised at the door to death, and only he can guide us in to pull that victim back from the brink."

Reporters on either side exchange skeptical looks but Bill is beyond questions. He does not so much ignore his colleagues as rise above them like a soul cut loose and floating outside himself, observing from the top left-hand corner of the press booth. Did he see the dog's eyes back then or did he only imagine it?

Does it see him?

Do I?

He whirls. Dear God!

"Don't you see?" the officer trills, rolling into the finale. "Now we know who to rescue first!"

All over the auditorium, hands fly up: questions.

"Of course you want to know how we discovered his power. Science is an exact discipline but to tell the truth, it was an accident."

Bill leans forward as she describes a routine training exercise, the black dog going through its paces like all the others until, without prompting, it stops cold. Sits down in front of the trainer. Refuses to budge. In spite of threats it sits like a rock until its original trainer—young man, too young to have a heart condition—clutches his throat and drops like a felled redwood. Infarction, the coroner says. It's nothing, the chief says. It's just coincidence.

"But I," the speaker says, "as an expert, I knew we were onto something big." She whispers into the microphone, "I took him home."

There the ambitious forensics officer devised a series of tests for the black dog . . .

Matter-of-factly, she details visits to hospitals and hospices, in which the dog paces the complex of halls like a moving shadow and then. Sits. Is present at the exact moment when the soul leaves the body. He is unfailing in his accuracy. The black dog is right every single time. Trainer and dog move on to wards where patients are more viable. Some will make it. Some may not. The dog sits down. Doctors send in the crash cart and save the patient, see how valuable this is?

Bill tunes out of her recital. What it took to get the commissioners' approval. Startup money. Training and experiments. The first disaster—factory explosion—in which medics follow the black dog into the ruins and make sensational, last-minute rescues. The building collapse in which at least a dozen are yanked back from the brink of death. Certain fires. The list goes on, but by this time Bill Siefert is thinking of one thing and one thing only.

He has to see the dog.

"In emergency situations like these," she says, "prioritization is imperative. Why rush to help people strong enough to make it until we get around to them when there are cases in which immediate rescue means the difference between life and death? Why lose hours excavating victims who are already corpses?"

Buzzing with pride, she moves on into the pitch. "Therefore, the response time of our disaster relief units and our success rates depend heavily on the services of the black dog. You can see it is essential to breed thousands like him." Now she romances the crowd in that deep, sexy whisper, "And that's where you come in."

As one, they nod. Yes yes. Oh, yes yes.

"At the moment, the black dog is unique, but I am happy to report that our veterinary unit has used genetic material from our black dog to impregnate thirty black bitches. We hope to replicate his genetic set. He is, after all, this year's gold star winner for valor under extreme circumstances in the Vidalia implosion and the West Virginia mine disaster. My triumph." She raises her voice like a ringmaster preparing to bring on the lions: *ta-da*. "The miraculous black dog."

Everybody cranes.

Speakers vibrate with the communal shout, "Bring on the dog."

She raises a hand like a traffic cop. "And with your support . . . "

But the crowd is waiting for the grand entrance. They squirm in their seats, straining to see the animal, but nothing happens.

Smiling, the glossy, imposing speaker dangles the bait. How much will they pay to see? "And once we receive your support . . . "

On the floor of the auditorium, city officials and invited guests shift in their seats, chanting, "bring on the dog." The cry starts as a ripple but gathers force, "The dog . . . " It rolls in like a long comber, growing until it breaks on the shore. "The dog!"

"Now, we are prepared to take your pledges."

Somewhere outside himself, fixed on something he can not see, Bill Siefert scours the shadows behind her, searching. He thinks he sees . . . He sees . . . No, he doesn't see . . . Where is it, he wonders, changed. What is it?

You don't want to know.

With a start, he returns to himself, shuddering.

Why is this so important to him?

It isn't just the sensational story: *Interview with the Black Dog.* Skeptical Bill Siefert, who came here to debunk, has been sucked in. He is changed and threatened by the possibility of something that he will never understand. Like a thousand others, he wants to see the animal, but the dog is nowhere present. And yet . . .

Yet

Bill's head jerks so abruptly that his neck snaps. He doesn't know it yet, but in the realm of colliding fates he has chosen the black dog, or the black dog has chosen him. For whatever reasons they are in communication. In a universe of particles, in an arena of conflating sights and sounds and stimuli, he and the black dog are yoked in a way that both draws and terrifies him. All at once and through no cause Bill Siefert can divine, he comprehends its size and shape, the yellow eyes burning. Without seeing, he knows.

A question boils inside him. **Name. What is your name.**

Words come in from somewhere new and strange. **What makes you think I have a name?**

"My God!"

The video teams on either side of Bill turn to stare. He shoves his knuckles into his mouth, sealing it shut.

The forensics officer is saying, "Now, I know many of you are wondering why we haven't brought our marvelous black dog onstage tonight, and under ordinary circumstances we would, but these are not ordinary circumstances and this is not an ordinary dog."

The audience grumbles.

She raises a stern hand. "You will have to content yourself with the video of his last rescue. As you will see, we fitted him with a collar cam and a pin spot to bring you this remarkable footage. You will not see the black dog today. In a minute my associates will pass among you with hand mikes because of course I am anxious to answer your questions," she says in a way that makes clear that she has no patience with questions. "Especially yours, Mr. Mayor, since I am here to seek your support for this ambitious project. Of course you deserve an explanation. You won't see the amazing black dog today, but if you will direct your attention to the monitors in the arms of the chairs where you are sitting, you can see one of the miracles he performs daily in the line of duty."

Murky videos blink to life on a thousand monitors. Because the camera is mounted on the collar the people who sat here so patiently won't see the dog tonight, not even on video. Still, the audience shivers as the camera rushes into tight spaces and through dark corridors on the back of something huge and powerful. Everybody but Bill Siefert will see, and everybody but Bill will hear the forensics officer's warning.

By that time he's bolted out of the press box ("pardon me, excuse me, excuse me, pardon me") and through the exit at the end of the corridor, down flight after flight of stairs into the belly of the place. He is running hard. Hunting the beast. He wants to lock his hands in its thick, leonine ruff so he can look it in the face while he asks certain questions.

Therefore he will not hear the forensics officer say, in conclusion, "We can not show you the black dog on stage here in the auditorium. This is for his protection. And for yours."

She says, "Believe me, this is for your own safety."

The crowd protests until she raises her hand for silence.

She says, "In a crowd this size, there are bound to be some . . . well, you can imagine. I mean, actuarial tables suggest that several of you are already. . . " Discreetly, she breaks off. "Think what that would do to him! Sensory overload, and before we can perpetuate the breed. And as for you. Well. Think what would happen if he sat down in front of one of you!"

There is a long silence.

"The presence of the black dog has terrible implications."

For the black dog, the responsibility is tremendous. In a ruined building or an arena full of strangers he must go to the feet of the dying like a bullet to the heart. No, to the first to die. He must sit quietly, when more than anything he wants to lift his head and howl to the heavens. Even here, deep in the belly of the building, he is painfully aware of the hundreds of hearts of hundreds of strangers rustling and thrumming in the vast auditorium above, the cumulative pressure of their failing bodies. There are too many to save!

This is the prodigious engine that drives him. Before they know, he knows.

Can the black dog predict the future?

No. The future predicts him.

Now every hair on his huge body shimmers and ripples over powerful muscles as he pads along the corridors toward the space under the stage where his mistress stands. He is heading for the sunken orchestra pit. Above, his mistress is speaking to all the sad, vulnerable humans. He can hear their ruined bellies crying out. Lungs failing. Hearts stuttering. He knows which will falter and stop.

In spite of his size the black dog goes silently with his great head lifted, scanning the corridor with yellow eyes. His jaws are clenched on the necessary.

He is carrying it in his teeth. *For her.*

Bill Siefert is already compromised, and, like Bill, you must proceed with caution. Stay back if you are anywhere in the vicinity. Be still. The black dog is approaching. No matter who you are or how strong or how arrogantly healthy, this is the time when you must be very, very careful.

Do not run if you see him coming because no matter what you try, whatever is going to happen next will happen.

Do not be afraid of the black dog. Feel sorry for him.

Imagine the burden of foreknowledge. The pressure. The choices he has to make. In this world there are billions of humans marching toward death, thousands are at the gate at this very moment, and he cannot reach them all.

He does what he can.

His mistress does not know that he is racing to save her. Nor can the forensics officer, strutting and preening to massive applause in her best Armani suit, guess that tonight her pet—no, her creation—is coming for her, trotting purposefully through the maze of corridors with the necessary tightly clamped in his soft mouth.

Stand back. Hold still. Stay out of his way. Be grateful he isn't coming for you.

There are so many! Earlier, a voice cried out to him. Nothing, he thinks, just something he heard. Voice. Yes. That will come, but in due time, because more important to the black dog than this new element in his troublesome cosmos is doing what the black dog does. The voice cries out. It is the other: searching. The dog's head comes up, but there isn't time. Asking, but the black dog does not brook questions. There are too many. There isn't time. There isn't time! For the black dog tonight, there is only one. Upstairs, she is still talking. Because she is his mistress, because in spite of her commanding, clinical approach, the black dog has grown fond of her in the way of all dogs.

She does, after all, forget sometimes and scratch his ears. Therefore instead of vaulting the ladder and bounding onstage to sit down at her feet, the black dog will wait down here. He will give her a chance to do what she does as he must do what he does. He may want to spare her public humiliation, if that's a concept the noble creature grasps. For the black dog, pride is irrelevant. All that matters is responsibility.

What he must do.

Of all the failing hearts and bodies in departure mode tonight, exuding death smells in the great, echoing coffin above, even in the realm of a hundred simultaneous deaths he would choose her. When his mistress comes down the ladder he will drop the cell phone at her feet so she has a minute to call 911. Then he will sit down. He'll sit with his flag tail thumping the floor and beg her to save herself.

The others, he will not necessarily save.

The black dog is heavy with foreknowledge. He does not exactly see the blood clot floating into his trainer's brain, but he knows it. When it strikes its mark and that part of the brain explodes the black dog will sense it in the way he knows what exactly is failing inside of you, which part of the mechanism you wear so proudly will break and cut you loose from whatever you think you are.

Until the black dog's handler began emanating death smells in the house today, the whole last-minute rescue thing was something she asked him to do, and being a good dog, he did as told. Ordinarily he does what he does in his own time, and as he has always done it, but it seemed to please her when he did as she said. She and the big, clumsy men she yoked to him on rescue missions rushed in with their medicine and electric paddles, jerking people back from death, and that is their business. The hero thing was her idea.

The black dog does what he does.

Overhead the applause crescendos and the auditorium floor thrums with the footsteps of a thousand people leaving. His mistress has started down, into the cavity. She descends in a funnel of light at the far end of the corridor. Long stretch: not much time. Must reach her. Drop the phone into her hand. Give her a minute. Sit. She'll know.

Running with his head lifted and every muscle taut with urgency, the black dog is fixed on the orderly progression, the necessary timing. First this. Then this.

Then all at once a human blunders out of a side passage and skids to a stop in front of him, flailing like a flagman on train tracks. It is barking and barking. "Is that you?"

The one he knows, and does not know why he knows it. The thing has a bad smell. It has an ugly bark.

The black dog growls. *Not now.*

It goes, bark bark. "Doggie, stop. I have to see you!" Dog hears: Blarg blarg blarg.

The black dog growls again. No time. *Move.*

It just keeps barking. "Doggie, I have to ask you a question."

Shut up so I can hear her breathe!

She's on the ladder! She's halfway down! He growls again but the human in his path is like a balloon, getting bigger and bigger until it fills the corridor. In times like this even a rescue dog must drop whatever he is carrying to bare his teeth.

"Come on, dog." The human's bark falters. "Please." Then it does the unthinkable. It lunges for the black dog's collar.

The black dog does what he has to. He rakes the human's arm with his fangs and grunts in recognition. He tastes blood, but only a little, and it is vile. At least he has distracted it so he can move on. Whining, the creature frets over its wound. The black dog puts his huge paws on its back to push it down, vaults over it and runs on, bent on rescue.

Too late. In the lost time his mistress dropped like a felled redwood; she is unconscious. Worse: while he was grappling with the human, the window of opportunity slammed shut. This isn't the black dog's fault, even though grief and frustration make him throw back his great head and howl his grief. It is the human's.

The creature with his mark on it made him drop the phone.

What was that? What is it? Trembling, Bill tries to sit up. Ahead, the black dog looks up from the body it has been nosing—Bill wonders *What happened? Did it kill somebody?*—whirls, and charges. He cowers as the great beast covers the distance between them in enormous, terrifying leaps. With its red jaws wide and its yellow eyes suffused with blood and turning a murderous orange, it comes.

"Don't! Don't kill me." Bill cries. Still the great beast rushes down on him, and as Bill Siefert collapses and waits for death, the black dog plants one huge paw on his chest, squeezing the breath out of him, and with an efficiency signifying complete indifference, stalks over him and moves on.

The form passing over Bill is huge, warm and heavily muscled, bigger than a Newfoundland with its thick, shimmering black fur soft and rich and every muscle and tendon humming with power. Its passage is swift but the sensation lingers. It is like being overshadowed by a lover.

Aren't you going to kill me? Bill gasps, struggling for breath as the black dog passes over him and goes on running.

Did it answer? Does he imagine it? In the instant when the enormous paw compressed his chest and its full weight landed on his heart, Bill thinks he heard or comprehended what the creature may have told him. **It isn't time.**

Right now no one in the auditorium knows what has happened down here in the pit, but the implications are prodigious. The forensics officer, its mistress, is dead. Nobody else can control the animal.

The black dog is on the loose.

"Wait!" the human barks as the black dog passes over it, but when he plants his paw in the creature's chest there is a shift in the air. He recognizes it at once. It is the human, pleading: Wait. He lifts his head, considering. Did it speak? **Oh please, please wait**. Fragile as the human is inside its thin pink skin, the creature is communicating.

A talking human? How? In time he will have to deal with the matter. The human asks, **what are you?** but the black dog has his own imperatives.

There is a brief flurry after Bill's story breaks. Since he was there when it happened, since he found the body, since he *saw* the thing, it is a big story. Blood clot to the brain, but that doesn't stop false charges against the animal. "I was there," Bill says breathlessly. "He tried to get me too. I alone am left," he says. "I alone am left to tell the tale," he says, and by the time he has told his story on every known talk show, he is temporarily famous and eminently employable.

There will be a statewide search and bogus reports of countless sightings. The spawn of the black dog—litters artificially inseminated and carefully reared—turn out to be depressingly devoid of powers and are destroyed. For a short time Bill makes news with his *Encounter With the*

Black Dog, but only for a little while. He quits his job to write an existential book under the same title, but by the time he has it finished the black dog is a dead issue. After a brief memorial service for the city's top forensics officer, felled by a cerebral embolism on the night of her triumph, the mayor and the police commissioner will forget. After corruption hearings and a series of firings, the city will forget. In time Bill Siefert will forget. Almost.

Meanwhile the black dog runs on. He will not forgive the human he left squirming in the corridor that night, nor can he know why he and it are somehow yoked, but they are. Never mind. In the realm of the black dog there are imperatives that supersede all else.

If their fates are intertwined, then everything will come down when it comes down. When is a matter of no particular importance to him. The time will come and when it does the black dog will know it. Until then, unencumbered by police handlers, harnesses and leashes and the mistress he almost loved, the black dog runs loose in the world. Not free, exactly, because he is still driven by imperatives. Even so he is free, with nobody to answer to.

Loose in the world, he does what the black dog does.

Bill is not a superficial person, but you can't go on dwelling on a mysterious moment in your past.

He used to think the black dog would make him rich, and if it didn't make him rich it would make him famous. All he had to do was figure out how. If he could find it again, if he could catch the thing, then he could follow his big story, *Encounter With the Black Dog*, with *Capture of the Black Dog*, to be followed by *Interview With the Black Dog* and finally, *Secrets of the Black Dog*, but he had no idea how to go about it. Or collect the reward. Then the police department gave up on the case and withdrew the reward, so that was the end of that.

Siefert never caught the black dog and he never got that book contract. His lecture, *Encounter With the Black Dog*, never made him rich and it didn't make him famous, but it did help his career. He is a local television anchor now. He married a nice girl from the valley, ten years younger. They just bought a house just over the hills, on the Hollywood side.

Still, Bill knows he must have tangled with the black dog for a reason. Like most people in the world, he has to proceed on faith, which in his own way he is doing. He used to think that if the encounter wasn't about fame or money, it must be about power. Years pass. That hope has come and gone, so Bill has to wonder whether whatever happened back there had left him marked in some other way. If only he could figure it out!

A family man now, Siefert tells himself he's finally let it go, but whether or not he knows it, he and the black dog are by no means done.

Even now there are nights when he sits up in bed and wonders. Sitting next to his sleeping wife with his knees drawn up and his arms locked around them, he gnaws on his bare kneecaps and wonders. What happened back then? Was the black dog trying to tell him something that night in the darkened corridor? What? Why were its yellow eyes turning orange, and if they turn red, what happens then? If he and the black dog were thrown together for a reason, it's no reason he can divine.

And the dog. Every year since his collision with the human, everything the black dog does takes a little longer to do. The slowing tempo is gradual but apparent. Whether it is the byproduct of that night, the black dog could not tell you. Is it that unwanted encounter with an unlike animal that is forever mysteriously linked to him? The unbidden memory of his lost mistress? The other human's bark-bark-bark, its smell, his own resent-ment? Insofar as it is the function of the black dog to wonder, he wonders.

Alone in his slowing body he lifts his head and howls without making a sound.

Bill Siefert is middle aged now, father of two, secure in his career and still happily married. There were years when he would have been thrilled to see the black dog, because he was ambitious and reckless and too young to be afraid of the creature. Even though he has more to lose now he has become—not careless, exactly, but less vigilant.

Then he goes to the E.R. with a bellyache and wakes up in a hospital room—a double—groggy and minus his appendix. No big. He'll be fine. A lump in the next bed, supported by ticking monitors and a welter of tubes and drains, tells him it's a double.

It is night in the room, and in the shadows, there is a deeper shadow. Twin lights wink and glow yellow.

Bill shudders. **Is that you?**

He gropes for the buzzer to get help, but it isn't anywhere that he can find. Nice wife, kids, they have a bigger house. He cries, "You can't be here for me, it's just an appendix!"

The black dog blinks but does not move. At least it's still standing.

He doesn't mean to whimper, but he does. "You don't get it, I'm up for the network anchor job!"

Blarg blarg blarg, why won't the human stop barking and communicate? The black dog creates the silence into which thoughts can fall. In time the creature in the bed quits flailing and lets the words out. *Don't take me.* The smell it gives off is feral, frantic. *Not me, I'm young! I have so much to lose.*

Exactly.

The human points to the next bed. **Take him.**

Still standing, the black dog considers. Nothing will happen until he sits down, and he is not ready.

Although his mission is preordained, he does not know what he will do now, now that they have come to the convergence, only that he and the barking human have been brought together for a reason.

Please.

It seems right to wait until he knows. **All right.**

He moves on to the other bed in the room and sits down. He sits until the old soul parts from the old body. For reasons the black dog is not built to contemplate, his bones rattle with foreknowledge.

Bill Siefert emerges from the hospital changed. He can't say what drives him now but he has lost his ambition. His children find him indifferent. His wife says he is drifting.

This is not precisely the case. He is troubled, distracted. He has become cruelly aware of the multitude of scents, miseries and toxic humors of the people around him: the lump in his wife's breast, the rales in the lungs of his producer.

It makes him frantic. Can he make her get a checkup so soon after the last one, and for no reason he can give her? Can he get his producer to the doctor in time to forestall his death and keep his job, at least for now? He does not know. The pressure is terrible, the responsibility tremendous.

His narrow escape from the black dog troubles him. He is not so much changed as sensitized. Where he used to be self-contained and live his life however, a chorus of outcries and farewell wails rolls in, filling his consciousness. It is like coming into a room where a million people are calling out to him.

Still, a man has to live his life and support his family, so painful as it is—the voices multiply, a million fingers clawing at his heart—Bill goes to New York with a DVD of his best newscasts for the last round of inter-views with the Manhattan network affiliates. Only a strategic cocktail party stands between him and that spot as weekend anchor. Not what he wanted as a kid, but better than he expected.

The black dog is dying. He knows it now. This explains everything, but in his life in service, the black dog has never stopped for explanations. For now, he will do what the black dog does.

The top of New York. Siefert has retreated to the penthouse balcony at the top of the glittering network tower. He told them he needed time to consider the offer, but it was the pain that drove him out here, the pres-sure of the unexpected. Alone for the first time since he arrived, he inhales air so cold that it's like breathing distilled brandy. Maybe he is a little drunk. That must account for it. When he sees the black dog sitting on the wide cement rail with the wind lifting its shimmering hair, he is not surprised. He isn't even frightened.

The black dog blinks its yellow eyes. **You know why I'm here.**

He does. He doesn't. **Time to die?** In a way, it would be a relief. He waits for the eyes to turn orange. Red. For it to finish him.

In your dreams.

He does not say, *Why are you here?* He doesn't have to.

You're not the agent I would have chosen.

"If it's about that time I ran into you in the hall . . . "

The black dog turns its magnificent head to taste the wind and lets out a wild, exuberant cry. **It's your turn**, the black dog either says, or doesn't say. Then it is gone.

It won't matter whether this last is spoken, dreamed or imagined. Siefert understands. Grimacing with unspeakable pain, he turns. Goes inside. Sits down in front of a network vice president.

WHAT SHE THOUGHT SHE WAS DOING
The Fictions of Kit Reed

by Joseph Reed

Kit Reed writes fiction about us, people we know, our world, but it is made strange both by the temporary circumstances and permanent realities her characters find themselves in. The reason it is so tempting to call Reed's short stories fantasy or something else is that she makes the extraordinary seem common. Yes, her characters have families: mostly they are alienated but not estranged from them. Everything has just gotten a little out-of-hand. Mom is a trial, Dad doesn't recognize anybody on the street, Harry Farmer loves his teeth, the gift (of a robot tiger) has started to look a little worn, a woman has just ordered a new model of herself. "A little" is a lot to Kit Reed because, the world her stories tell of is a plausible impossible; in the course of a short story "a little" can come to be an awful lot—inescapable, unavoidable, world-changing. Unexpected things are realized, corners are turned, chasms leaped, ordinary days begun. Two and two can come to a new sum in these stories. She has changed her world by the what her characters meet and how they react.

Many feminist critics have written about Kit Reed as a feminist writer. Much of her work is published as SF. In this context, speculative fiction: stories of the plausible impossible, the realm of what-if in which disbelief is willingly suspended. It is a mistake to call Reed's stories science fiction, strictly fantasy, or even by the new term SF. They are sometimes published in SF magazines because these magazines know Reed is unique. SF is the best collective term: but in the case of Kit Reed SF does not mean science fiction in the ordinary sense. Reed has always refused to be a part of any literary ghetto—not the Southern, the Roman Catholic, or the Science Fiction. She's not Southern (her mother was). She doesn't do rocket ships or hard science. She writes about people. Kit Reed writes what she writes because she writes it. She doesn't think writing is necessarily rewarding, but she "does it because she does it because she does it" (this is a frequent Reed answer in Q&A or interview). There is a kind of determinism to all this, neither fatalistic nor entirely Christian. But it is stubborn, determined, and directed. It is Kit Reed.

John Clute in his encyclopaedic manner tells what it is. "It is about . . . women . . . whom motherhood and sisterhood has wired up strange; women whose estrangement from their fate gives them a weird at-bay gaze; it is about the high wire and circuitry of being a woman and a human person in the Suburbia Deserta of an America where the Hard Rain falls . . . Some . . . utilize fabulation or SF or fantasy to shape and give air to sharp tensile plucking insights into the human condition.

. . . She has . . . a Braille sensitivity to the anguish and mutual self-incriminations characteristic of relations between mothers and daughters." (John Clute, *Excessive Candour*)

Clute is, as usual, definitive: the stories, as he says, scan the horizon of an odd country which seems a lot like early America—that is, America between 1955 and Armageddon. They are not women's stories, but they center on women, the war between women and men, women and their families. The premise of each takes an odd pitch that throws the horizon, the whole spiritual geography into question, creating the Kit Reed Story.

It's difficult to say exactly what a Kit Reed Story is: this essay is an attempt to analyze Kit Reed's short fiction as a type unto itself. Sometimes SF, usually about a woman and family but not always, funny but sometimes it makes us nervous to call it that: unexpected, sudden, and tangibly engaging.

Kit Reed was born in San Diego to Lillian Hyde and John Rich Craig, a naval officer (U. S. Naval Academy, '30). They made their home at various duty assignments: New London CT, Pearl Harbor in Hawaii and the U.S. Canal Zone in Panama. She began to write at five, the adventures of her stuffed rabbit named Harbor (after Pearl) called *Harbor Plots Her Plans*. She dictated it to her mother, who dutifully wrote it down without offering to correct it: somehow she knew better.

In 1943 her father, in command of the submarine *USS Grampus*, was lost in enemy action in the Coral Sea. "A woman was expected to have a man. Overnight, my mother and I were disenfranchised." (Introduction *Weird Women, Wired Women*)

Kit and her mother began a series of forced marches from one place to another, later (when her mother took up managing an officers' club) back to a Marine base at Parris Island. She is relentlessly realistic about her mother: "A tentative person at best, sweet and uncertain, my mother responded with a combination of toughness ("We have to do this alone") and terrifying vulnerability. She was the only person I had left, the one person I had that I knew I could count on; I was the only thing about her world that she could hope to control. She loved me but, One Woman Alone, she worried." (KR *WWWW*)

Reed had many schools where she always found herself a stranger in a strange school. Her closest friends were other Navy juniors, subject to the same rules of change. She found herself at Beaufort (SC) High School and then at Georgetown Visitation Convent, then Baltimore and the College of Notre Dame of Maryland, run by the School Sisters of Notre Dame. She took a sensible attitude towards nuns as: "academics who had been spared the exigencies of housekeeping and child rearing, I came up believing I could do anything I wanted... Before feminism, the nuns were the first feminists." (KR *Women* xiv)

Of course women were men's equals, and nuns were smart (if one picked them right). At Notre Dame she wrote a senior thesis of short stories. Sister M. Maura, SSND, a poet, was her tutor.

The important discipline in writing came later; Reed taught herself to write fiction with the help of city editors of two metropolitan dailies and a thorough reading of F. Scott Fitzgerald and Evelyn Waugh, William

Faulkner, Graham Greene and John Cheever along with everything else she's ever read. From them came her taste for offbeat characters who turn out to make perfect (and serious) sense later on, the landscape (as in Faulkner's Yoknapatawpha County), intimate knowledge of fictional places that seem like home, just down the road from where we live. And to this she added what she knew and they didn't: how much time being a mother, a daughter—and a wife can take up.

The salient ingredient of Reed's taste in subject-matter was not the classroom but the newsroom. She still reads the newspaper with this strange bent: the 30-pound cat, the newspaper-collecting recluse, spontaneous human combustion. The newsroom component, she summed up in a very practical note: "In newsrooms, reporters used to compose on the typewriter. I hammered at my lead, typing and retyping until I had it right, and something about the process opened up the rest of the story for me: sentence by sentence, graf by graf. For me, the process transferred to fiction writing and I destroyed several forests' worth of copy paper before the computer delivered me. I find out what I have to say while I'm figuring out the best way to say it." (KR, conversation)

Both her father and mother came from Jacksonville, FL. Jack Craig's mother was the first white child (that is, non-Indian) born in Deland, Florida, and Clarabelle Rich's family had come there to found the town, by steamer or overland, from Beaufort, South Carolina. Kit and her mother drifted into—no, washed up in a town her father, years before, had chosen as a place unlikely to be disturbed by war with Germany and Japan, St. Petersburg, Florida.

After college, she went to work at the *St. Petersburg Times* where she was church editor for a minute and a half (she wrote this stint as Fidelia Kirk); TV editor and feature writer. The sand, the sun and skies show up all over the fiction, but perhaps more significant are the women. In the context of the St.Petersburg social world Reed's alienation from what women had to do, their various "appearances," hardened. The stranger in a strange school came to the fore.

"Most of us write better about what we hate and fear than about what we love, and it would appear that at some level I have always been afraid of my sisters' expectations, from the day in high school when I understood that I would never fit in with the girl gang to the moment when I pushed back from the bridge table with the sense that I'd blundered into a territory where I did not belong." (KR)

At the bridge table she was alone, so she pushed back and went to the typewriter. But the women are still there playing bridge and talking pretty mean. And they go on, like the sun, sand, and sky.

Over the years St. Petersburg would become Fort Jude a geographical hunting-ground for her dissimilar but sometimes angry, sometimes countercultural, always out-of-whack stories: imagining something happening in Fort Jude would work a localizing transformation on the mundane stuff of dreams, the alluvial sludge of humanity that might at this turn produce debutante or recluse, dingbat or hawker of patent medicines, imprisoned child or captive adult.

In 1955 she married Joseph Reed whom she met on a blind date while they were still in college—a Yale graduate, a Boswell, Faulkner, and film scholar. They had two sons and a daughter and, having it all, are still married, three in-law children and four grandchildren later.

As a daughter becoming a mother she has written in a story, "nobody ever told me I would have to be a mother this long." And she writes in "The Mothers of Shark Island," "Unlike pneumonia, motherhood is an irreversible condition. Motherhood is forever." Reed's mother gave her grief, but what is important about the pneumonia statement is that Kit Reed opted for this irreversible condition and chose to have children. As she has also written, "Biology may not be destiny, but it is certainly a pain in the ass."

After their marriage the Reeds moved first to Waukegan Ilinois, where her husband finished a stint in the Navy and Kit Reed wrote the house newspaper for the District Public Works Office at the Great Lakes Naval Training Center. In that office, she wrote short stories—including "The Wait," her first published story (some unpublished stories from this period are archived at Yale). Another move took them back to Connecticut where Reed worked for a trio of weekly newspapers for three long months. These led her to the *New Haven Register*. There she interviewed

Josef Albers, Cary Grant, Thornton Wilder, Eleanor Roosevelt, wrote features and covered juvenile court (the *Register* was the first paper to do this). This led to her prizewinning series, "The Road to Crime." Four youths killed a man for small change. Reed's series on it won the New England Newspaperwoman of the Year award.

Reed wrote fiction at night and on weekends and began to submit stories to national magazines: regular mailing, return envelopes for each story, mailing flew thick and fast. She had by this time worked through the city editors, Waugh, Faulkner, and Cheever; the apprenticeship was over and the career had begun.

Her first story to be published was "The Wait" in the *Magazine of Fantasy and Science Fiction* (then edited by Anthony Boucher): high school girl is used as a pawn by an insecure mother intent on fitting into a new society.

A friend with an insider's knowledge of psychiatric establishments said, "'You're very brave to write about your mother like that.' Wuow, is that what I was doing?" (KR *WWWW* xv)

The story is a retelling of two tales from Herodotus about Old Babylon. There is a central plaza in which the ailing mother waits, even as her daughter waits less willingly for a suitor to wind up the colored string threading through a nearby field and leading straight to her lap so he can have his way with her. One critic describes it as: "a piece about the fear of sex that was a revelation to me when I read it in a now-forgotten anthology as a teenage boy—an unexpected and profoundly sensitizing experience. I had never read anything quite like it." (Simon Ings in *infinity plus*, UK, 18 June 1999)

"The Wait" is a talismanic hallmark of a story, a touchstone, as good for ending as for starting off a career. Often anthologized, it is a story everyone knows. It has everything Kit Reed will find for her best stories: mom, daughter, strange customs, mortality, sex, and waiting, waiting, waiting. Her first story defines the Kit Reed Story. It's all there but not comic, as are many of the stories that follow.

In rapid succession came more stories: by 1961 Reed had sold seven, most (again) to the *Magazine of Fantasy and Science Fiction*. which has continued to publish her work to the present), and by 1962 seven more, but, significantly, two of these appeared in *Cosmopolitan*, one in *Seventeen*. More important, at least three typically Kit Reed Stories, "Piggy," "Mr. da V." and "The New You" appeared—somewhat brash, smart, funny fictions, tending to cultural satire (or at least sophisticated knowingness). In a typical Kit Reed story: "a housewife is disenfranchised from society by widowhood or divorce, and . . . in her desperate desire to belong again, sacrifices her innocent, cumbersome child . . . These are stories driven by personal demons, not by pre-articulated political arguments. In modern parlance, therefore, they are not 'political' stories—because no one believes any more that you can be honest and political at the same time." (Louise Wicks)

In "Piggy" would-be poets who sit astride the flying hog discover they utter verse. In the *New York Times Book Review*, Enid Shomer anatomizes Reed's characters—parents, children, in-laws, friends, women who pursue what they think might turn out to be happiness—and themes: entrapment, death and those near death, isolation, disease. Reed calls such stories "speculative fiction."

The mainstream novels (outside the scope of this essay) treat their settings with love, and construct rules for their enclaves (the particular field or culture or trap this fiction makes) with respect to this central line. Although short fictions do not have novelistic scope, both Reed's novels and short stories turn on odd accidents outside the range of the story's premises—events that have brought just these people to just this place at just this time—not exactly the hand of Fate, but certainly more than dumb luck or the flip of a coin. In other words both novels and stories clearly come from the same writer.

Like the novels, the short stories tend to be "character-driven": people confronting the inevitabilities of living with combinations of grace and despair. To some readers this makes the stories rationally frightening. Like Henry James, the territory she makes her own carries with it an "imagination of disaster."

"The "imagination of disaster" in Kit Reed's stories is vivid. These stories creep up on you, unnerve, make you nervous. Over and over again in seemingly innocuous middle-class lives, Reed images a monster . . . that devours desire, good looks, marriages, children, lives . . . Mortal dangers are hauntingly described as characters are drawn into physically and emotionally enclosed space; mismatches, misapprehensions, mistakes, misunderstandings, miscommunications, unidentified feelings." (Patricia Laurence in *Review of Contemporary Fiction*, fall 1993)

"The reliance the reader places on Reed's characters is absolute, and character determines action even as story determines form. "Reed is the only writer living to have mastered Henry James's dictum that action is character and character, action." (Patricia Laurence, *ibid*)

We can see this in standout stories ("Automatic Tiger," "The New You," "Songs of War," "The Wait," "The Vine," "Pilots of the Purple Twilight," "Bride of Bigfoot," and "Winter.")

What attracted anthologists of all kinds to her was the recognizable entity of the Kit Reed Story (it could be satiric or chilling, or both). The fact that these stories were very funny but serious at the same time is a hallmark. In "Queen of the Beach" the heroine is funny but she doesn't really know what she's saying, and this is very serious. In "The New You," the protagonist unwraps the new you as it comes from the factory (funny), but the old husband just won't go away (serious).

The maguffin (the plot gimmick—like the uranium in the wine bottles of Alfred Hitchcock's *Notorious*) is never at the end of that story, nor is it the *raison d'être*. It comes in the middle, pushes a character into a particular state of mind: the subsequent *actions* of that character carry the story's significance. She depicts a broken world, not somewhere you'd want to visit, but you recognize it at once, and then you think Oops, here I am ... These stories disturb for they suggest so many things that we cannot put a name to: among others, a mind afraid of its own death. (Patricia Laurence, *ibid*)

The individual track history of some of the best of these stories traces the importance of anthologies, the backbone of SF. "The Wait," was anthologized by Boucher's *Best from F&SF* (1959), went to the French edition of *F&SF* (1961), as "To Be Taken in a Strange Country" in Harry Harrison's *Apeman, Spaceman* (1967), a Japanese translation (1968), *Town* in the UK (1967), and in 1970 there was a Spanish translation in *Antologia de*

Novelas de Anticipacion. "Automatic Tiger," first published privately in 1964, came out in *F&SF*; then Judith Merril (anthologist, critic and historian of SF, who may have invented the term, "speculative fiction") picked it up (1965) for the *10th Year's Best*, there was a Japanese translation (1968). "Automatic Tiger" was first published privately; then in *F&SF* (1964), Judith Merril's *10th Year's Best* (1965) p.9; Japanese translation (1965); Avram Davidson's *Best from F&SF* (1965), and appeared as "El Tigre Automatico" in *Minautauro* (Argentina) (1984), "Le Tigre Automatique" in Paris *F&SF* and "Tigre Automatico" in *Magazine de Ficçâo Cientifica* (1971). *Best from F&SF* 1965, as "El Tigre Automático" in Buenos Aires: *Minotauro* (1984) under the title "Le Tigre Automatique," Paris: *Fiction*; and; as "Tigre Automatico" in *Magazine de Ficçâo Cientifica.*

"The Vine" was first published in *F&SF* (1967), then taken by *Best SF* 1968, (Harrison/Aldiss), there was a Japanese translation (1968); it also appeared in *Anthropology through SF* (1974). "Winter," a horror story, came first in *Winter's Tales* (UK1969), *Argosy* (UK1970), *Year's Best Horror Stories* (1971), Damon Knight's *Happy Endings 15 Stories by the Masters of the Macabre* (1974).

Ten volumes of short stories (including *What Wolves Know* and the 2005 collection, *Dogs of Truth*, as well as *Seven for the Apocalypse*, which contains one novella) represent a remarkably diverse constellation of narrative.

Including a Kit Reed story in a nationally recognized anthology, one editor wrote: "Kit Reed has one of the liveliest imaginations now at work in our fiction. With alchemical conversions she makes what is horrid amusing and what is commonplace dreadfully creepy. Her satire gains a dimension to become an extravaganza of superhuman theatrics. The sheer range of subject matter in these stories is disciplined by something like the snap of a ringmaster's whip guiding all her creatures in their paces around a singular and marvelous ring." (R. V. Cassill, *Norton Anthology of Contemporary Literature*)

Contents of Reed collections are not determined by theme or thematic organizing principle, but by the way the stories available at the time of gathering the collection hang together. *Weird Women, Wired Women* features both weird and wired: this was not the reason for the book, but the nature of the contents once assembled.

Two collections of Kit Reed's stories first appeared in the United Kingdom. *Mr. da V. and Other Stories*, her first published collection (London: Faber and Faber, 1967) contained (among others), her first published story, "The Wait," and "The New You." The latter does a comic take on radical makeovers now popular on television; in this case it is America's ready-to-wear, buy-it-in-a-box culture, but offhand retail ease takes on darker overtones once the story gets going and it (and the heroine) wonder what to do with the leftovers.

The Killer Mice (London: Victor Gollancz, 1976) was published only in the U.K. It contained one of Reed's most controversial stories, and subsequently gave critics the most frequent opportunities to reconsider it. "Songs of War" is the story of women living on the edges of an endless war (the five-mile traffic jam and the endless war are staples of Reed's imaginary landscape), and women who wait or suffer on the margins. It was included in *Weird Women, Wired Women*, a collection nominated for the 1998 Tiptree Award for best science fiction stories and books written by women that year.

One critic described the consternation in the Tiptree jury: "Everyone admired "Songs of War"; and it made us all uncomfortable . . . To quote Candas Jane Dorsey, 'It was such a relentless indictment of a certain era of social prejudices that reading . . . [it] was like watching a torture session, hearing scream after scream . . . ' " (Elizabeth Hand *F&SF,* fall 1998)

One such *mea culpa* is remarkable, but two is almost unbelievable: "I remember the first time I read "Songs of War" by Kit Reed . . . in 1974. I was fresh out of college . . . all fired up about the Women's Liberation Movement, eagerly anticipating the Revolution . . . I was sure was on the horizon. I kind of assumed Kit Reed must feel the same . . . "Songs of War" shocked me not because it was not what I expected, but because I didn't know what it was. It sure wasn't politically correct feminism ("'As soon as it's over we dump the housewives,' Rap said") . . . but it wasn't anti-feminist, either . . . It was an attempt to joke about a subject too important to be joked about." (Lisa Tuttle, New York *Review of Science Fiction*. July 1999, p. 18,).

This was not so much Reed changing her mind, no *volte-face*, but a growing realization. As she put it in "What I Think I Was Doing," "Other people went to consciousness-raising groups. I wrote 'Songs of War'." (KR, *WWWW*, xvi)

"In Behalf of the Product" is another take on similar behavior but from a different angle. The subject is the product; she speaks: "I am a weeny bit too frank to be a typical Miss Wonderful Land of Ours, he says I have too many regrets, but just as soon as I get down from here and they run the last commercial, they're going to take care of that. He says I'll be ready to begin my nationwide personal appearance in behalf of the product just as soon as they finish the lobotomy." ("In Behalf of the Product," 1973.)

She's referring to the producer of the national beauty pageant, the narrator is their product. The story comes to a climax in its last line. Irving Malin (in *Review of Contemporary Fiction*) asks incredulously if a lobotomy is called for. He writes, "Does Miss Wonderful really need one? Does she have a brain?" Maybe she doesn't, but the story calls for one because Miss Wonderful's calm acceptance is why it's there. And without her acceptance it isn't a Kit Reed story.

Kit Reed stories not only take on familiar outlines of cultural convention and cliché, gender roles, but they also deal with contemporary shibboleths of belief. She is a feminist, like many others, too busy writing the texts of feminism to go out and burn anything. "If satire is the instrument of rebellion," writes Kit Reed in her introduction to this elegantly produced collection of stories, "I was loaded for bear." (KR, *WWWW*)

Reed refuses to think about fiction in terms of "themes," genres and subgenres or "serious and light." "Themes are for high school lit teachers," she has said. In *The New York Times Book Review*, one critic citing Reed's darkly comic rants, calls them: "less fantastic than visionary, uncovering humor and horror where others have seen only clothes, makeup and recipes snipped from then newspaper." (Enid Shomer, *NYT Book Review*, 10 July 1998).

Other Stories and The Attack of the Giant Baby (Berkley Books,1981) is an American edition of the 1976 Gollancz *Killer Mice* collection with several stories added. In "Pilots of the Purple Twilight" (title from Tennyson) wives from many wars wait at a motel for their dead husbands to return.

According to one critic, it is: ". . . a touching and beautifully written story about loss, and the strange sort of non-life many women have accepted for generations while the American war machine has relentlessly ground our young men into dust." (Tim Sullivan in *The Washington Post's Book World*).

Added to this edition is "Winter" (1969), much anthologized and subsequently included in *The Norton Anthology of American Literature*: Two sisters who live in the northern boondocks, hungry for both food and affection, take in a young soldier gone AWOL. Frequently critics praise Kit Reed for "the Gothic"; again here (as in Faulkner's "A Rose for Emily") the grim denouement is kept from us until the story's last line. "So we et him.'"

"The Food Farm" (1967), frequently anthologized, is another addition not included in the UK volume. Again it's about eating, but this is not a rice-diet spa but a farm devoted to fattening up women (not all that far removed from tonight's evening news). Diet fads and fat have been subjects Reed has written about again and again and in 2004 Tor published her novel, *Thinner than Thou*, about a diet evangelist and body image as a new religion.

Reed's collection *The Revenge of the Senior Citizens **PLUS* included her take on Kafka, titled, "Sisohpromatem, "which is, of course Metamorphosis spelled backward. Although this is what Reed calls a "one-idea" story, it has great vitality.

"I, Joseph Bug, awoke one morning to discover I had become an enormous human." Sometimes when Reed says something is a one-idea story, the story surprises her: "Hubbies, an Introduction" (like "Automatic Tiger" and "The Wait" before it) makes unexpected twists as it goes along. The Hubbies are not just useless, they're everywhere. They are like Al Capp's Shmoos: they clog the landscape. Kit Reed once had to read on a program with a Romance novelist on a long night. She read last, and, looking the Romance writer in the eye, introduced her story as "It's a kind of romance. It's called, 'The Bride of Bigfoot.'

Reed gives precedence to "Chicken Soup" as her best story of matriarchal violence: "The resulting tension and ambiguity drive much of my work, perhaps most obviously "Chicken Soup," a horror story about the ultimate mother. An editor had asked me to 'write about the thing that frightens you most'." (KR)

The thing that frightens her most (mothers) is a constant in Kit Reed Stories ("The Wait," "Cynosure," The Weremother," "Queen of the Beach," and "The Mothers of Shark Island." "Last Fridays" introduces a group of eight, all mothers of convicted serial killers). It's not that unnamed horrors inhabit these stories of mothers, it's that what you most fear is drawing near and it looks like Mom—doesn't look dangerous, turns out to be lethal. So, malls are dangerous, makeovers tend to end badly; helpful men and women have a vicious day-jobs; youth is not innocent, but knowing; age is not mellow but rancid; don't, whatever you do, go to the suburbs; try to avoid superhighways; and if someone offers you a vacation, say no, thank you.

Significant as the first of Reed's collections to be published by a university press, *Thief of Lives* (University of Missouri Press, 1992) took 25 years to assemble. The stories are predominantly "mainstream," published in periodicals like *The Tampa Review, Winter's Tales, Voice Literary Supplement,* the *Yale Review,* and the *Transatlantic Review* (or first printed in this volume). Critics were getting more respectful. These are stories of loss, but the loss is couched as not the action of natural forces, but of the "human psyche." Some of these stories were aptly compared to those of Raymond Carver. "Pure dazzlement" (Ann Slegman in *New Letters Book Reviewer* 18) is not an ordinary phrase in a review; "pain can be instructive" (James Kaufmann in *Minneapolis Star Tribune*) isn't either.

And where did the stories begin? "Voyager" began when one of the aides at the place Reed had moved her mother to remembered a torrential rainstorm: ". . . years before, when a hurricane flooded the point where the retirement community sat, the frail inhabitants were bussed to shelters in downtown churches. Some of them were fine, some were Not

Quite Right and kept wandering off. I compressed everything I knew and imagined, and made the story." (KR, introduction, *Seven* xi).

Domestic anguish, the Kit-Reed-Story staple, becomes individual and personal in a story of entrapment in a sunken submarine in her story, "In the *Squalus*." A former serviceman is haunted his life long by the death of a buddy.

In "Journey to the Center of the Earth" the search for the father ends in a down-at-the-heels religious cult taking refuge from What Is to Come in an empty underground storage tank. The son tries to save the father but he insists he's *been* saved. The power of the story derives from the language: Father and son talk simply each to the other, but without either exchange or explanation. The encounter is not so much a reunion as it is an underground trainwreck.

To many critics Reed's stories are rationally frightening. "Queen of the Beach" has lived too long, made too many decisions, come to too many forks in the road to change now. She confronts the present with a surprisingly placid assurance, in spite of all. She advises her daughter, "'It's not what happens to you that makes the difference. It's the way you handle it"; and "Save everything you have to say," "Take care of yourselves," "prepare for it," and "protect" ("Queen of the Beach").

In *Thief of Lives* Kit Reed, on the offensive, moves her quirky domain closer to the mainstream. Turns out "Songs of War" wasn't an antifeminist pamphlet but a feminist warcry. "In the *Squalus*" didn't just apply to the missing father (never far from Kit Reed's fiction); but to mourning as a way of life. "Voyager" wasn't just a tragic tale of Alzheimer's but a continuation of a favorite emblem of the Kit Reed Story: isolation and despair. One critic (Greg Johnson in *NY Times Book Review*) says *Thief* "is ... distinguished by several masterly examples of the form" (17 January 1993). That these stories and the collections also managed to escape the strange boundaries of SF, sci-fi (or "skiffy" as students now call it) was clear in this collection: the tales are off-the-wall, outlandish, shocking, non-PC, but in this volume Reed's fiction was finding a place free of genre where she could just let her garden grow.

Another thing that needs to be said (and the critics say it again and again): Kit Reed's prose is sometimes so good it takes your breath away.

From the volume's title story: We already know things are not wonderful between the Warriners because of the presents they give each other. Last Christmas she gave him a copy of the OED with a magnifying glass and he gave her a set of snow tires"'" ("Thief of Lives"). Or in "The Hall of New Faces": "Amazements take place in the Hall of New Faces, but like life itself, the miracles are only temporary; some things refuse to stay done.

American novelist, poet and critic George Garrett, in his summary of that year's new fiction quotes from "Songs of War": "This gathering of twenty "womanist" fantasies, written from 1958 to 1996 . . . are richly various in form and strategy, linked by the author's voice and irrepressible, ironic, often mordant wit." (George Garrett in 'The Year in Fiction' in *DLB Yearbook*, 1998).

He quotes as follows: "The women had collected twigs and they were first about to set fire to Patsy and Andy when Sheena came out, closely followed by Dr. Ora Fesenden and a warlike Rap. Everybody started shouting at once, and in the imbroglio that followed, Patsy and Andy escaped. They would surface years later in a small town in Minnesota, with an ecologically alarming number of children; they would both be able to pursue their chosen careers in law because they worked hand in hand to take care of all the children and the house and they would love each other until they died." (George Garrett in 'The Year in Fiction' in DLB Yearbook, 1998).

Garrett indicates the change in critical climate for the Kit Reed Story from shock to deep respect. He does not comment on the quotation, but simply hands it to us. We'll know what he means.

Reed is refreshingly straightforward about her sense of her art: "The stories I wrote in the late fifties and early sixties ("Empty Nest," "Cynosure," "The New You") are about women defined by their roles—the mother who loves her young no matter how hideous, the housewife who will do anything to protect her hardwood floors, the woman who will do anything to keep her man. In ads the woman's face was pretty and wholesome, but wait: Was her upper lip always filmed with the sweat of anxiety, or was it only mine?

"In the early Seventies my friends' lives caught up with the women's movement; women who had been living according to their mothers'—or was it their partners'?—expectations were in full rebellion by that time. So, fine, and welcome. What took you so long? Career was an issue; so was the place where feminists stood in relation to other feminists. Lives changed. Marriages started to blow apart, and in the lexicon of extrapolation it seemed logical for antagonists of both sexes to take to the streets with buns and clubs . . .

"What has followed over the last three decades plus is a fairly accurate representation of my attitudes in what I think of as pre-feminist and post-feminist (as in post-modern) times. I can't stand back far enough to mark the spikes on the graph of the national feminist consciousness, but my sense is that I came early to the feast, sat at a reserved distance from the table, and stayed long enough to see the dinner guests start squabbling among themselves—another story I need to write some day." [KR].

A critic later quoted this passage and added that Reed's mother: "had to struggle . . . constantly worried about appearances. The daughter grew up determined to have it all and did—and also to write social criticism in the form of satire and speculative fiction." (Lisa Tuttle, *NY Review of Science Fiction* July 1999, p.19)

Weird Women, Wired Women (Wesleyan University Press, 1998) was the second collection published by a university press. It was dedicated to the memory of Reed's mother "who would have been proud. And horrified. And proud." The collection contains almost forty years' worth of stories centered on women and their concerns as well as a look at American society from a feminist perspective.

Seven for the Apocalypse (Wesleyan University Press, 1999) the third collection from a university press, derives its title from the novella, *Little Sisters of the Apocalypse*, short-listed for the Tiptree Prize. In the novella, a coven of biker nuns on the edge of chaos zips about doing its religious work. *Little Sisters* was originally published as a chapbook in the Black Ice series of *Fiction Collective Two* in 1994.

The collection features a variety of narratives similar to that in *Thief of Lives*: in "Voyager" a wife drifts off from the moorings of reason; in "River" a computerized security system attempts to protect "her" family from its own failings. "In the Palace of the Dictator" is a surreal excursion into Totalitarianism. There is also a ghost story, "The Singing Marine" (which was a best short story nominee in the World Fantasy Awards that year).

"Reed has a mean way with aphorisms ("When the world ends, the last person standing will be a woman") . . . "The Singing Marine," is black and nightmarish and eerily satisfying. . . It leaves the reader thirsty for more, which is a good way, maybe the best way, to end any book." (Elizabeth Hand in *F&SF*).

Part of what Hand is saying is also demonstrated in what is perhaps Reed's most quoted line (also in "The Singing Marine"): "When you have been dead and buried many things worry you but nothing frightens you."

An eighth Reed collection, *Dogs of Truth* (the epigraph reads: "the Hound of Heaven is hard on the heels of the Dogs of Truth") came out from Tom Doherty Associates (Tor) in 2005, and like many of her books, was reviewed in *The New York Times*

"Reed has a prose style that's pure dry ice, displayed in dystopian stories that specialize in bitterness and dislocation."—*The New York Times Book Review*

Writing about the collection for Keith Brooke's *Infinity Plus*, John Toon wrote: "Can't live with 'em, can't live without 'em. The family is the predominant theme of the stories in Kit Reed's collection *Dogs of Truth*— the dark side of it, the desire to escape, the terrible adventures of those who do. 'Escape From Shark Island' is a fine example, and the story out of this collection that has persisted the most strongly in my mind. In it, a mother insists on keeping her large family permanently together in one enormous bed and exhibiting them on their own TV show, so that the nation can bask in their exaggerated family values. The eldest kids find out what happens to those who try to escape the Family Bed. It's a harsh and grotesque examination of traditional family values."

Also writing about *Dogs of Truth*, a reviewer at *Publishers Weekly* touched on the dynamic that drives all of Reed's short stories.

"Reed (*Thinner Than Thou*) transforms the ordinary into the extraordinary in this impressive story collection . . . No matter how absurd, these horror stories still sting with truth and ring with humor, often ending with an odd happiness." (*Publishers Weekly*)

In her forward to *Weird Women, Wired Women*, Connie Willis writes, "Kit Reed's true genius lies in her ability to see straight through to the center of things. It's this clear-eyed ability to get below the surface and down to the reality—more than her flair for detail and dialogue, her quirky insights, her fantastical stage settings—that makes Kit Reed stories unique. She sees straight . . . to the truth. And understands just how complicated that truth is." (Introduction, *Weird Women, Wired Women*).

Proofreading and re-reading four decades' worth of stories for that collection made Reed speculative, and she issued a rare bit of introspection, indulging in the kind of thinking her characters so frequently find themselves engaged in: "We don't only become what we behold. We who are writers behold what we have become. And motherhood? If we behold what we become, we also become what we behold. In some of our best moments, my friends and I used to sit around discussing our mothers. We vowed that we'd do anything to keep from being like that. When I look around I see that we are close to our adult sons and daughters. In fact, although my grown kids delight in telling me just what about their childhood—moments when I lost it, eggplant Parmesan, certain cakes—was weird, we're pretty good friends. Still, I saw myself in 'The Weremother': and I recognize myself in 'The Mothers of Shark Island . . . nor do I need a psychiatrically sophisticated friend to point out exactly who those women are poised on the cliff outside *Chateau D'If*, wondering what heinous crime against society put them there. One of them is me." (KR Women xvi-xvii).

BOOKS

Mother Isn't Dead She's Only Sleeping (Boston: Houghton Mifflin, 1961)

At War as Children (NY: Farrar, Straus & Co.,1964)

The Better Part (NY: Farrar, Straus & Giroux, 1967; London: Hutchinson, 1968)

Mister da V. and Other Stories (1967)

Armed Camps (London: Faber & Faber,1969; NY: E. P. Dutton & Co., 1970)

Cry of the Daughter (NY: Dutton, 1971)

Tiger Rag (NY: Dutton, 1973)

Captain Grownup (NY: Dutton, 1976)

The Killer Mice (London: Victor Gollancz, 1976)

The Ballad of T. Rantula (Boston: Toronto, 1979)

Other Stories and The Attack of the Giant Baby (NY: Berkley, 1981)

Blood Fever [as Shelley Hyde] (NY: Pocket Books [paper only],1982)

Magic Time (NY: Berkley Publishing Group, dist. by G. P. Putnam's Sons, 1980)

Fort Privilege (Garden City: Doubleday & Co. Inc., 1985)

*The Revenge of the Senior Citizens **PLUS* (Garden City NY: Doubleday, 1986)

Catholic Girls (NY: Donald I. Fine Inc., 1987)

Gone: A Novel of Psychological Terror [as Kit Craig] (NY: Little Brown, 1992)

Thief of Lives (Columbia: University of Missouri Press, 1992)

Twice Burned [as Kit Craig] (NY: Little, Brown, 1993; London: Headline, 1993)

Little Sisters of the Apocalypse (Boulder CO: Black Ice Books)

Strait [as Kit Craig] (London: Headline House, 1995)

J. Eden (Hardscrabble Book: Hanover and London: Univ. Press of New England, 1996)

Closer [as Kit Craig] (London: Headline, 1997)

Some Safe Place [as Kit Craig] (London: Headline, 1998)

Weird Women, Wired Women (Wesleyan University Press, 1998)

Seven for the Apocalypse (Wesleyan University Press, 1999)

@expectations (New York: Forge: Tom Doherty Associates Book, 2000)
Thinner than Thou (New York: Tor: Tom Doherty Associates, 2004)
Dogs of Truth (New York: Tor: Tom Doherty Associates, 2005)
The Baby Merchant (New York: Tor: Tom Doherty Associates, 2006)
The Night Children (New York: Tor Starscape; Tom Doherty Associates)
Enclave (New York: Tor; Tom Doherty Associates, 2009)

To date Kit Reed has published more than 110 short stories in periodicals: (in the UK), *Argosy, Fashion, F&SF, Nova, Ingenue, Town & Country; Fiction,* (Argentina) *Minotauro;* (U.S.) *Asimov's SF, Chronicles, Cosmopolitan, The Critic, Ellery Queen's Mystery Magazine, Fantastic Universe, Ladies Home Journal, F&SF, OMNI, Redbook, Rod Serling's Twilight Zone, Seventeen, Timbuktu, Voice Literary Supplement, Yale Literary Magazine; Missouri, Tampa, Texas, Transatlantic,* and *Yale Reviews,* and in 2009 and 2010, *The Kenyon Review.*